Also by Jennifer L. Schiff

For Whom the Shell Tolls

A Sanibel Island Mystery

Jennifer Lonoff Schiff

Shovel
& Pail
Press

FOR WHOM THE SHELL TOLLS: A SANIBEL ISLAND MYSTERY
by Jennifer Lonoff Schiff

Book Eight in the Sanibel Island Mystery series

http://www.SanibelIslandMysteries.com

© 2021 by Jennifer Lonoff Schiff

Cover design by Kristin Bryant

Formatting by Polgarus Studio

ISBN: 978-0-578-92852-4

Library of Congress Control Number: 2021913632

No man is an island,
Entire of itself.
Each is a piece of the continent,
A part of the main.
If a clod be washed away by the sea,
Europe is the less.
As well as if a promontory were.
As well as if a manor of thine own
Or of thine friend's were.
Each man's death diminishes me,
For I am involved in mankind.
Therefore, send not to know
For whom the bell tolls,
It tolls for thee.
—John Donne, "For Whom the Bell Tolls"

PROLOGUE

Bonnie and her husband Clyde pulled into the Bailey Tract just as the sun was rising. Clyde was a wildlife enthusiast, and every Saturday he and Bonnie would explore one of Sanibel's many nature preserves in search of birds and other fauna (though Bonnie was more partial to seeking out shells on Sanibel's many beaches).

A solitary car was parked in the lot. No doubt someone else who had come to walk the Bailey Tract in search of alligators, river otters, kestrels, and moorhens. Clyde ignored the other vehicle, busily checking his binoculars. But something about the car made Bonnie pause.

"Hey, Clyde," she called, taking a few steps towards the sedan.

"Hm?" he said, still adjusting his binoculars.

"That car over there," she said pointing. "I think there's someone inside."

Clyde glanced over at the car, then looked over at his wife, who was still staring at the parked car.

"Probably getting ready to go for a walk."

Bonnie frowned.

"Looks more like he fell asleep."

"Leave him be, Bonnie."

But Bonnie didn't move.

"What if something's wrong?"

Clyde sighed.

"I'm sure he's fine. Now let's go."

He walked to the entrance, but Bonnie didn't follow.

"I'm going to go see if he's all right."

Clyde frowned.

Bonnie peeked in the passenger-side window of the parked car. The man inside was slumped over the steering wheel. She tapped on the window.

"Bonnie, leave the poor man alone," called Clyde.

Bonnie ignored him and tapped again on the window.

"Hello? Are you okay?" she called.

The man didn't move.

Clyde came over and took a look.

"He's probably just a heavy sleeper. Now leave him be."

He tried to pull her away from the car, but she wouldn't budge.

"I think something's wrong."

Clyde sighed.

Bonnie knocked on the window again, louder this time.

"Hello?" she said, practically shouting. "Are you okay?"

Again, the man didn't move. She tried the door, but it was locked.

"What are you doing?" said Clyde.

"I'm telling you, Clyde, something's not right. He may need help."

She went around to the driver's side and knocked on that window. Again, no response. She tried the door, but it too was locked. She frowned.

"I'm calling the police."

"Is that really necessary, Bonnie? I'm sure he's just a sound sleeper."

But Bonnie had already pulled out her phone and dialed 911.

Clyde sighed a third time. So much for their early morning wildlife walk.

A few minutes later, they heard a siren and watched as a

Sanibel Police car pulled in. The doors opened and a uniformed officer and a man in plain clothes got out.

"Detective O'Loughlin," said Bonnie, addressing the man in plain clothes. "Thank you for coming."

The detective looked over at the two cars, which were parked on opposite sides of the lot.

"It's that one," said Bonnie, pointing to the silver sedan. "I knocked on the windows, but there was no response, and the doors are all locked."

The detective took out a pair of blue nitrile disposable gloves and fitted them over his hands. Then he went over to the silver sedan. He tried the driver's side door, but it was locked, just as Bonnie had said. He rapped on the window, but there was no response.

"Sir, are you okay in there?" he called loudly.

The man didn't move.

The detective turned to the uniformed officer, who looked barely out of high school.

"Officer Pettit, get me the rod."

The young officer nodded and quickly returned with a long metal rod.

"You want to do the honors?" asked the detective.

Officer Pettit went over to the locked door and managed to jimmy it open. A foul smell permeated the air, causing Officer Pettit and the detective to cover their noses and take a step back.

"Is he…?" asked Bonnie, peering around them. But judging by their expressions and the smell, she already knew the answer.

"Please step back, ma'am," said Detective O'Loughlin looking grim.

"Is he okay?" asked Clyde, who was standing several feet away.

The detective didn't answer. Instead, he turned to Officer Pettit.

"Call nine-one-one and get an ambulance here."

Officer Pettit nodded and walked over to the police car while the detective examined the vehicle and the body.

"Any idea who he is?" asked Clyde, walking over to the vehicle to see what the detective was up to.

"Please step back, Mr. …"

"Barnes. Clyde Barnes."

"I knew something was wrong," said Bonnie, still staring at the car.

Officer Pettit came back over.

"They're on their way," he informed the detective.

The detective didn't reply. He continued with his examination, only stopping to make notes in a little tan book. When he was done, he turned to Officer Pettit and told him to photograph the scene. Then he turned to Bonnie and Clyde.

"What time did you say you arrived here?"

"A little before six-thirty," said Bonnie.

"You see any other cars?"

"No, just that one."

"And you said you knocked on the windows?"

"I did, but there was no response. That's when I tried the doors. But they were all locked."

The detective was writing in his notebook again. He was about to ask another question when they heard the sound of sirens and a few seconds later the EMTs pulled in.

CHAPTER 1

"It was just awful," said Bonnie, addressing the other ladies who had gathered at their friend Shelly's house to paint shells for the National Seashell Day treasure hunt.

The hunt had been the brainchild of the Lee County Visitor & Convention Bureau and the Sanibel & Captiva Islands Chamber of Commerce as a way to celebrate National Seashell Day, which took place on June 21. Sanibel was famous for being the Seashell Capital of the United States. So what better way to celebrate the holiday than with a treasure hunt where all the clues were seashells? And who better to paint all the shells than the Sanibel Shell Fairies? A group of talented artists and shell lovers, the Shell Fairies painted local shells with tropical scenes, animals, and flowers, then hid them around the island for others to find and enjoy—and post on Facebook.

Bonnie was more of a shell seeker than a shell painter, but she had joined the Shell Fairies a couple of years ago at the insistence of her friend Barbara. Now she and Barbara and their friends Linda and Janice were at their friend Shelly's place, painting shells for the hunt. Though so far they had done more gossiping than painting.

"And you have no idea who it was?" asked Barbara.

Bonnie shook her head.

"Detective O'Loughlin shooed us away when the ambulance arrived, and you know Clyde. He was eager to go birding."

"I don't know how Clyde could possibly go bird-watching after that," said Linda.

"You don't know Clyde," Bonnie replied.

"Substitute *fishing* for *bird-watching* and Steve would be the same way," said Shelly.

Barbara and the other ladies nodded their heads.

Guin had only been half-listening before Bonnie spoke. She was there to cover the shell-painting party for the local paper, the *Sanibel-Captiva Sun-Times*, but she had been spacing out. Now, however, she was all ears.

"Can you describe the man?" Guin asked Bonnie.

"Not really. All I know is he had darkish hair. He was slumped over the steering wheel, so I wasn't able to see his face."

Guin made a mental note to ask Detective O'Loughlin about the body when she saw him that evening. The two of them had been dating. Though *dating* didn't seem the right word. Seeing each other? Sleeping together? (Though little sleep was involved.) She didn't know what to call their relationship. Four months ago, she had feared that whatever it was was over. Then, after not returning Guin's calls or texts for several weeks, the detective had asked her out to dinner. And they had been seeing each other ever since.

"Guin?"

It was Shelly.

"Hm?" she said. She had been so busy thinking about the detective, she hadn't heard her friend's question.

"I asked if you had heard anything, about the body."

"Nope, not a thing. This is the first I've heard about it. Though I plan on asking the detective about it when I see him later."

"How much later?" said Shelly, giving Guin a sly look.

Guin glared at her friend. While Shelly knew about her on-again, off-again relationship with the detective, as did Bonnie, she didn't want to discuss her private life with the

Shell Fairies. After all, she was here on business, not to gossip.

"Well, let us know if you find out anything," said Bonnie, sensing Guin's discomfort.

"I will. But you know Detective O'Loughlin. He only supplies information on a need-to-know basis."

"But you're with the paper!" said Janice.

Guin looked over at her.

"I'm afraid that doesn't matter to the detective."

"Well, someone's bound to know who the man was," said Linda.

Guin cast a pleading look at Shelly.

"Okay, everyone. We came here to paint, not gossip."

A couple of the ladies grumbled, but they got the hint.

"Thank you," mouthed Guin, as the Shell Fairies picked up their brushes.

Guin stayed at Shelly's for another hour, taking photos (making sure not to reveal what was painted on each shell) and making notes. She envied these women their talent. She had tried painting shells shortly after she had moved to Sanibel. But she had quickly given up, not having what it took to wield a tiny paintbrush or the patience. But these five women were all artists.

The Shell Fairies continued to paint as Guin said her goodbyes, Shelly putting down her paintbrush to walk Guin to the door.

"Have fun tonight!" she said with a mischievous grin. "You two going out or will you be dining in?"

Shelly continued to grin, and Guin thought about lying. But she had never been a good liar.

"We're having dinner at his place. He's cooking."

Shelly sighed.

"Gotta love a man who cooks."

"Hey, Steve cooks!"

"Steve grills. There's a difference."

"I'm sure he'd cook you dinner if you asked him to."

"Last time he tried, he served me raw chicken. I swear, you'd think a man who knew how to grill could figure out how to use an oven."

She shook her head and Guin smiled.

"Call me tomorrow and let me know how dinner went," said Shelly. "And if you find out who the dead guy is... or was."

Guin said she would, then left.

Guin arrived home a short time later and immediately went to her office. She had started to type up her notes from the party, but her mind kept wandering to the body Bonnie found over at the Bailey Tract. Who could it have been? She was tempted to text the detective, even though she was seeing him in a few hours. But he was unlikely to reply. Though, surely, someone on the island, other than the police, must know something.

She picked up her phone and speed-dialed her colleague Craig Jeffers. If anyone on the island knew something, it would be Craig. Craig was officially the paper's fishing reporter, but before he had moved to Sanibel, with his wife Betty, he had been an award-winning crime reporter in Chicago. And he had helped Guin solve several murders.

He picked up after three rings.

"Jeffers."

"It's me," said Guin. She paused. "So, uh, you hear about a body being found over at the Bailey Tract this morning?"

"I was out fishing this morning." Guin waited. "But I may have heard something."

"What did you hear? Do you know who it is—or was?"

He didn't answer right away.

"I suppose you'll be hearing about it soon enough."

Guin waited for him to continue.

"It was that lawyer."

"Which lawyer?"

"The one with all the billboards, who has those ads on TV."

There were several lawyers in the Fort Myers area who advertised on TV and had billboards up and down Route 41.

"Could you be a bit more specific?"

"You know the one. He has that stupid slogan: 'If you want action, call Jackson!'"

"You mean Jackson Brennan?"

"You know another Action Jackson?"

She did not.

Guin was dumbfounded. Jackson Brennan was dead? He was so young. Barely fifty. She frowned.

She had no love for Brennan—she had hired him to help her with a real estate matter, and he had come onto her, grabbing her and kissing her. Then when she had told him to cut it out and threatened to report him, he told her he was dropping her case and sent her a bill for double the fee they had agreed on. So while she was shocked to hear he had died, she couldn't say she was sorry.

"Do you know how he died?" she asked Craig.

"Not yet. They're doing an autopsy. The report should be out sometime this week."

"Anything else?"

"Nothing official."

Guin hoped he'd say more, but he didn't.

"You talk to Ginny?"

Virginia "Ginny" Prescott was the publisher and editor of the *Sanibel-Captiva Sun-Times* and their boss.

"She called me earlier."

Of course.

"She ask you to cover the story for the paper?"

"She did."

Guin silently fumed. She understood why Ginny had asked Craig to cover the story. After all, he was the award-winning crime reporter. But Guin felt she had proven herself over the last couple of years. Hadn't she helped solve the case of the missing junonia and several murders?

"Well, if you need any help…"

"I'm sure if you asked Ginny, she'd be fine with us working together."

Guin knew that was probably true. But she was still sore that Ginny hadn't come to her first.

"Hey, kid, I need to go."

"Oh, you and Betty have plans?"

"We're having an early dinner, then seeing a movie."

"Well, have fun."

"What about you? Any plans?"

"I'm having dinner with the detective."

Craig didn't say anything.

"Well, I should let you go," said Guin. "Let me know if you hear more about Action Jackson."

He said he would, and they ended the call.

Guin stared at her monitor. She started to type, then stopped. A black cat jumped into her lap. Fauna. She stroked the purring feline, who had curled herself into a ball.

"Don't get too comfortable, pussycat. I need to get up in a few minutes."

She continued to pet the cat, then gently placed her on the floor.

"I need to get ready for my date."

Though calling it a date seemed a bit silly. Chances are they would be spending the evening watching the Red Sox game.

The detective was a huge Boston sports fan, being from the area. And his office and apartment contained a trove of Red Sox, New England Patriots, and Boston Bruins memorabilia. Guin wasn't as big a sports fan as the detective, though she was okay watching sports, or at least baseball and football. She had grown up rooting for the New York Mets and the New York Giants, her father's teams, and still watched games when she could.

So what do you wear to watch a baseball game with your boyfriend?

Guin stood in her walk-in closet, gazing at her clothes. She doubted the detective cared what she wore. But she wanted to look nice, even if he spent more time looking at the TV than at her.

She pulled out a sundress and slipped it on. Then she went into the bathroom. She gazed at her mop of curly strawberry-blonde hair and pulled it back into a ponytail. Then she stared at her face. Were those more freckles or were they age spots? She thought about putting on makeup to hide them but nixed the idea. She knew the detective didn't care. But she did apply some mascara and lip gloss. Then she took her hair out of the ponytail and looked at herself in the mirror again.

As she did, she felt something furry rub against her legs. She looked down and saw Fauna looking up at her.

"I think I know what you want," said Guin.

The cat meowed, then followed Guin to the kitchen.

"I may be back late tonight," she told Fauna as she poured some dry food into her bowl.

But Fauna wasn't listening. She was too busy scarfing down her food.

Guin watched for a few seconds, then went to get her bag and keys.

CHAPTER 2

"Mm... something smells good."

Guin had followed Detective O'Loughlin into his kitchen and saw two large pots resting on the stove, alongside a sauté pan.

"The clams should be done," he said, opening the pot and looking inside.

Guin peered over his shoulder.

"What are you going to do with them?"

"Put them over some linguini."

Guin watched as he moved around the kitchen, removing the clams from their pot, putting linguini into the other pot, and creating a garlic white wine sauce to go over everything.

"So is this another one of your grandmother's recipes?"

"Yup. Learned how to make it when I was ten."

Although his last name was O'Loughlin, the detective's mother and grandmother had been Italian, and he had grown up in his grandmother's kitchen in the North End of Boston, helping her to cook (when he wasn't outside getting into trouble with his friends).

Guin continued to watch him, mesmerized.

"So when do we get to eat it?"

"When the pasta's done."

"And when will that be?"

"Another six minutes."

Guin's stomach let out a low growl.

"If you're hungry, we can start with the salad."

"That's okay," said Guin. "I can wait."

The six minutes felt like sixty, but finally the pasta was ready.

"You want to bring it to the table? I'll grab the salad and the wine."

Guin nodded and took the bowl of pasta to the table, the detective following behind her with the salad and a bottle of white wine.

"Almost forgot the garlic bread."

He returned to the kitchen and came back out with a small loaf of garlic bread.

"You make it?" asked Guin.

"The bread's from Mario's. I just added the butter and garlic."

"Well, it smells amazing."

They took their usual seats and the detective poured them some white wine. They each took a sip.

"Go on, help yourself. You don't want it to get cold."

Guin didn't have to be told twice. She grabbed the bowl of linguini and heaped some on her plate. Then she placed some salad on her salad plate and broke off a piece of garlic bread.

She twirled her fork in the pasta, making sure to stab a clam, and placed it in her mouth.

"Mm…" she said, letting the garlic, butter, and white wine coat her tongue. "It's delicious. Your *nonna* would be proud."

"She'd probably say there wasn't enough garlic," he replied.

Guin stared at him. The dish was swimming in garlic.

They continued to eat and drink.

"Is that a new shirt?" Guin asked when they were nearly done. "I like it. It really brings out your eyes."

The detective eyed her suspiciously.

"What do you want?"

Guin looked at him innocently.

"Can't a woman give a man a compliment?"

"This shirt is five years old and has a stain on it."

Guin felt her cheeks warm.

"But I don't think you've worn it before."

He continued to eye her.

"Okay, fine," said Guin, putting her napkin on the table. "I want to know whose body Bonnie Barnes found over at the Bailey Tract this morning."

The detective frowned.

"Was it Jackson Brennan?"

"Where'd you hear that?"

"It doesn't matter. Is it true?"

He continued to look at her, his face revealing nothing. Then he gave her an almost imperceptible nod. Guin started to grin, then quickly adopted a more serious expression.

"Do you know the cause of death?"

"Not yet."

He got up and started to clear the table. Guin followed him into the kitchen.

"But you must have a guess or a theory."

He made to go back into the living area, but Guin blocked him.

"Looked like a suicide."

"Suicide?" she said, following him back to the dining table and absently picking up the salad bowl. She couldn't believe Jackson Brennan killed himself.

"You asked me what it looked like."

"No, I asked if you had a theory." She waited for him to say something, but he continued to busy himself with the dishes. "You don't really think Brennan killed himself, do you?"

He stopped what he was doing and looked at her.

"Off the record?"

She nodded.

"Off the record."

"It looked like he killed himself, but something about it didn't feel right."

"How so?"

The detective glanced at the kitchen clock.

"Game's on."

"You didn't answer my question."

He ignored her and headed into the living room, turning on the television.

"What about the dishes?"

"They can wait."

She thought about going back into the kitchen. She usually helped him do the dishes when he cooked. But instead she sat next to him on the couch.

The second inning began, and he turned to her.

"You want a beer?"

"Do *you* want a beer?" she asked him. That was a silly question. He always had a beer while watching the game. "I'll go get us a couple."

She went into the kitchen and emerged a minute later with two beers, handing him one. She knew it was a bad idea to drink beer after she had had nearly two glasses of wine, but she didn't care.

Guin hadn't realized she had fallen asleep until the detective gently shook her awake. Clearly, she should not have drunk that beer, though she had only drunk half of it.

"You missed the ninth inning," he informed her.

She gazed at him sleepily.

"Did the Sox win?"

"They did."

"Sorry, I missed it." She glanced around. "What time is it?"

"A little after ten."

"I should go."

He gazed at her, the look on his face causing Guin to feel warm again.

"Stay," he said.

Guin opened her mouth to tell him she needed to work the next day, but he had leaned over and begun kissing her. The next thing Guin knew, he was leading her back to his bedroom.

Guin opened her eyes and noticed the space next to her in the bed was empty.

"Bill?" she called. There was no answer.

She got out of bed and went into the bathroom. There was no sign of him.

She went into the kitchen. There was coffee in the carafe with a note next to it. It said, "Gone fishing." No endearment or "I'll text you later." But that was typical of the detective. He was a man of few words. Though Guin couldn't believe she hadn't heard him get up or leave. She wasn't typically a heavy sleeper. Though they had been rather busy last night—and again early that morning. She smiled at the memory. The detective wasn't usually that amorous. Not that she minded.

She felt the carafe. The coffee was still hot. So he must not have left that long ago. She got down a mug and poured coffee into it. She took a sip, not bothering to add milk or sugar. It was strong, just the way she liked it. She took another sip, then went to get dressed.

Guin was greeted at her front door by Fauna, who mewed loudly and then trotted to the kitchen. Guin followed her.

The cat dish was empty, so Guin grabbed a can of wet

food and scooped the contents into it. Fauna lunged.

"Take it easy," Guin admonished her. "You don't want to throw it up."

The cat ignored her.

"I should probably eat something too," Guin said, staring at the feline.

She rummaged in the pantry and grabbed a protein bar. She took a couple of bites then reached for her phone. But it wasn't in her back pocket. She went to get her bag and found it. A minute later it began to vibrate. It was her mother. She thought about letting the call go to voicemail but picked up. Her mother never called her this early.

"Hi, Mom. Is everything okay?"

"Thank goodness. You're alive. I was beginning to wonder."

Guin sighed inwardly. She knew she hadn't called her mother in a while, but she had been busy.

"I tried reaching you yesterday and left you a message, but you didn't reply."

"I was out yesterday."

"Still, you could have called me back or sent me a text."

Guin found herself silently counting to ten.

"Well, you've got me now. Is everything okay?" she asked again.

"Everything's fine. I've just been worried about you, what with everything that happened."

"That was months ago, Mom. And I told you, I'm fine."

Guin knew what her mother was really worried about. It wasn't that Guin had been shot and then called off her wedding to Bertram "Birdy" McMurtry, the famous wildlife photographer and ornithologist.* Though she knew her mother had been upset by both things. It was the fact that Guin was single and hadn't given her any grandchildren. Not

---

* See Book 7, *A Perilous Proposal.*

that either of those was her fault.

Guin had wanted to have children. At least two of them. But she and her ex-husband Arthur had tried for years and had been told they suffered from unexplained infertility. Then Art had gone and screwed their hairdresser. And that was the end of that.

"If you're fine, why haven't you called? Your brother calls or texts me nearly every day."

Guin rolled her eyes. She knew her older brother Lance was their mother's favorite. And she was fine with that. But she hated when her mother compared them.

"I told you. I've been busy."

"Doing what? I thought Sanibel was dead this time of year."

"It's almost National Seashell Day, and I'm covering it for the paper."

"National Seashell Day? Is that an actual holiday?"

"Around here it is."

"Well, I hope in your busyness you haven't forgotten about Lavinia's eightieth."

How could I? thought Guin. Her mother had mentioned it practically every time they had spoken over the last six months and had even mailed her a plane ticket. Not that Guin would have forgotten. Lavinia was her stepfather Philip's sister and lived in Bath. And when Guin was a teenager, she had spent a summer with Lavinia and her family, Lavinia's son and daughter being just a bit older than she was.

"I'll be there, Mom. It's on my calendar."

"Good. It's been years since we all got together. And you know how important this is to Philip."

"I know, Mom. I said I'd be there, and I will."

"Lance said you'd be staying with him and Owen, though I was hoping you'd stay with us."

Lance had rented a two-bedroom cottage and insisted

Guin stay with them. Not that Guin needed much convincing. She had no desire to stay with her mother and stepfather at their hotel, even though they wouldn't be sharing a room.   •

"I appreciate the offer, but I prefer not having to dine out every meal. And it will be nice to spend some time with Lance and Owen."

Her mother sniffed.

"Well, if you change your mind, your stepfather and I will be staying at the Royal Crescent."

"Duly noted. So, is there anything else?"

"No. I just wanted to make sure you were okay. I worry about you."

"I'm fine, Mom. Really. And I promise to give you a call next week."

"Very well. Just do me a favor and try to stay out of trouble."

"I'll do that," she said. "Give my love to Philip."

They said goodbye, and Guin slumped against the counter. Speaking with her mother was exhausting. And she was already tired. She thought about taking a nap, but she needed to get Ginny her article on the shell-painting party. But to do so, she would need more coffee.

CHAPTER 3

Despite her fatigue, Guin had managed to bang out a first draft of her article by late afternoon. She would go over it the following morning, then send it off to Ginny. She glanced at the clock on her monitor. It read 5:55. A part of her just wanted to go to bed, but she knew she would wake up at two a.m. if she did.

She glanced out the window. *May as well go for a walk.*

She thought about walking down to the beach, but she was too tired for a long walk. So instead she opted for a quick stroll through the neighborhood, just to give her legs a bit of exercise. Half of her neighbors were snowbirds, who had flown or driven back up north for the summer. But she saw a few of the permanent residents out walking their dogs and smiled and said hello.

When she got back, she made herself some mac and cheese and took her bowl of cheesy goodness into the living room. She plopped down on the couch and turned on the TV. She scrolled through the TV guide and saw that there was a *Murder, She Wrote* marathon on the Hallmark Movies and Mysteries channel. Perfect.

She was half paying attention to what Jessica Fletcher was saying when the show cut to a commercial. And there was the ad for Action Jackson, personal injury attorney. Guin stared at the television screen. A part of her couldn't believe he was dead. And suicide? She knew plenty of seemingly confident people were secretly depressed, but she couldn't see that applying to Jackson Brennan.

She wished she could rewind the ad, but she couldn't. Though she had seen it enough times she practically had it memorized. *Murder, She Wrote* came back on, but Guin was no longer interested in watching a fictional mystery. She wanted to solve the real one in front of her.

She looked down at her bowl of macaroni and cheese. There were a few bites left, but she was no longer hungry. She was also no longer that tired. She washed the bowl, then went to her office. She woke up her computer and did a quick search to see if Jackson Brennan's death had been reported. There was nothing. Though the *San-Cap Sun-Times* and the local papers would no doubt run something soon.

She typed a quick note to Ginny, saying she had spoken to Craig and that the two of them would be investigating Brennan's death, then hit "send."

Monday morning Guin opened her eyes to see light filtering through her shades. She glanced over at her clock. It was a little after six. She got up and peeked out the window. Although it was barely light, it looked like it was going to be a nice morning, no rain. She quickly went into the bathroom, then threw on a pair of shorts and a t-shirt. Less than fifteen minutes later, she was on the beach.

The beach was quiet, with only a few beachcombers and a solitary fisherman. That was one of the things Guin loved about living on Sanibel in June, how you could walk for miles and barely see another soul.

She headed west and immediately came upon a pile of shells the tide had swept in overnight. Guin was not a fan of shell piles. She had no patience to dig for hours in hopes of finding a junonia or an alphabet cone, but she couldn't resist taking a look. There were hundreds, perhaps thousands, of clam shells, scallop shells, kitten paws, ark shells, ceriths, and other common shells. But with a little digging, she was able to find several banded tulips, lettered olives, small horse conchs, and apple and lace murexes, which she placed in her shelling bag.

She was on the verge of moving on, having spent nearly twenty minutes moving shells around with her feet, when she felt her phone vibrating in her back pocket. She removed it and saw she had a new text message. She hoped it was from the detective, whom she hadn't heard from since he had left her that "Gone fishing" note. But it was from Craig.

"Preliminary autopsy report should be out end of day," he had written.

"That was fast," Guin typed back. "Any idea what it says?"

"No," he replied.

Guin knew Craig had contacts in the medical examiner's office. But they were only willing to reveal so much.

"OK. Keep me posted," she texted him. Then she put her phone back in her pocket.

She stared down at the shell pile, but her mind was on Jackson Brennan.

"You find anything?"

Guin jumped, then turned to see a slightly hunched man in his seventies looking at her.

"Lenny! You scared me!"

"Didn't mean to. You were looking pretty intently at those shells. Find anything good?"

Lenny was one of the first people Guin had met on Sanibel. A retired middle school science teacher from Brooklyn, he loved to spend his mornings on the beach, teaching people about seashells and ecology.

"Not really. Though I did find an alphabet cone. I was actually about to leave the pile and head west."

"Mind if I join you?"

"Of course not! Though don't you want to dig through the pile?"

"Meh. Shell piles aren't really my thing. Too much work."

Guin smiled. She totally agreed.

They headed west, both quiet as they focused their attention on the shoreline, stooping to pick up the occasional shell. Guin stopped just past Beach Access #7.

"I should probably turn around and head back."

"Everything okay with you?"

"Yeah, just need to finish an article about the treasure hunt." She paused. "Did you enter?"

In order to participate in the hunt, you had to apply, as the city didn't want hundreds of random people driving all over the island in a mad hunt for buried treasure.

"Nah, I'm too old for stuff like that."

"You are not too old!"

Lenny waved her off.

"Don't you want the five-hundred dollars and your picture in the paper?"

Lenny scowled.

"Just what I need, my picture in the paper."

Guin smiled. Lenny was a bit of a curmudgeon. But that's what she loved about him.

"What about you?"

"Can't. People who are involved with the hunt aren't allowed."

She looked down at the water. Then she saw it. A glint of red. Could it be? She darted in before the tide could drag the shell back out and nearly missed it, grabbing it at the last second. She held it up for Lenny to see. It was a bright red true tulip shell.

"Nice," said Lenny.

Guin examined it and noticed that it had a small piece missing. She frowned. She was a bit of a perfectionist when it came to shells, usually not taking broken ones. But the color was so pretty, and she loved true tulips, so she placed the shell in her bag.

She was about to say she needed to go when she felt her phone vibrating again. It was another text message. This time it was from the detective.

"Get over to the SPD," it read.

That didn't sound good.

"I'm on the beach," she replied.

"When can you get here?"

Guin thought.

"An hour?"

It would take her close to half an hour to get home. Then she needed to change. And the Sanibel Police Department was a good ten minutes from her house.

"OK," the detective typed back.

"Is everything OK?" Guin asked him. But there was no reply.

She frowned.

"Is everything all right?" Lenny asked her.

"I don't know. Detective O'Loughlin wants me to come to the Sanibel Police Department ASAP."

"You find another dead body?"

"No, thank goodness." *Though Bonnie did,* she was tempted to say. Guin tucked the phone back into her pocket. "I should get going."

They said goodbye, and Guin had started walking east when Lenny called out.

"If he throws you in jail, I'd be happy to bail you out!"

Guin stopped and turned. She could see that Lenny was smiling.

"Thanks! I may take you up on that."

Then she turned back around and headed home.

Guin rinsed off her feet, then went inside to change. Ten minutes later, she was on her way to the Sanibel Police Department.

She parked her car in the lot and trotted up the stairs.

"I'm here to see Detective O'Loughlin," she told the woman seated behind the plexiglass partition, someone new she didn't know. "He's expecting me. Guinivere Jones."

The woman asked to see an ID. Guin slid it through the partition. The woman examined it, then returned it to Guin.

"You know where his office is?"

Guin nodded. She had been to the Sanibel Police Department multiple times over the last two years and could have found the detective's office with a blindfold on.

The woman buzzed Guin back, and Guin made her way to the detective's office.

His door was ajar, and she could hear him speaking to someone on the phone. She knocked, then poked her head inside. The detective gestured for her to come in and have a seat.

"I have to go, Mike," he said into the phone. "Thanks for the heads up."

He hung up and looked over at Guin.

"Is everything okay?" she asked him.

"You've been covering the Shell Fairies for the paper."

It was somewhere between a question and a statement.

"I have." She paused. A sense of dread crept over her. "Don't tell me one of them was murdered!"

The detective gave her a sarcastic look.

"Anyone ever tell you that you have an active imagination?"

"Besides you?" said Guin.

He ignored the comment and continued.

"They found a shell on Jackson Brennan's body, in his pocket. It was one of those painted shells."

"So?"

People were constantly finding painted shells on Sanibel.

"This one was painted black with a white skull and crossbones."

"Like a pirate flag?"

"Or poison."

Guin was getting a bad feeling again.

"It also had the words *Time's up!* written on it, on the inside."

"*Time's up?*"

He nodded.

"You happen to know if one of the Shell Fairies painted it?"

Guin didn't recall seeing anyone painting a shell with a skull and crossbones at Shelly's, but someone else could have painted it.

"Do you have a photo?"

The detective took out his phone and showed Guin a picture of the shell.

She took the phone and examined the photo. It was a clam shell, painted black with a white skull and crossbones, just like the detective had said. The painting was very neat, no fuzzy lines or stray blobs of paint. Clearly, whoever had painted it was an artist or had painted on shells before.

"I haven't seen a shell like that," she told him. "But I can ask around."

The detective frowned.

"That's okay."

"It's no trouble," said Guin, who was now eager to find out more about the shell. "If it was painted for the treasure hunt or by one of the Shell Fairies, it should be easy to find out who painted it. I know the head Shell Fairy."

"The head Shell Fairy," said the detective, his lips curling up.

"You know what I mean. Come on, let me help. One of the Shell Fairies must know who painted the shell." She paused. "Wait. Do you think the shell is connected to Brennan's death?"

His face took on a neutral expression, what Guin often referred to as his poker face.

"Maybe."

Guin eyed him.

"What aren't you telling me?"

The detective continued to wear his poker face.

"I heard you on the phone with Mike. Could that have been Mike Gilbertie, the medical examiner?"

Guin knew that the detective and Gilbertie were fishing buddies.

"Were you eavesdropping?"

Guin scowled.

"You were on the phone with him when you told me to come in." They stared at each other. "Come on, Bill. I'm going to find out eventually."

The detective looked like he was thinking it over.

"They found cyanide in Brennan's system."

"Cyanide?"

The detective nodded.

"So that's what killed him?"

"We're still waiting on the official autopsy report. Mike—Mr. Gilbertie—just called to give me a heads up."

Guin's wheels were turning. She knew people took cyanide to kill themselves. At least in the movies. But she couldn't picture Brennan doing it.

"So, you think he killed himself? Or…" She looked at the detective. "Do you think someone forced him to take it?"

The detective didn't reply.

"You know, Craig and I are covering his death for the paper. Ginny's going to want to know."

The detective scowled. Guin tried another tack.

"You speak with Brennan's wife and his assistant?"

He gave her a look, the one that said, *What do you think?*

"Did they say he was suicidal?"

"No. But…"

"But what?"

"We found a note."

"What kind of note? You mean a suicide note?"

The detective looked like he had swallowed something sour.

"Come on, Bill. Spit it out. Did the guy leave a suicide note?"

"In his pocket."

"What did it say?"

Again, the detective looked reluctant to speak.

"It said, 'Sorry for all the pain I've caused.'"

"That's it?"

"That's it."

"Was the note handwritten or typed?"

"Typed, on his letterhead."

"Doesn't that seem a bit odd to you?"

"Why? Is there some kind of etiquette to suicide notes?"

Now it was Guin's turn to frown.

"So what does Gilbertie think?"

"He thinks it was suicide."

"And what do you think?"

"I think it's too soon to say."

"So you don't think he killed himself."

The detective's phone rang. He immediately picked up.

"O'Loughlin." He listened and nodded his head. "I need to call you back." He hung up and turned to Guin. "Talk to the head Shell Fairy. But don't tell her why you're asking. Be discreet. I just want a name."

"Got it. You can count on me!"

"And don't look so excited."

Guin hadn't realized she was grinning and immediately adopted a more serious expression.

"Got it."

"Now if you'll excuse me?"

Guin knew she was being dismissed.

She had opened her mouth to say something, but the detective had already reached for his phone, so she let herself out.

As soon as Guin was back in the parking lot, she took out her phone and called Craig, hoping he wasn't out fishing. He picked up after several rings, just as she was about to leave a message.

"Where are you?" she asked him.

"Walking in the door."

"You going to be home for a bit?"

"I was planning on it. Why?"

"Okay if I swing by?"

"You know you're always welcome. You have breakfast? Betty made bran muffins."

Guin smiled. Craig's wife Betty was always after Craig to eat better and constantly made him healthy, low-calorie, low-sugar foods. Bran muffins, which she studded with raisins, were one of her favorite things to make. However, Craig thought they tasted like sawdust and often tried to pawn some off on Guin.

"I'll be right over," she said.

CHAPTER 4

Craig led Guin into the kitchen.

"Here, have a bran muffin," he said, holding out a plastic container.

"Thanks," said Guin, taking one, though she wasn't hungry.

"Can I get you some coffee?"

"I'm good," she replied. (Craig and Betty drank instant decaf, which Guin couldn't abide.)

"Shall we go out to the lanai?"

Guin nodded and followed him out.

"So," he said, taking a seat, "what's up?"

"I was just at the Sanibel Police Department, meeting with Detective O'Loughlin. He practically ordered me over there," she added.

"And?"

"Would you believe he actually wanted my help?"

Craig smiled.

"Sounds like you finally won him over."

"Eh. I think it had more to do with the subject matter."

Craig looked confused.

"He asked me to identify a shell."

"Why didn't he look it up on the Shell Museum's website?"

"It wasn't that kind of a shell. It was a painted shell." Craig waited for her to go on. "They found it on Brennan."

"So?"

"It was painted with a skull and crossbones and had the words *Time's up* printed on the inside."

"I'm still not following."

"A skull and crossbones is a symbol for poison, and the medical examiner thinks Brennan died from cyanide poisoning."

"And the detective thinks they're connected?"

"He didn't say, but it would be a pretty odd coincidence. And he did ask me to find out who painted the shell."

"Interesting."

"There was also a note."

"What kind of note?"

"A suicide note, supposedly. It was typed on Brennan's letterhead."

"What did it say?"

"Sorry for all the pain I've caused."

"That's it?"

Guin nodded.

Craig was frowning.

"So they think he killed himself?"

"Sounds that way, but…"

"But you're not buying it."

"No. I mean, I know how it looks, but Brennan was a successful attorney with a beautiful wife and daughter. And he didn't seem the least bit depressed or suicidal. Though I didn't really know the guy."

"You know looks can be deceiving. And Brennan was on a bit of a losing streak."

"He was? How do you know?"

"I hear things. I also heard he was planning on running for the open House seat."

"Brennan was planning on running for Congress?"

Craig nodded.

"So if he was planning on running for Congress, why kill himself?"

"Why indeed?"

They sat on the lanai contemplating that for several seconds.

"So, did you know who painted that shell?"

"No, but it should be pretty easy to find out if it was one of the Shell Fairies. I'll give Mary Ann Pinkham a call. She's one of the administrators of the group and the treasure hunt liaison."

"And if it wasn't painted by one of the Shell Fairies? Then what?"

Guin frowned. She hadn't thought of that.

"I can make some private inquiries."

"You speak with Ginny?"

"About the Brennan story?" Craig nodded. "I sent her an email. Why, did you hear from her?"

As if on cue, Craig's phone began to ring. It was Ginny.

"Speak of the devil." He swiped to answer. "Virginia, how good of you to call. I was just talking about you."

Guin watched as Craig listened to Ginny and bobbed his head.

"I was actually the one who suggested it," he told her. "With the Boca Grande Tarpon Tournament, I don't really have time to look into the Brennan matter this week. And Guin's more than capable."

He listened again and bobbed his head.

"I promise," he said, then ended the call.

"So?"

"Ginny said it was fine to work together."

Guin felt relieved. Not that she really thought Ginny would say no. But Brennan was a local celebrity of sorts. So no doubt bigger papers would be looking into his death. And Ginny hated to be scooped.

"And what's this about a tarpon tournament in Boca Grande?"

"You don't know about it?"

Guin shook her head.

"I don't fish, remember?"

"How can you live on Sanibel and not fish?"

"How can you live on Sanibel and not be into shells?"

"Touché," said Craig.

"So when's the tournament?"

"It starts Thursday, but we're heading to Gasparilla Wednesday."

Boca Grande was located on Gasparilla Island, just north of Sanibel.

"So Betty's going with you?"

"Yup. Said I wasn't going without her."

Guin smiled.

"Well, have fun." She paused. "So, how do you want to work the Brennan story?"

"I was planning on looking into his business dealings. You want to speak with the wife and his assistant?"

"Sure."

Though Guin wasn't sure how much information she would get out of Brennan's assistant, Wanda. Wanda tended to guard information as though it was precious, which to a lawyer like Brennan it probably was. No doubt he had instructed her to be stingy with it. Though maybe now that Brennan was dead, Wanda would be more helpful.

She got up and Craig followed suit.

"Let me know when you're back and we can compare notes."

"Sounds good," he said, following her back inside. "Though who knows? You may have cracked the case by then."

Guin stopped and turned.

"Doubtful." She glanced around. "Where's Betty?"

"Playing bridge."

"Ah. Well, tell her I said hi and thanks for the bran muffin."

"I will. Though you didn't touch yours."

Guin looked down at her hand, which was still clutching the uneaten bran muffin.

"I'll eat it when I get home."

Craig walked her to the door.

"Have fun at the tarpon tournament!" she called.

He smiled and waved goodbye.

As soon as she got home, Guin called Shelly. She was going to call Mary Ann, but as Shelly was also a Shell Fairy and knew all the Shell Fairy gossip, she figured she'd ask her about the shell first.

She picked up after a few rings.

"Ooh, a phone call! To what do I owe the honor?"

"I call you plenty," said Guin.

"You usually text first."

"Should I hang up and text you?"

"Don't be silly. What's up?"

"Do you happen to know if anyone painted a shell with a skull and crossbones for the treasure hunt?"

"A skull and crossbones, like a pirate flag?"

Guin nodded.

"Yeah."

There was silence on the other end of the line for several seconds.

"I don't recall seeing any shells like that, though it's a great idea. Perfect for the treasure hunt. You ask Mary Ann?"

"Not yet. I figured I'd ask you first."

"Ask Mary Ann. She'd know."

"I will. Thanks."

"So, while I have you on the phone, you want to grab a bite later this week? Steve's going out of town on business."

"Sure. Just say when."

"Great. I'll text you."

They ended the call and Guin decided to check out the Shell Fairy Facebook page before calling Mary Ann. It was unlikely someone had posted a picture of the shell, as the shells for the treasure hunt were supposed to be top secret. But in case the shell hadn't been intended for the treasure hunt…

She clicked on the page and began to scroll.

There were lots of beautifully painted shells, but there wasn't one painted with a skull and crossbones.

She picked up her phone to call Mary Ann, then sent her a Facebook message instead. If Mary Ann didn't get back to her by the end of the day, she would call her.

And speaking of painted shells, she had nearly forgotten about her article. She pulled it up and began reading through it.

By the time she was done going through it one last time, it was after noon, and Guin could feel her stomach grumbling. She opened her email and sent the article to Ginny. Then she went into the kitchen and made herself a peanut butter and jelly sandwich.

Guin looked at the clock on her monitor. How did it get to be four o'clock? She had planned on going to Jackson Brennan's law office that afternoon, but it typically closed at four. And she had no idea if anyone would even be there. She picked up her phone and dialed the number, but the call went straight to voicemail. She thought about emailing Wanda but decided she needed to speak with her in person. She gazed out the window and sighed. She had a feeling this story would not go easily.

She turned back to her computer and typed in the name of Brennan's wife's boutique, Paradise Found, which was located on the East End of Sanibel, near the lighthouse. It was supposedly open until six. Though would Beth even be there? Guin had interviewed Beth Brennan the year before, just after she had opened the boutique. It was a cute place, as Guin recalled, with resort wear and beach- and Sanibel-themed tchotchkes and souvenirs. But she hadn't been there in months, rarely visiting the East End, except to go the lighthouse.

She dug up her article, which had featured a smiling image of Beth. She was around Guin's age, maybe a few years older, with blonde hair and blue eyes. Brennan had given his wife the money to open the store, and Guin was pretty sure he had been funding it. What would happen to the boutique now?

Guin then went to Paradise Found's Facebook page to see if the store had closed in light of Jackson Brennan's death. There were lots of pictures and general information but nothing about the store being closed.

She clicked on the link to send a message and started to type. Then she deleted what she had written. She would call there in the morning and see if they were open—and when Beth might be there. If she had taken time off, Guin could always try her at home.

CHAPTER 5

A little after six, Guin received a Facebook Messenger notification on her phone. It was from Mary Ann.

"Just saw your message. The shell sounds familiar. Can I get back to you? I don't remember off the top of my head who painted it."

"Sure," Guin wrote back. "Thanks."

She had just closed the app when her phone started to vibrate. It was her friend Glen.

Glen was a photographer with the paper, technically a freelance photographer, and had helped Guin finish the renovation of her house. (In a previous life he had worked as a carpenter and handyman and still liked to fix things.)

Like Guin, Glen was in his forties and divorced. He had moved to Fort Myers from New York City to help care for his aging parents. And the two of them had instantly clicked.

But there was nothing romantic between them. At least not on Guin's side. Sure, Glen was good-looking and funny and a talented photographer. But he reminded Guin a little too much of her ex, Art. And besides, Guin was with the detective.

She swiped to answer.

"Hey, Glen, what's up?"

"You want to grab a bite to eat?"

"When?"

"Now. Well, technically around forty-five minutes from now."

Guin thought. It wasn't like she had plans or a lot of food in her fridge.

"Where are you?"

"I'm up on Captiva, just finishing up an assignment."

Guin was mulling it over.

"Come on. I'll meet you someplace on Sanibel, my treat."

"You don't have to treat me."

"Just say you'll have dinner with me."

"Fine. Where were you thinking?"

"You want to meet me over at the Clam Shack? We could get a couple of lobster rolls, some beer... It's a beautiful evening, and they have live music."

"How can I refuse?"

"Excellent. I'll meet you there at seven. Grab us a table if you beat me there."

"Will do."

"So, what were you doing up on Captiva?"

They were seated on the Clam Shack's deck, drinking beer and listening to guitar music.

"Doing some pre-wedding shots for a couple whose wedding I'm photographing this weekend."

"At South Seas?"

Glen nodded.

"Nice couple?"

"Nice enough."

Wedding photography was one of Glen's side hustles.

"I imagine you have a fair amount of wedding photography this time of year."

"Not really. But that's fine by me."

Their lobster rolls came out, and they dug in.

"So, what does Ginny have you working on?"

"Some treasure hunt stuff and some headshots mostly." He took a bite of his lobster roll. "You hear about Jackson Brennan?"

She was surprised he knew. Then again, Sanibel was a small town.

"What did you hear exactly?"

"That he killed himself."

"Where'd you hear that?"

"Around." He took a sip of his beer and eyed her. "You know something, don't you?"

Guin glanced around, to make sure no one could hear them.

"Not really. At least not yet. Craig and I are covering his death for the paper."

He was still looking at her.

"You don't think it was suicide?"

"I don't know. But doesn't it seem odd to you that someone like Action Jackson would just up and kill himself?"

Glen smiled.

"Those billboards and ads always crack me up. 'If you want action, call Jackson!'"

Guin smiled at the imitation.

"They are a bit over the top."

"A bit? You ask me, it was all an act."

"An act?"

"I knew guys just like Brennan back when I worked on Wall Street. Always acting like they were hot stuff when in reality they were knee-deep in debt with their wives about to leave them."

"You think Brennan was in debt and his wife was about to leave him?" Though Guin wouldn't have blamed Beth. Brennan had a wandering eye—and she doubted that she was the only client he had grabbed and kissed.

"I don't know, but it wouldn't surprise me. Now how about we change the subject?"

"Fine by me. You going to get away at all over the summer?"

"As a matter of fact, I'm off to the Hamptons in a few

weeks to photograph a friend's wedding."

"Nice. They paying you?"

"No, it's my gift to the groom—and the bride."

"Must be a good friend."

"He is. What about you? Any plans?"

"I'm going to my step-aunt's eightieth birthday celebration in Bath."

"That should be fun."

"Oh, yeah."

The way she said it indicated otherwise.

"You not get along with your step-aunt?"

"She's fine. Mostly. It's more my mother. Lavinia's kids are both happily married with kids of their own. Whereas poor Guin is all alone and childless," she said in a pouty voice.

Glen looked at her.

"Come with me to Italy."

"Excuse me?" said Guin, taken aback. "I thought you said you were going to the Hamptons."

"I am. Then I'm going to Italy to attend a cooking course."

"I thought you didn't like to cook."

"That's because I wasn't very good at it. But I've been watching videos on YouTube." Guin smiled. She could just picture Glen learning to cook by watching YouTube videos. "And then Bridget invited me to attend her cooking course in Tuscany. And, well…"

"Who's Bridget?"

"A friend from my Wall Street days. She went to Italy on vacation, met a butcher, and stayed. Now she teaches a cooking course in Chianti a few times a year, and she invited me to attend."

"Nice. When is the class?"

"July twelfth through the eighteenth. When are you going to Bath?"

"The third. Then I fly back the following Thursday."

"Perfect. Just fly to Tuscany instead."

"You serious?"

"I am. It'll be fun. You should come."

"Won't the class be booked?"

"I'm sure Bridget could squeeze in one more."

Guin wasn't so sure about that.

"Thanks for the offer, but…"

"Don't say no yet. Let me send you the info, then you can decide. Besides, Sanibel is dead in July."

"Tell that to Ginny."

"You want me to speak with her? I will, you know. Actually… You and I could do a piece on the course. I bet our readers would eat it up. I mean, who doesn't dream of spending a week in a Tuscan villa learning how to cook?"

"I don't know…" said Guin. Though it wasn't the craziest idea she had heard. And it was tempting.

"Just think about it."

"Okay, I'll think about it."

Glen grinned.

They finished their lobster rolls and listened to the guitar player.

"Would you two like some dessert?" asked the server.

"I'm good," said Guin.

"Just the check," said Glen.

A minute later the server returned with the check, which Glen insisted on paying.

Guin was watching the Food Network when she received an email from Glen with a link to the Tuscan cooking course.

She clicked on the link and was immediately transported to the hills of Tuscany. The class took place at a restored Tuscan villa located in the Chianti region, in a small town called Greve that Guin had never heard of. The villa, now a boutique hotel, was perched on a hillside and had a gorgeous pool with views of the rolling countryside and a garden.

There was information about Bridget and her course too. As Glen said, Bridget was a former Wall Streeter with a passion for cooking who had gone to Italy on vacation and stayed, marrying a butcher who owned a restaurant. After working with him for a year, she decided to begin teaching cooking classes, using local ingredients and recipes. Then she had partnered with a local boutique hotel to offer guests a unique culinary experience.

Guin thought it sounded like a dream come true and sighed. If only she didn't have to go to Bath.

She was staring at her phone when it began to vibrate. It was Glen.

"You click on that link I sent you?"

"Yes, you evil man."

She could tell Glen was smiling.

"It sounds pretty good, doesn't it?"

"It sounds amazing. But I can't go."

"Why not?"

"I told you why not."

"Those weren't good excuses. Come on, let me speak to Ginny."

Guin wavered.

"I need to think about it."

"Well, don't think about it for too long."

"Good night, Glen."

"Good night, Guinivere."

She ended the call and looked down at the pictures of the cooking course on her phone. Cooking in Chianti did have a nice ring to it.

CHAPTER 6

That night Guin dreamed she was in Tuscany. She was having a wonderful time, eating delicious food, visiting a vineyard, checking out the local shops, sunning herself by the pool. Then it was time for her to go home. But her ride to the airport was late. Then they got lost. And she wound up missing her flight. In a panic, she went in search of another flight, but they were all booked.

Guin could feel her anxiety rising. Was there no way for her to get home? Just then she felt a tap on her shoulder and jumped. She woke up to find Fauna pawing her. There was light coming through her shades, so she knew it must be after six. Fauna pawed her again and mewed.

"Okay, okay," said Guin. "Just give me a minute to calm down."

She closed her eyes and placed a hand over her heart, slowly taking a deep breath in, then releasing it. She did that two more times, then opened her eyes to find Fauna looking at her.

"I need to pee. Then I'll feed you."

She went to the bathroom, then headed to the kitchen, Fauna trotting behind her. She opened a can of wet food and dumped the contents in Fauna's bowl.

"There. You happy now?"

Guin watched as Fauna inhaled bits of turkey, then turned and headed back to her bedroom to get dressed.

It was gray and cloudy, a bit like her mood, but Guin headed to the beach anyway. She liked being on the beach just before a storm. As she walked, breathing in the sea air, she could feel the tension melting away.

She thought about her dream as she walked, wondering what it meant. She had clearly enjoyed being in Tuscany, but the terror of not being able to get home… Though not like being stuck in Tuscany was a bad thing. What was she afraid of?

Before she knew it, she had walked past Beach Access #1. She looked around. The beach was practically empty. And was that a raindrop? She looked up at the sky. It had grown ominous. If it wasn't raining yet, it soon would be.

Guin turned around and quickly headed west, not bothering to look for shells. As she walked in the door, it began to pour. She had made it home just in time.

By nine-thirty the rain had ended. Perfect timing. She would go to Jackson Brennan's office to speak with his assistant, Wanda. Guin had spent the morning searching for information about the attorney, something that might indicate why he had killed himself. If, in fact, he had. Guin still wasn't convinced. Everything she had found online attested to Brennan being a success. Though she didn't trust the internet. She would need to take a deeper dive later.

She drove east on Periwinkle Way, Sanibel's main thoroughfare, until she arrived at the office of Brennan & Associates. She pulled in and parked her purple Mini in the lot. She locked the car, then jogged up the stairs. The lights were on inside the office, and she saw Wanda at her desk.

Guin knocked on the plate glass window and waved, but either Wanda didn't hear her or was ignoring her. Guin went to the door and found it unlocked.

She knocked, then poked her head inside.

"You open?"

"What do you think?" said Wanda, glancing over at her, a scowl on her face.

Guin stepped inside, then walked over to Wanda's desk. "Do you have a minute?"

Wanda stopped what she was doing and looked up at Guin.

"No. But you clearly have something you want to ask."

"I was sorry to hear about Mr. Brennan," she lied. Wanda didn't say anything. "I imagine it was quite a blow."

Wanda continued to look at Guin, not saying anything.

"I gather he left a lot of work," said Guin, seeing the stack of folders on Wanda's desk.

"Is there something I can help you with, Ms. Jones? I appreciate your concern, but as you can see, I'm rather busy."

"Of course," said Guin. "Is there someone helping you?"

"Mr. Dewey and I are managing."

"Mr. Dewey?"

"Mr. Brennan's partner."

"Mr. Brennan's partner? I wasn't aware Mr. Brennan had taken on a partner. When did that happen?"

"A few months ago."

"And his name is Dewey?"

Wanda nodded.

"What's his first name?"

"Tom."

Tom Dewey. The name sounded familiar, but Guin couldn't place it.

"Is he from around here?" Guin asked.

"No, Chicago."

"Could I speak with him?"

"He's not here," said Wanda. "Now, if you would excuse me?" She glanced down at the pile of folders.

Guin knew that was her cue to leave, but she still had more questions.

"I understand Mr. Brennan lost some cases recently," Guin said, not taking the hint. "That must have been upsetting. Would you say Mr. Brennan was depressed before he died?"

Wanda stopped what she was doing and looked up at Guin.

"Are you asking me if I think Mr. Brennan killed himself?"

Guin nodded.

"I'll tell you what I told that detective," said Wanda, looking more annoyed than upset by the question. "Mr. Jackson Brennan was the last person who would take his own life."

"Because he was Catholic?"

"Because he wasn't the type."

"And what type is that?" asked Guin, curious to know the answer.

"Mr. Brennan may have lost a couple of cases, but he didn't sit around moping about it like some people would." She looked at Guin. "He was a fighter."

"So you don't think he killed himself?"

Wanda gave Guin the same look the detective would give her when he thought the answer to a question was obvious.

"So if he didn't kill himself…" Guin trailed off. "Do you think someone—maybe an angry client—could have killed him and made it look like suicide?"

"What I think doesn't matter. Now if you would excuse me, I've got work to do."

Guin was about to see herself out when the front door was flung open and a well-dressed woman, who looked to be in her fifties, stormed in. Guin recognized her. It was Audra Linwood, one of Sanibel's top real estate agents.

Audra marched over to Wanda's desk, placed her hands on the edge, and leaned over, completely ignoring Guin.

"I need those files, Wanda."

Wanda looked unphased by the angry woman leaning over her.

"I told you, Ms. Linwood, that's up to Mr. Dewey."

"Before he died, Jack told me he would hand over the files. They're mine! I paid for them!"

"That may be, but you need to speak with Mr. Dewey," said Wanda calmly.

Guin watched as the two women stared at each other, neither giving an inch.

"Fine. You'll be hearing from my lawyer," said Audra. Then she noticed Guin. "Who are you?"

"Guin Jones. I work for the *Sanibel-Captiva Sun-Times*."

Audra eyed her.

"You covering Jack's death for the paper?"

"I am."

"We should talk."

"I'd be happy to. I take it you were a client of Mr. Brennan's?"

"Was," said Audra. "I ditched his no-good ass months ago."

Guin was surprised by Audra Linwood's tone and word choice.

"How come?"

"He was a loser."

Wanda tsked.

"Doesn't say much for you. You're just sore because of that land deal. And you know that wasn't Mr. Brennan's fault."

Audra sneered.

"You would say that. Then again, you always took his side. Hope he paid you well."

Guin heard a phone ringing. It was Audra's. Audra removed it from her bag and frowned. Then she looked over at Wanda.

"I need to go. But I expect those files to be turned over to me by the end of the week."

She turned and stormed out.

Guin watched her leave, then looked at Wanda.

"What was that about?"

Wanda was looking at the door, shaking her head.

"Ms. Linwood's just angry that she and her partner didn't get the land that was up for sale over on the West End."

"What land?"

Wanda looked at Guin.

"The parcel over on Wulfert."

Guin racked her brain. Then she remembered.

"You mean the land SCCF acquired over by Ding Darling?"

SCCF stood for Sanibel-Captiva Conservation Foundation, and Ding Darling was how locals referred to the J. N. "Ding" Darling National Wildlife Refuge.

Wanda nodded.

"What did Mr. Brennan have to do with it?"

"He was working with the developers, Ms. Linwood and her partner."

"Ah," said Guin.

She was about to ask who Ms. Linwood's partner was, but Wanda cut her off.

"Good day, Ms. Jones."

Guin knew she would get no more out of Wanda, at least today. But she had one more question she needed to ask.

"When will Mr. Dewey be in?"

"I don't know."

"Well, would you ask him to get in touch with me when he gets back?" She took out a card and placed it on Wanda's desk. "He can email, text, or call me, whatever's easier."

Wanda looked down at the card, then up at Guin.

"I'll let him know."

"Thank you," said Guin. She stood there awkwardly for a few seconds, then turned and left.

As she went down the stairs, she wondered if Wanda would pass along her message to Tom Dewey. The odds were fifty-fifty… or maybe forty-sixty. If she didn't hear from him, she'd follow up.

She reached the bottom of the stairs and unlocked the Mini. It was strange that she hadn't known about Brennan taking on a partner. Though the name Tom Dewey rang a bell. Again, she couldn't place it. She would have to look him up when she got home.

She got in her car and thought about her next move. Paradise Found was just a short distance away. Might as well drive over.

CHAPTER 7

Guin parked in the lot and made her way to the shop, which was located at the end of the small strip mall. The door tinkled as she opened it.

A young woman behind the cash register was checking her phone.

"Excuse me," said Guin, trying to get her attention. "Is Beth in?"

"She's in back," said the young woman, still looking at her phone. Guin waited for the young woman to look up. Finally, she did. "Can I help you with something?"

"Could you let Ms. Brennan know that Guin Jones from the *Sanibel-Captiva Sun-Times* is here to see her?"

"You doing an article on our one-year-anniversary?"

Guin thought about lying.

"Actually…"

But before she could say more the young woman had picked up the phone.

"Hey, Beth, I have a reporter here to interview you about the big one-year celebration." She nodded. "Okay, I'll tell her."

The young woman put down the phone.

"She'll be right out."

"Thanks," said Guin.

She glanced around the shop as she waited. A few minutes later, Beth Brennan appeared.

"Guin! How nice to see you again!" she said, a smile on her face.

"Nice to see you too, Beth. I was so sorry to hear about Mr. Brennan."

Beth's smile turned into a frown.

"Thank you. We were all pretty shocked."

"I'm sure. Actually, I'm a bit surprised you're here."

"I know. But this store is my baby, and I couldn't leave it unattended."

"But surely you have help."

The young woman at the front desk was once again typing on her phone, oblivious to the conversation going on nearby.

"Yes, but..." Beth glanced at the young woman and frowned. "Come. Let me give you a tour. We've made a number of changes since you were last here."

Guin allowed Beth to show her around. She would need to have a word with Ginny later about doing a piece on the store's one-year anniversary.

When they were done, Beth turned to her.

"So, what do you think?"

"The place looks great," said Guin. And it did.

Beth beamed.

"I'm so glad you think so! I've put my heart and soul into this place." She paused. "Do you have any questions for the article?"

"Actually," said Guin, again feeling a bit uncomfortable. "I do. But they concern your husband." Beth frowned. "Is there somewhere we can talk... privately?"

"Let's go to my office."

Beth turned and led Guin to a room near the back of the store. It was cramped, with barely room for a desk and a small table. And there wasn't really anywhere for Guin to sit as the lone chair was covered with clothing. Beth hastily moved the clothing aside and indicated for Guin to have a seat. She then sat in the chair by her computer.

"So, what is it you want to know?"

Again, Guin was struck by how calm Beth was. Though maybe she was in shock? She knew grief affected people differently.

"The medical examiner believes your husband took his own life."

"Cyanide poisoning, I know. But as I told Detective O'Loughlin, Jack would never kill himself."

"And why is that?"

"He wasn't the type. And he was about to announce his run for Congress."

So the rumor was true.

"So the loss of those cases and the land deal didn't bother him?"

"Oh, they bothered him all right. But they only made him want to fight harder, not give up."

"So what do you think happened?"

"I don't know."

Guin didn't really believe that, but she didn't want to push Beth too hard.

"Is it possible he could have taken the cyanide accidentally… or that someone gave it to him?"

Guin watched Beth's face. It looked as though she was mulling something over.

"Are there any clients who were unhappy with him? What about those cases he lost?"

"Well, there was that landscaper. He was pretty angry when Jack lost his case."

"Landscaper? Do you recall his name?"

Beth scrunched her face, trying to recall it. Then she lit up.

"It was Martin! No, wait. He pronounced it Mar-TEEN."

"What happened?"

"He hired Jack to help him with a personal injury lawsuit. He was maimed by a client's dog."

"And Jack lost the case?"

Beth nodded.

"He was very upset. Claimed Jack told him he never lost, that the case was a slam dunk. Then when Jack lost, Martín refused to pay the bill. Said Jack told him he only charged if he won."

"That wasn't the case?"

"Jack doesn't work for free."

Guin frowned. She knew that many personal injury lawyers took a percentage of the award if they won and didn't charge the client if they lost. But she didn't know if that was how Brennan operated. She would need to ask Wanda or Tom Dewey. Though why would the landscaper lie? She would need to talk to him too.

"So did this landscaper make any threats against your husband?"

Beth nodded.

"He did, but Jack didn't take them seriously."

"I see," said Guin. "Is there anyone else who might have been unhappy with your husband?"

"Well, there's Audra Linwood. She and that partner of hers were pretty steamed when that land deal fell through."

"The one up on Wulfert?"

Beth nodded.

"Audra was furious. She fired Jack right after and said she would make him regret screwing her." Beth snorted, and Guin wondered what was so funny.

"You said Audra had a partner?"

Another nod.

"Some guy from New York named Tony Mandelli."

Beth looked like she had just eaten something sour. Guin tried not to stare.

"I'm sorry. Did you say Tony Mandelli?"

"Yes. Why? You know him?"

Now it was Guin's turn to nod.

"I do."

Guin had met Anthony Mandelli shortly after moving to Sanibel, when she had been looking into the death of a prominent Captiva real estate developer. Mandelli was the man's silent partner, and he had tried to seduce Guin—and then nearly raped her when she resisted his charms.

"Did he hit on you?"

Guin tried not to stare.

"How did you know?"

"He hit on me too. Guys like that think they're God's gift to the world and that every woman wants to sleep with them."

"But you're married."

"Please," said Beth.

"And your husband was doing business with him."

Beth snorted.

"Like Jack would care."

Guin didn't know what to make of that.

"Do you think Mandelli could have had something to do with Jack's death?"

"It's possible. I wouldn't put it past him. Though I don't think Jack had seen him since right after the land deal went south."

"Is there anyone else who might have wanted to harm Mr. Brennan or bore a grudge? What about his assistant?"

"Wanda?"

Guin nodded.

"Wanda was fiercely loyal to Jack. He hired her right after she fled here from Haiti, took her in and helped her get her green card. She's the last person who would want something bad to happen to him."

"What about his new partner, Tom Dewey?"

"Tom? Tom wouldn't hurt a fly."

So that left the landscaper and Audra Linwood—and Tony Mandelli.

Guin was about to ask Beth another question when there was a knock at the door, and the young woman from up front poked her head in.

"I'm sorry to disturb you, Beth, but I need your help with a customer."

"I'll be right there, Paris."

Paris left, and Guin turned to Beth.

"Her name's Paris? Like the city?"

Beth smiled.

"She was actually named for Paris Hilton."

Guin could believe it. She even looked a bit like her namesake, as well as a younger version of Beth.

Beth got up and Guin followed her to the front of the store.

"Thank you for your time," said Guin as they neared the register. "And I'll speak with Ginny about an anniversary piece."

"I'd appreciate that," said Beth.

"And if you think of anyone else who might have had an issue with your husband, please let me know."

Beth took the card Guin held out to her.

"I will."

Paris was silently indicating the customer Beth was to speak with, and Beth excused herself. Guin watched as Beth smiled and calmly dealt with the woman. No one would know Beth's husband had just died. It sent a small shiver down Guin's spine. Guin stayed for a few more seconds, then left.

She was about to get in her Mini when Paris came racing out.

"Ms. Jones!" she called. Guin stopped and turned.

Paris stopped in front of the Mini, admiring it.

"Is that your ride?"

"It is."

"Sweet."

"Is there something I can help you with, Paris?"

Paris looked conflicted.

"It's about Mr. Brennan."

"What about him?"

Paris fidgeted.

"I should go back inside. Do you have another card?"

Guin reached into her bag and produced one.

"I'll text you," said Paris. Then she turned and ran back into the boutique.

Guin watched her go, wondering what that was about.

CHAPTER 8

As the *Sanibel-Captiva Sun-Times* office was on her way home, Guin decided to stop by and pay a visit to Ginny. She was one of only a handful of people who actually worked out of the office. All of the writers and photographers worked remotely.

Guin entered, but there was no one at the front desk. (During the season, which ran from October to May, the paper employed a college intern, who usually sat in that spot.)

"Hello?" she called. "Anybody home?"

A dog began to bark, and a few seconds later Peanut, the creative director's miniature labradoodle, bounded out. Guin bent down and petted the pup.

"You on reception duty today, Peanut?" she asked him.

Peanut barked and wagged his tail. Guin laughed.

"Sorry about that!" said Jasmine, emerging from the back. "He gets so excited whenever someone shows up."

"No worries," said Guin. "Is Ginny in?"

Jasmine nodded.

"She's in her office."

"You think it's okay to go back?"

"I don't see why not."

"She's not on the phone or in a meeting?"

"Ginny's always on the phone. But I'm sure she'd be happy to see you." Jasmine turned to her dog. "Come on, Peanut."

The dog obediently followed his mistress, and Guin headed back to Ginny's office.

Ginny's door was ajar, and Guin didn't hear anything. But just in case, she knocked.

"What is it now?" Ginny called.

Guin poked her head in. Ginny was studying something on her computer.

"I was in the neighborhood and thought I'd say hello."

Ginny turned and looked over at Guin.

"Guinivere." Guin hesitated. "Don't be shy. Come on in and take a load off."

Guin stepped inside and glanced down at the two chairs across from Ginny's desk. As usual, they were piled with folders, papers, and magazines. Guin removed one of the piles and sat.

"So, how goes it?" asked Ginny. However, before Guin could answer, Ginny spoke again. "I read over your piece on the shell-painting party. Not bad. A shame we can't actually include pictures of the finished shells."

Guin agreed, but they both understood why they couldn't.

"Speaking of shells and the treasure hunt," said Guin. "Did you know that a painted shell was found on Brennan's body? It had a skull and crossbones on it, with the words *Time's up!* on the inside."

"You think it could have something to do with his death?"

"I don't know, but it would be an odd coincidence, considering that a skull and crossbones is a symbol for poison and Brennan was poisoned."

Ginny looked thoughtful.

"Well, only one way to find out. You talk to Brennan's wife and colleagues?"

"I have, albeit briefly. But I didn't ask them about the shell. I also communicated with Mary Ann Pinkham, to find out who might have painted it."

"Good thinking. Well, let me know what you find out."

"About Brennan… Do you really think he killed himself?"

"If you had asked me that a week ago, I'd say no. But…"

"But what?"

"But you can never really know why someone decided to end it," said Ginny.

"I heard he had lost a couple of cases recently," said Guin. "And you know what a big ego Brennan had."

"True, but I can't picture him swallowing cyanide just because a couple of verdicts didn't go his way. He struck me as the type to lie about it, not die."

Guin had to agree.

"Though there was also the land deal that fell through."

"You mean the land up on Wulfert?" Guin nodded. "I confess, I was a bit surprised that SCCF managed to snag it, considering. But again, I wouldn't have thought Brennan was the type to kill himself over a failed real estate deal."

"And he was planning on running for Congress. Though, do you think he had a real shot?"

Ginny shrugged.

"I wouldn't have voted for him. But you never know. He certainly had the name recognition. Anyway, you and Craig should keep digging. In the meantime, I have another assignment for you." Guin waited as Ginny shuffled through some papers on her desk, then looked back up. "A new restaurant just opened over by Bailey's, the Savoury Spoon."

"I know the couple who runs it," said Guin. "If it's the same people who had a stall at the farmers market."

"It is. So, you've had their food?"

Guin nodded.

"Many times. I'm addicted to their waffles on a stick and smoothies."

"Good. So this should be an easy assignment. Even though you've had their food, you should still check out their new place. Running a restaurant's not the same as running a stall at the farmers market."

"Of course. And I will be totally objective. When do you want the review?"

"I'd like to run it before the Fourth. So get it to me as soon as you can."

"You got it. Anything else?"

"Why, you got too much time on your hands?"

"Hardly. Just asking. And don't forget, I'm leaving on the third."

"Got it on my calendar."

Guin thought about asking Ginny about taking a second week off but chickened out.

"I guess I'll be going then," she said, getting up.

Her hand was on the doorknob when Ginny called, "And sorry to hear about O'Loughlin."

Guin stopped and turned.

"Sorry? Did something happen to him?"

She had just seen him.

"He didn't tell you?"

"Tell me what?"

"That he's leaving Sanibel."

Guin stared at her boss.

"He's leaving Sanibel? Like forever?"

"I don't know about forever, but I heard he handed in his resignation."

"He resigned? Why?"

"Don't know. I only know he handed in his resignation and they're looking for a replacement."

"When did this happen?"

"Pretty recently. I just heard. I'm surprised you hadn't."

Guin was too.

"Do you know when he's leaving?"

"No. I think he's planning on sticking around until they find his replacement."

Guin didn't know what to say. She was too stunned.

"I should go."

She turned and left Ginny's office, not bothering to say goodbye to Jasmine on her way out. She got to the Mini, then began to pace.

How could he resign without saying anything? Did it have something to do with me or with us?

She pulled out her phone and was about to call him when she speed-dialed Craig instead.

"Did you know Detective O'Loughlin resigned and was leaving Sanibel?"

There was silence on the other end of the line.

"Oh my God, you did know. And you didn't say anything?! Does everyone know?" *Except me?* she added silently.

"I don't think it's public yet. And I only just found out. I thought you knew."

"Well, I didn't. Ginny just told me."

Silence again.

"Why did he resign? I thought he was happy here."

"I don't know."

Guin stopped pacing and closed her eyes. Then she took a deep breath and slowly released it.

"Are you okay?" asked Craig.

"No."

"You want to come over?"

"That's okay." Guin tried to control her emotions. *Focus on work*, she told herself. "Did you know that Brennan had a partner?"

"I did not. What's his name?"

"Tom Dewey."

"Like the former governor of New York?"

Guin didn't reply.

"You know, the guy who narrowly lost to Roosevelt and then Truman."

Again, nothing from Guin.

"Don't they teach kids U.S. history anymore?"

"Sorry, U.S. history wasn't my strong suit."

Craig sighed.

"So, you speak with this Tom Dewey?"

"Not yet. He wasn't there when I stopped by the office. I also paid a visit to Brennan's wife."

"What did she have to say?"

"She gave me some names of people who were unhappy with her husband, including one Anthony Mandelli."

"The same one that...?"

"The same, unless there's another Anthony Mandelli from New York who invests in real estate. Apparently, he and Brennan and Audra Linwood were hoping to buy that big tract up by Wulfert and build condos there. And neither he nor Audra was thrilled with Brennan when the deal fell through."

"Understandable. But you don't really think they killed him over a failed deal?"

"It was a pretty big deal."

"So you still don't think he offed himself."

"I don't. It just doesn't make sense."

"Suicide often doesn't."

"I know, but Brennan's wife also mentioned that her husband had gotten into it with one of his clients, a local landscaper named Martín. Martín had hired Brennan to help him with a personal injury case. Brennan had told him it was a slam dunk and would only charge him if he won. Then he lost, and Brennan sent him a bill. A pretty big bill, I take it. And the landscaper was furious."

"Furious enough to kill him?"

"I don't know. But one of us should speak with him."

"What about Mandelli? One of us should talk with him too."

Guin bit her lip. The last thing she wanted to do was

speak with the man who had nearly raped her. But she would if she had to.

"Why don't I speak with him?" said Craig, sensing her apprehension.

"Thank you. But what about the tarpon tournament in Boca Grande?"

"I think I can do both."

Of course he could.

"That would be great. And I'll speak with the landscaper and Audra Linwood."

"You sure?"

"Yeah, no problem."

"I already put some feelers out regarding Brennan. I'll let you know if I find out anything."

"Sounds good. When will you be back from Gasparilla?"

"Friday afternoon or else Saturday."

"Okay. Have fun. And let me know if you catch any tarpon."

"I'm purely there as an observer."

Yeah, right, thought Guin. She knew Craig wouldn't be able to resist doing a little fishing.

They said goodbye and Guin ended the call, feeling much calmer. Then she unlocked the Mini and got in. She had only driven a short distance when she passed the sign for Audra Linwood's real estate office and made a U-turn.

A young woman was seated at the reception desk. She smiled at Guin, and Guin smiled back.

"May I help you?" she asked cheerfully.

"I'd like to speak to Ms. Linwood."

"Do you have an appointment?"

"No. I'm with the *Sanibel-Captiva Sun-Times*, and…"

As if summoned from a magic lamp, Audra Linwood appeared.

"You're here from the *Sanibel-Captiva Sun-Times*? Did Ginny send you to do an article about me?"

"I, um…" said Guin at a loss for words.

"Come, I'll give you a tour. Then we can chat. About time Ginny sent someone."

Guin didn't move.

"You coming?"

"Sorry. I'm not here to interview you. I mean, I am, just about Jackson Brennan."

Audra frowned.

"It should only take a few minutes," said Guin. "And I can ask Ginny to have our real estate reporter contact you after we chat," she added.

Audra sighed dramatically.

"Fine, but make it quick."

CHAPTER 9

Guin was seated across from Audra in Audra's coastal chic office.

"So, what is it you wanted to know?"

"I understand Jackson Brennan was your real estate attorney."

"*Former* attorney," said Audra.

"Is that because of the land deal, the one that fell through?"

"That and other things."

"I imagine it must have been upsetting to have lost your bid."

"Upsetting is putting it mildly. Tony and I were furious. The Royal Poinciana was to have been the crown jewel of the West End, the first new luxury condo and single-family community on Sanibel in years. We had already sold fifty percent of the units. Then those eco-warriors stepped in and said the land should be protected."

"You mean SCCF?"

She nodded.

"They launched a big fundraiser to buy the land out from under us. Though Jack assured me they would never raise the necessary funds." She gave a hoarse laugh. "Silly me for believing him."

"So you blamed Brennan for the deal falling through?"

"He could have stopped it."

Guin wasn't so sure about that.

"What about your partner?"

"Tony? What about him?"

"Did he lose a lot of money?"

"What do you think?"

"And did he also blame Brennan?"

"Of course he did. Who else was there to blame? Jack was handling the transaction and said it was in the bag. If we had known SCCF would swoop in and steal it, we wouldn't have gone ahead and pre-sold units. And Tony wouldn't be in a bind."

"A bind?"

"Tony had already invested the money from the pre-sales. He never imagined he'd have to give it all back."

"What about those files you wanted?"

Audra looked confused.

"The other day, in Jackson Brennan's office? I was there when…"

"Oh that. Jack had promised to turn over all of my files to me after we parted ways. But he didn't. I simply wanted what was mine."

"Files of deals he'd helped you with?"

"Yes. But he was dragging his feet, and that assistant of his now refuses to release them."

"Why?"

"She claims they belong to the firm, even though they concern my deals."

"What about Mr. Brennan's partner? Have you spoken with him?"

"Only briefly. He's always in a meeting or out."

"Getting back to Mr. Brennan… Were you surprised to learn he was dead?"

"Very. I thought I'd misheard."

"Why is that?"

"The great Jackson Brennan dead? It didn't seem possible."

"So you don't believe he took his own life?"

Audra snorted.

"Please. The man loved himself way too much."

"But the land deal, and he had lost a couple of cases…"

"Both of which he was already spinning to make them sound like they were no big deal." She paused and eyed Guin. "You ever meet Jack?"

Guin nodded.

"Then you know there was no one on Sanibel with a bigger ego. A man like that doesn't go and kill himself because of some minor setbacks. And I heard he was planning on running for Congress. Not that he would have won."

"So if he didn't kill himself, what do you think happened?"

"I haven't the foggiest," said Audra, sitting back.

"Is it possible someone killed him, made it look like he committed suicide?"

Audra stared at her.

"You serious?"

"If he didn't kill himself, what are the other options?"

Audra looked thoughtful.

"It's true that Jack rubbed some people the wrong way. He could be a bit… abrasive. Not everyone appreciated his methods."

"Anyone in particular he rubbed the wrong way?"

"I imagine the attorneys he beat or those clients whose cases he lost."

"What about you?"

Audra leaned forward.

"If I wanted Jack dead, I would have put a bullet in him and claimed it was self-defense."

Guin tried to hide her shock.

"What about your partner, Tony Mandelli?"

"I'm sure he wanted to kill Jack at the time, but he's been in the Hamptons."

Guin made a mental note to verify that.

"Have you spoken to Jack's wife?" asked Audra.

"Beth?"

"Unless he has another one, which, by the way, I wouldn't put past him. Jack did so like the ladies," Audra sneered.

"You think Jack—Mr. Brennan—was cheating on her?"

"I'd be surprised if he wasn't."

Guin would have been too.

"So there was some trouble between them?"

"Please. You'd have to be a saint to put up with Jack's shenanigans. And Beth is no saint."

Interesting, thought Guin.

"So why didn't she divorce him?"

"They're Catholic."

Guin was about to ask Audra another question when there was a knock at the door and the receptionist poked her head in.

"Your clients are here, Ms. Linwood."

"Tell them I'll be right out." She turned to Guin. "I'm afraid our time is up." She got up and escorted Guin out. "Good luck with your article—and be sure to tell Ginny to send her real estate reporter next time."

Guin replayed everything Audra had said in her head as she drove home, but she was finding it hard to concentrate. What she needed was food. She thought about stopping at the Savoury Spoon, but what she was really craving was one of Jean-Luc's famous turkey, brie, and Granny Smith baguettes.

She pulled into the lot by the bakery and headed inside. Jo, one of the young people who worked there, smiled at Guin as she entered.

"What can I get for you today?" she asked Guin.

"One of Jean-Luc's turkey, brie, and Granny Smith baguettes and a sparkling water, please."

"For here or to go?"

"For here."

Jo took a sandwich out of the case and placed it on a plate, then handed it to Guin along with a can of sparkling water. Guin paid, then found a seat.

She had only taken a few bites when Jo came over with a mocha éclair, Guin's favorite.

"I didn't order an éclair, Jo."

"It's on the house. Last one left, and we'll be closing soon."

Guin hesitated.

"Go on. Jean-Luc won't mind. He hates when we have to throw away food."

"Well, in that case," said Guin, smiling as she took the plate. "But I insist on paying."

"You don't have to."

"I know," said Guin. "But I want to."

She reached into her wallet and pulled out a five, handing it to Jo.

"Thanks."

Guin finished her sandwich but was too full to eat the éclair.

"Hey, Jo, could I get a to-go box?"

Jo brought over a small pastry box, and Guin thanked her. She placed the éclair inside, then waved goodbye as she headed out.

Even though she had eaten, Guin was still finding it hard to concentrate as she sat in front of her computer. Her thoughts kept bouncing between Jackson Brennan and Detective O'Loughlin. Why hadn't the detective told her he was leaving Sanibel?

She reached for her phone to call him, but she stopped herself, putting her phone in a drawer instead. It was no use though. She couldn't stop thinking about him. She sighed and looked out the window. Maybe a walk would clear her head.

She changed into a pair of shorts and a t-shirt and headed out.

It was a typical June afternoon, warm and humid, but at least there was a slight breeze by the shore, and it appeared to be low tide. Although she hadn't planned on looking for shells, she couldn't help herself.

She spied a large ponderous ark shell with a black and white exterior and picked it up. Something about it reminded her of the shell Detective O'Loughlin had shown her, the one that was found on Jackson Brennan. She picked it up and examined it. There was nothing special about it. Just your average ponderous ark. She glanced at it for a few more seconds, then tossed it in the water and continued her walk.

The Gulf was on the calm side, with the water so clear you could see the sandy bottom. Guin watched as the water lapped against the shore, then looked out at the horizon. In the distance was a sailboat, sailing from east to west. She wondered where it was going. Overhead, a squadron of brown pelicans flew by. Though they probably weren't called a squadron. A posse of pelicans? She would have to look it up when she got home.

She stood there, looking out across the Gulf, breathing in the sea air, then turned around and headed back.

By the time she got home, she felt less anxious and more focused. She had decided she would pay another visit to Wanda and Beth. She would also call Mr. Martín, the landscaper, and pay a visit to the Savoury Spoon.

As for the detective, she would wait for him to reach out to her. She just hoped she wouldn't have to wait long.

Guin took her phone out of the drawer where she had left it and saw that she had received a text from an unfamiliar local number. It was from Paris, the young woman who worked at Paradise Found. "Call me when you get this," she had written. The message had been left less than fifteen minutes before.

Guin immediately called her.

"This is Paris."

"Hi, Paris," said Guin. "This is Guin Jones from the paper. You wanted to speak with me?"

"I did. Thanks for calling me."

"No problem. I just…"

"Can you hold on a sec?" said Paris, interrupting her.

Guin could hear voices in the background and was about to hang up (after waiting for what seemed like several minutes) when Paris finally came back on the line.

"Sorry about that," she said.

"That's okay. So what did you want to talk to me about? Is this about Mr. Brennan?"

"It is," said Paris. There was a pause. "I know he's dead and all, but I thought you should know."

"Know what?"

"He sexually abused me."

"He sexually abused you?"

Paris nodded (though Guin couldn't see her).

"He was always touching me, telling me how beautiful I was."

That was definitely inappropriate behavior, but Guin wasn't sure it fell under the heading of abuse.

"Did you say something to Beth?"

"Are you kidding me? What was I supposed to say to her, please tell your husband to stop harassing me?"

Yes, thought Guin. But she understood Paris's hesitance.

"Why didn't you quit?"

"I thought about it."

"Did you tell him to stop, that you weren't interested?"

There was a long pause.

"He told me he could help me."

"Help you how?"

"He said he could get me a job in Miami. That he had a friend."

"And what did you say to him?"

"I …"

"Why are you telling me this, Paris?"

Guin didn't mean to sound sharp with the young woman.

"I just thought you should know since you're doing a story on him."

"Thank you for coming forward," said Guin. "I'm sorry you had to deal with that kind of behavior."

"That's it? You're sorry?"

Guin wasn't sure what else to say.

"The man practically raped me!"

"He raped you?"

"Practically. He would have if…"

"When did this happen?"

"The day he died. He came to the store and attacked me."

"He attacked you at the store?"

Guin wanted to believe the young woman but was finding it hard to imagine Brennan going to his wife's store and attacking an employee in broad daylight.

"I was in charge of closing," said Paris. "Jack came in looking for Beth. I could tell he was upset. He asked where she was, and I told him she wasn't there. But he didn't believe me and marched back to her office.

"I followed him, to make sure he didn't mess with anything. He seemed pretty steamed. He was yelling her name, telling her they needed to talk. I told her she wasn't there and that he should go. Then he grabbed me. The next thing I knew, he had me pinned against the wall and was kissing me. If Marcus hadn't shown up, I don't know what would have happened."

"Marcus?"

"My boyfriend."

"What happened?"

"He heard Marcus calling my name, and I managed to escape."

"Where'd you go?"

"To the front of the store."

"And Mr. Brennan?"

"He stayed in Beth's office."

"Did you tell Marcus what happened?"

"No way."

"Why not?"

"Marcus would have killed him. Look, I have to go. I just wanted you to know what kind of man Jackson Brennan really was."

Guin was about to ask her how she could get in touch with Marcus, but Paris had already ended the call.

CHAPTER 10

Guin was staring out the window, replaying her conversation with Paris. If true, it was very disturbing. Though why would Paris lie? Guin chastised herself. She didn't know Paris, but she knew Jackson Brennan. Still, why tell Guin and not the police? Or maybe she had.

It was the perfect excuse to phone the detective. But she hesitated. Instead, she called Craig.

"I just had an odd conversation with a young woman who works for Beth Brennan."

"Odd how?" asked Craig.

"She claimed Brennan tried to rape her."

Craig whistled.

"Yeah."

"His wife know?"

"I don't think so. She said it happened the evening he died, and that Beth wasn't at the store."

"You believe her?"

"I don't not believe her."

"You check with the police?"

"I thought about it but…"

"You got dinner plans?"

"Excuse me?" That was not what she had expected Craig to ask her.

"I asked if you had dinner plans."

"Aren't you guys heading to Boca Grande?"

"Not until tomorrow. Come on. Betty would love to see you."

"Did you ask her if it's all right?"

"Hey, Betty!" Craig hollered. Guin covered her ear. "Okay if Guin joins us for dinner?"

Guin couldn't help smiling.

"She says it's fine."

"I didn't hear her."

"You want me to put her on the phone? Hey, Betty!" he hollered again.

"That's okay," said Guin. "So, can I bring something?" Not that she had much in her refrigerator. But she could always pick up something.

Craig scoffed.

"Please. We have enough food to feed a small army— and we're going to be away for a few days. You're doing us a favor by eating our food."

Guin was skeptical, but she did enjoy having dinner with Craig and Betty. They had become like family. And frankly, she preferred having dinner with them over her own family.

She looked at the clock on her monitor. It was after six.

"I'm surprised you haven't eaten already."

"Hey! We don't always eat early."

Guin smiled.

"What time should I come over?"

"Can you come now?"

"I'll go grab my bag."

Betty was bringing food over to the table as Guin walked through the door, as though she had been keeping it warm until Guin arrived.

"You didn't have to wait for me," said Guin.

"Nonsense," said Betty. "Now have a seat."

Guin sat, and they passed around the food. Betty had

made a roast chicken with roasted potatoes and a salad.

"Thanks for inviting me," Guin said, helping herself to a piece of chicken.

"We loving having you," said Betty.

Guin sensed that Betty missed her children, all of whom were grown and lived far away.

As they dug in, Guin asked them about their trip to Gasparilla and Boca Grande. Betty was very excited as it had been years since she had visited the island—and said she was looking forward to visiting the lighthouse and the museum. When Betty was done, Guin asked Craig about the tarpon tournament. Then it was Craig's turn to ask Guin questions.

"So you were saying about this young woman, the one who works for Brennan's wife…"

"Right." She turned to Betty. "I assume Craig told you we're covering Jackson Brennan's death for the paper?"

"He did. I didn't know the man, but what a horrible way to die."

Guin didn't disagree.

"Are you done, dear?" Betty asked her.

Guin was.

Betty then began to clear the table.

"Can I help?" asked Guin.

"I've got it," said Betty. "You two go ahead and talk shop."

Guin felt a bit guilty but didn't argue.

"So about this young woman," Craig repeated. "Why do you think she called you?"

"Well, she knew I was interviewing Beth Brennan about her husband for the paper, and she said she wanted me to know what kind of man Jackson Brennan really was."

"And she told you he tried to rape her?"

Guin nodded.

"In Beth's office. Said he had come to the store looking for his wife, that he was angry, and then forced himself on her."

"I see," said Craig.

"She said the only reason he stopped was that her boyfriend showed up."

"You speak to the boyfriend?"

"Not yet. I was going to ask her for his information, but she ended the call before I could."

Craig looked thoughtful.

"You believe her?"

"I want to, but…"

"But?"

Guin sighed.

"Something about her story… And she referred to Brennan by his first name."

"That doesn't necessarily mean anything."

"I know. I just wish I could have seen her face. Then I would know if she was telling me the truth."

"You should talk to the detective."

"I know."

"You two want some dessert?" called Betty. "I have ice cream."

"Thanks," said Guin, "but I should go. Besides, don't you two need to get ready for your big trip?"

"Not much to do," said Craig. "You're welcome to stay."

"That's okay," said Guin getting up. "You sure I can't help with the dishes?" she asked Betty.

"I'm all set."

Guin went over and gave Betty a hug.

"Thanks for dinner."

"Our pleasure," said Betty.

"Have a great time in Boca Grande," said Guin. Then Craig walked her out.

The next morning Guin took a walk around the neighborhood, then drove to the Savoury Spoon, which opened at nine. There was a line to get in, a good sign, especially in June. Clearly, their farmers market patrons had followed them to the new place.

Guin stepped inside five minutes later and greeted the owners, Nick and Savannah, who were busy making waffles and smoothies. Finally, it was her turn.

"One Belgian waffle on a stick with bacon and a Sanibel Sunrise smoothie, please!"

"Coming right up!" said Nick.

"How've you been?" asked Savannah. "I don't think I've seen you since we opened."

"Busy," said Guin.

She didn't tell them she was covering the restaurant for the paper. Though they might figure it out after she had dined there a few more times.

"Looks like you've been busy too."

"Oh yeah," said Savannah, making Guin's smoothie. "It's been nonstop. A lot of our customers from the market followed us over here."

"So business has been good?"

"So good that we need to hire more help already. You wouldn't be interested, would you?" she said grinning.

Guin smiled back at her.

"Thanks, but I already have a job. Though I'm tempted," she said, smelling the bacon.

"One Sanibel Sunrise smoothie!" said Savannah handing it to her. "The waffle should be ready in just another minute."

Guin took a sip of the smoothie and waited off to the side. A minute later, Nick handed her the waffle on a stick. She thanked him and made her way outside, taking a seat at one of the picnic tables. She had just taken a bite of the waffle when she felt someone looming over her. She looked up to see the detective staring down at her. She took a sip of her smoothie, trying to act nonchalant.

"May I join you?" asked the detective.

Guin shrugged.

"It's a free country."

He sat down across from her, and Guin continued to eat her waffle, though she barely tasted it.

"Is something wrong?" he asked her.

She looked up at him.

"You tell me."

He seemed genuinely confused.

They continued looking at each other until Guin gave in and spoke.

"When were you planning on telling me you were leaving Sanibel?"

He ran a hand over his face.

"I…"

She cut him off.

"Don't bother."

"I can explain."

She waited.

"It's complicated."

"It's always complicated with you."

"This time is different."

Guin waited for him to go on.

"Look, I can tell you're upset."

"Oh, really?" said Guin, trying to keep her emotions in check and failing. "Gee, I wonder why?"

The detective frowned.

"I don't want to discuss it here."

"Then where? Or maybe you were just going to slink out of town without telling me."

Now the detective looked annoyed.

"Of course I was planning on telling you."

"When?"

The detective's phone was ringing. He immediately answered.

"O'Loughlin." He listened and nodded. "I'll be right there."

Guin was watching him.

"I have to go."

"Of course you do," said Guin.

The detective sighed.

"We should talk."

"I'm all ears."

"Not now."

Guin waited for him to say more.

"Go on," she said, making a shooing motion with her hands. "Don't want to prevent you from arresting someone going over thirty-five."

The detective frowned, then turned and left.

Guin watched him go and slurped her smoothie. It was only when he had gotten into his car that she realized she had blown her opportunity to ask him about Paris.

CHAPTER 11

Guin finished her smoothie, then threw the cup in the garbage and headed to the Mini. She thought about following the detective to the Sanibel Police Department. Though she didn't know if that's where he was headed. She kicked herself for letting her emotions get the best of her.

She sat in the Mini, debating what to do. What she really needed was someone to talk to, a friend who would listen and not judge her.

Guin arrived at Shelly's house five minutes later. She had no idea if Shelly was home and realized she should have called or texted first. But she was there already.

She got out of the Mini and rang the doorbell. Shelly opened the door a minute later.

"Is everything okay?" she asked Guin.

"May I come in?"

Shelly invited her inside.

"You didn't find another dead body, did you?"

Guin shook her head.

They headed into the kitchen.

"You want something to drink?"

"I'm fine," said Guin.

"So, what's up? Your car break down?"

"No. I just needed some advice."

"Is this about a certain detective?"

Guin nodded.

"What did he do this time?"

"He's leaving."

"Leaving?"

Guin nodded again.

"He's leaving Sanibel."

Shelly gaped.

"What do you mean he's leaving Sanibel? Like, for good?"

"He handed in his resignation."

"But why? I thought he liked it here."

"No idea. And I did too."

"He didn't tell you why he was leaving?"

"He didn't tell me anything. I heard about it from Ginny."

"Could she be wrong?"

Guin shook her head.

"Craig confirmed it. He's leaving as soon as they find a replacement."

"Wow," said Shelly. "Well, I don't know about you, but I could use a drink after hearing that news." She opened the refrigerator and pulled out a bottle of white wine. "You want some?"

"Thanks, I'm good. I just had breakfast at the Savoury Spoon."

"What did you have?"

"A Belgian waffle on a stick and a smoothie."

"Were they good?"

Guin nodded.

Shelly looked at the bottle of wine and put it back in the fridge.

"Probably not a good idea." She turned back to Guin. "So, you have no idea why the detective is leaving?"

"None."

"I can't believe he didn't say anything."

But Guin could. The detective always kept information to himself.

Shelly reached over and took Guin's right hand.

"You know I'm here for you."

"I know."

"So, you going to talk to him?"

"I don't know."

"You need to confront him."

"You know I hate confrontations."

"So, what, you're just going to let him slink away?"

"No, but…"

Shelly straightened.

"Give me your phone."

"Why do you want my phone?"

"Just give it to me, though unlock it first."

Guin hesitated.

"Come on. Unlock it and give it to me."

Guin did as she was told, and Shelly snatched the phone away from her. A few seconds later, she was busy typing.

"What are you doing?"

"What you should have done." She finished typing and grinned. "There."

"What did you do, Shelly Silverman?"

"I wrote to Detective O'Loughlin."

"You didn't."

"See for yourself."

Guin was horrified. She grabbed her phone and looked down at the screen.

"The man owes you an explanation."

The phone began to vibrate in Guin's hand. It was the detective, texting her back.

"Fine, let's talk," he had written.

"What do I say to him?" Guin asked Shelly, who was looking over her shoulder.

"Invite him over for dinner."

"Invite him over for dinner?"

"Why not? Give him some wine and a good meal and he'll be spilling his guts."

Shelly clearly didn't know the detective, but it wasn't a bad idea.

"When should I invite him over?"

"No time like the present. You got plans tonight?"

"No, but…"

"Invite him over. The worst he can say is no."

Guin paused, and Shelly reached for her phone. Guin pulled it away.

"Fine," she said and began typing. She hit "send" and looked at Shelly. "Happy now?"

"Ecstatic."

A few seconds later, Guin's phone began vibrating again. The two women looked at each other.

"Is it him?" asked Shelly.

Guin looked down at her phone and nodded.

"What did he say?"

"He asked, what time?"

She looked at Shelly.

"Well, what time do you two normally eat?"

"Seven?"

"Then tell him seven."

She watched as Guin typed.

"What should I make him?"

Shelly rolled her eyes.

"Do you need me to go over there and cook for you?"

Guin felt embarrassed.

"That's okay."

"What does he like to eat?"

"Italian food. But he makes it all the time."

"So make him something he'd like that he wouldn't make for himself."

Guin wasn't sure what that was.

"Now, I don't mean to be rude," said Shelly, "but I have work to do, and you probably do too."

"Thanks for listening," said Guin, as Shelly walked her to the door.

"Any time. And let me know how dinner went."

"I will."

Guin paused at the door.

"You think it will be okay?"

Shelly looked at her friend.

"You want my honest answer, or do you want me to tell you what you want to hear?"

"You know what they say, honesty is the best policy."

Shelly snorted.

"Whoever said that was a liar."

Guin smiled.

"So my honest answer is, I don't know. But you two need to have a talk, get things out in the open. Now go. And text me tomorrow."

She gave Guin a hug, then sent her on her way.

Guin sat in her Mini, staring out the window.

"Focus, Guin!" she admonished herself. "You have work to do."

She got out her phone and looked up the number for Martín Landscaping. She entered the number and listened to it ring. The call went to voicemail. She left a message, asking Mr. Martín to call her.

Now what? Should she speak with Beth Brennan again or try to see if Brennan's new partner was in? She decided on the latter and put the car in gear.

Guin parked in the lot for Brennan & Associates and was about to climb the stairs when she noticed a painted shell hidden next to a tree root. She picked it up and saw it had a picture of a turtle on it. She turned it over and saw the Shell Fairy mark on the inside. Had the shell found on Jackson Brennan also had a Shell Fairy mark? She couldn't remember but didn't think so. (Only shells painted by a Shell Fairy were allowed to include the Shell Fairy mark, a wand with a star on top.) She would need to ask the detective. Yet one more thing to ask him.

She glanced at the shell again. She was tempted to keep it but decided to leave it for someone else to find. Though that reminded her: she had yet to hear back from Mary Ann.

She sent Mary Ann a quick text, asking if she had found out who had painted a shell with a skull and crossbones. Though that assumed it had been painted by one of the Shell Fairies. She waited a few seconds, then put her phone away when there was no reply and climbed the steps.

She peered through the large plate glass window and saw Wanda working at her desk. Guin entered and went over to her. Wanda continued to type, ignoring Guin. Guin waited a few more seconds then cleared her throat.

"Is there something I can help you with, Ms. Jones?" asked Wanda.

"As a matter of fact, there is. Is Mr. Dewey available?"

"He's not. Now if you would be so good as to make an appointment…"

Guin interrupted her.

"Do you know what Mr. Brennan was doing at the Bailey Tract Saturday morning?"

Wanda regarded her.

"I have no idea."

"So you have no idea if he was meeting someone there?"

"I just told you, I had no idea what he was doing there."

"It wasn't on his calendar?"

"No."

"What about Friday? Was he meeting with anyone that afternoon or evening?"

"Just that landscaper."

"Do you mean Mr. Martín?"

"That's the one."

"Where was he meeting him?"

"At his office."

"In Fort Myers?"

Wanda nodded.

"What time was the meeting?"

"I don't remember."

"You can't pull up his calendar?"

Wanda frowned.

"Is there a point to this interrogation, Ms. Jones? I'm rather busy."

"I just have a few more questions."

Wanda pursed her lips but didn't say anything.

"What time did he leave the office on Friday?"

"I wasn't looking at the clock."

"Approximately."

"Five?"

"And do you know if he was meeting with someone after he met with the landscaper?"

"How should I know?"

"You are his assistant."

Wanda frowned.

"What about Mr. Dewey?"

"What about him?"

"Does he know what Mr. Brennan was up to Friday evening or Saturday?"

"You would have to ask Mr. Dewey. And before you ask, he's unavailable the rest of the day."

"Will he be back later?"

"He's in Estero."

As if that was an answer.

Guin tried to control her frustration.

"Would you please ask him to get in touch with me when

he gets back? I left my card…"

"I have your information," said Wanda, cutting her off.

Guin had turned to go, then stopped and turned around.

"Do you know anything about a shell with a skull and crossbones painted on it? One like that was found on Mr. Brennan's body."

Wanda looked up. She was frowning.

"I told him that shell was bad news."

"Bad news how?"

"Do you know what a *wanga* is, Ms. Jones?"

"A *wanga*?"

Guin had never heard of a *wanga*.

"A *wanga* is an object imbued with evil spirits."

"Evil spirits? That sounds a bit like voodoo."

Wanda pursed her lips.

"In Haiti, people take *wangas* like that shell very seriously."

"And did Mr. Brennan believe the shell to be a *wanga*?"

Wanda continued to frown.

"No. He said I was being superstitious. Instead of getting rid of it, like I told him, he put it in his pocket and said it was his good luck charm."

Guin liked to think she wasn't superstitious, but as Wanda explained about the shell, she shivered.

"So do you think the shell had something to do with his death?"

Wanda didn't reply.

"When did he find it?"

"Thursday morning."

Just two days before he died.

"Do you know where he found it?"

"Outside the office."

"And he showed it to you?"

"As soon as I came in."

"And you told him it was a *wanga* and to get rid of it?"

Wanda looked like she was losing patience.

"Did you tell the police?"

Wanda gave her a look.

Guin took that as a no.

"Now, if you would excuse me, Ms. Jones?"

Guin knew her time was up.

"Thanks for your help, Wanda. Next time, I'll arrange an appointment."

Wanda sniffed, and Guin saw herself out.

CHAPTER 12

Guin pulled out her phone at the bottom of the steps and looked up *wanga*. As Wanda had said, a *wanga* was a magical object or charm that, according to Haitian Vodou, was thought to bring the bearer bad luck. But could the shell found on Jackson Brennan have really been a *wanga*? Who besides Wanda, at least on Sanibel, even knew what a *wanga* was?

Guin stared at her phone for a few more seconds, then put it away and went over to the Mini. She unlocked it and paused, deciding what to do. Paradise Found was only a few minutes away. Should she have another conversation with Beth? Probably not a bad idea. This time, however, she would call first.

She entered the number for the boutique and a cheerful-sounding woman answered. Guin asked if Beth was available, but the woman (who didn't sound like Paris) said she was out.

"Would you like to leave a message?" asked the woman.

"That's okay," said Guin. "I'll try later."

She ended the call and put her phone back in her bag. Now what?

Guin was driving home when instead of turning left onto Casa Ybel Road she continued straight on Periwinkle Way, turning right onto Palm Ridge Road. A mile later, she pulled into the Bailey-Matthews National Shell Museum. Bonnie was a volunteer there, and Guin had a few questions she hoped Bonnie could answer.

She parked the Mini, then jogged up the steps. There was a family buying tickets at the front desk, so Guin waited, glancing over at the gift shop. Then she saw him. He was speaking with Olive Gerhard, the executive director of the museum. But it couldn't be him.

"May I help you?" asked the woman seated at the front desk.

"Hm?" said Guin, still looking at the man speaking with Olive. She hadn't realized the family had gone into the museum.

"Would you like to visit the museum?" asked the woman.

Guin finally turned to look at her.

"Sorry, what did you say?"

"I asked if you were interested in visiting the museum."

Guin reached into her bag and pulled out her wallet, producing her membership card.

"I'm a member," she said.

The woman examined the card.

"Welcome, Ms. Jones. There's a tank talk beginning in a few minutes if you're interested."

"Thanks, but I'm actually looking for Bonnie Barnes. Is she here today?"

The woman smiled.

"She's giving the tank talk. You can take the elevator to the lower level or…"

"I'll just take the stairs," said Guin, cutting her off.

She glanced over to where Olive and the man had been chatting, but they were no longer there. Guin turned back to the woman at the front desk.

"That man speaking with Olive Gerhard a minute ago…" she said, trailing off.

"You mean Dr. Hartwick?"

So it was him.

"Do you know why he's here?"

The woman glanced around, making sure no one could hear her.

"It hasn't been officially announced yet, but Dr. Hartwick's the new science director!"

"What?!" said Guin, a bit too loudly. "What happened to Dr. Gutiérrez?"

"He had to go back to Peru. Family emergency."

"So Dr. Hartwick is just the acting science director?"

"No, he's the new one. At least that's what they told us at the staff meeting."

Guin sagged. So Ris was back.

Ris, aka Dr. Harrison Hartwick, Ph.D., was a handsome marine biologist who had been a professor at Florida Gulf Coast University and the acting science director at the museum just over a year ago. He had also been Guin's beau. She had broken up with him after he had asked her to move to Australia with him, and she had felt guilty about it for months. Until Ris showed up at her wedding[*] with his hot Australian girlfriend, who was pregnant with their child. Guin had been shocked and a bit jealous.

She thought they had gone back to Australia. Had something happened?

"Just don't tell anyone I told you," said the woman.

"I won't," said Guin. *Except for Shelly.*

The woman looked over at the clock.

"You better get downstairs if you want to hear the tank talk."

"Right," said Guin. "Thanks."

She turned and headed to the door that led to the lower level.

---

[*] See Book 7, *A Perilous Proposal*.

Guin stood in the back, listening politely as Bonnie delivered the live tank talk. There were two families occupying the front rows, the children mesmerized by the colorful mollusks in the two tanks.

Most people visiting Sanibel didn't realize that shells were in fact the exoskeletons of mollusks such as snails, clams, scallops, and oysters. Hence the tank talks, the museum's way of explaining to people that shells weren't just pretty objects to be collected but homes for living, breathing creatures.

The talk concluded, and the children went up to the tanks to get a better look at the various mollusks. Bonnie patiently answered their questions, then the parents thanked her and shooed the children out. Guin smiled and went over to her friend.

"Great tank talk!" she said.

"I always get a bit nervous when I have to do them," Bonnie replied.

"Well, you did just fine."

"So, what brings you here? You've probably heard the tank talk a dozen times."

Guin smiled again.

"Never hurts to hear it again. Actually…" She glanced around. "I just saw Ris Hartwick speaking with Olive. Did you know he was the new science director?"

Bonnie nodded.

"I just found out."

"Do you know if his fiancée is with him?" Though Ling could now be his wife.

"I don't. I didn't even know he was engaged."

"Do you need to get upstairs, or do you have a minute?"

"I can spare a couple of minutes. What's up?"

"It's about Jackson Brennan."

"You writing about him for the paper?"

Guin nodded.

"You know I'd like to help, but as I said at Shelly's, I

didn't even know it was him."

"I know, but I was wondering if maybe you saw something that morning, something you may not have thought was important at the time."

"I'm not sure what that could be but ask away."

"Well, did you see anyone else at the Bailey Tract when you got there? Not necessarily another car but a bicycle or someone on one of the trails."

Bonnie looked thoughtful.

"I remember seeing a cyclist, but I don't know if he was coming from the Bailey Tract."

"Was he heading south on Tarpon Bay or north?"

"South."

So he could have come from the Bailey Tract.

"And you didn't see anyone inside the tract, walking on one of the trails?"

"There may have been someone, but we didn't see anyone. There are several trails, and you can't even see someone ten feet ahead of you in some places."

True. So the killer could have lurked somewhere, waiting for them to leave, thought Guin.

"And when you first noticed Brennan, you thought he was asleep?"

"That's what Clyde said. But I wasn't buying it."

"And did you notice anything odd about him?"

"Other than the fact he was slumped over the steering wheel?"

"Yes."

"Not really."

"Did you happen to notice if there was anything on the seat next to him?"

Bonnie looked thoughtful again.

"Sorry, Guin. I don't recall. I'm afraid my memory isn't as good as it should be. And Detective O'Loughlin shooed me away."

"That's okay," said Guin. "I just have one more question. Do you recall seeing a clamshell painted with a skull and crossbones?"

"For the treasure hunt or in general?"

"Either."

Bonnie twisted her lips.

"I don't think so. Why?"

"Just wondering."

"Did you ask Mary Ann about it?"

"I did, but she hasn't gotten back to me."

Bonnie glanced up at the clock.

"I need to head upstairs."

"I'll go with you," said Guin.

It was after noon when Guin left the Shell Museum, and she could feel her stomach rumbling. She thought about going back to the Savoury Spoon, but it was too soon. Instead, she went to Bailey's and picked up a sandwich, along with some cooked shrimp, a steak, and a bag of fingerling potatoes for dinner.

She put the steak and shrimp in her refrigerator when she got home, then ate her sandwich at the kitchen island. She stared out the window as she ate, thinking she should really get some outdoor furniture. Though it was too hot and buggy to eat outside right now.

She finished her sandwich and went to her office. She worked for an hour or so, but she was finding it hard to concentrate. She tried to distract herself by reading the news, but that wasn't working either. She kept thinking about the detective. Maybe a walk would help.

It was hot and humid out, but it still felt better to be outside than staring at her computer screen. Guin was perspiring by the time she got back nearly an hour later, but she felt much calmer. She downed a glass of water and glanced up at the clock on the microwave. She had just enough time to take a shower and wash her hair before she needed to start making dinner.

Freshly washed and dressed in one of her favorite sundresses, Guin went back into the kitchen. She removed the shrimp from the refrigerator and arranged them on a plate. Then she poured some cocktail sauce into a small bowl. Next, she took out some cheese and arranged the two wedges on a cutting board along with some crackers. That done, she began cutting up potatoes.

At five after seven, the doorbell rang. Guin could feel her heart racing as she made her way to the front door. She opened it to find the detective standing there, dressed in a pair of chinos and a light blue button-down shirt. He was holding a bottle of red wine.

"Here," he said, handing the bottle to Guin.

"Thanks," she said taking it. "Won't you come in?"

She led him to the kitchen, neither of them saying anything.

"Help yourself," she said, gesturing to the food she had laid out. "Dinner should be ready soon. I'm making steak and roasted potatoes."

The detective picked up a shrimp and dipped it in the cocktail sauce.

Guin glanced over at him.

"Would you like something to drink? I have beer in the fridge. Or we can open that bottle you brought."

"I'll get the corkscrew," said the detective.

He pulled it out of the drawer where Guin kept it and opened the bottle, while Guin took out two wine glasses. He poured.

"Cheers," she said, holding up her glass.

"Cheers," he replied.

Guin took a sip.

"It's good."

The detective smiled, or what passed for a smile on him. Then his expression turned, and he put down the wine glass.

"About what you heard, about me leaving..."

Guin waited for him to go on. Clearly, this was hard for him.

"I know I should have told you. It's just..." He ran a hand through his closely cropped hair. "It wasn't an easy decision."

Again Guin waited. When he didn't speak after several seconds, Guin spoke.

"But why resign? I thought you were happy here."

"I am happy here. It's just... It's Joey."

Joey was the detective's adult son, who lived in Massachusetts.

"Is something wrong with Joey?"

"With Joey? No, he's fine. It's the baby."

"Is something wrong with the baby?" asked Guin, a look of worry passing over her face.

Joey's wife had given birth to a baby boy at Christmas. The detective had been ecstatic and had gone to Massachusetts several times to visit the newborn and his family.

"The baby's fine. It's just..."

"Is Heather okay?"

Heather was Joey's wife, the baby's mother.

"Would you let me finish?" snapped the detective.

Guin held her tongue. She could tell he was nervous, which was unusual. The detective was rarely nervous.

"I wasn't the best father," he began. "I worked all the time and didn't have much time to do the normal dad things, though I tried."

Guin knew this already but didn't say anything.

"Then Molly took Joey. Said my work was too dangerous. Didn't want her son living around guns. Though she knew I was a cop when we had him, and that I would never do anything to endanger him."

Guin knew that too.

"I've tried to make it up to Joey, but it's been tough, what with us leading separate lives and him being up there and me being down here. But when they had Frankie, I knew what I had to do."

"And what was that?"

"I needed to take care of him."

Guin stared.

"Take care of Frankie?"

"Who do you think I was talking about?"

"When you say take care of him, you mean, like, be his nanny?"

"Something like that."

Guin was trying not to stare. But she couldn't picture the detective being anyone's nanny, let alone an infant's.

"They don't have childcare?"

"Molly's been helping out, but..."

"So if Molly's helping out..." Guin paused. "Can she not help out anymore? If it's a matter of not being able to afford someone, can't you just offer to pay?"

The detective frowned.

"I need to be there."

"But why?" said Guin. This made no sense.

"I wasn't there for Joey when he was a kid. But I can be there for him and Frankie now."

"But what about your job?"

"I'm over fifty. I've got benefits coming to me."

"That's not what I meant. I thought you loved being a detective."

"Maybe I love my grandson more."

Guin didn't know what to say to that.

"What do Joey and Heather think about you retiring and becoming their nanny?"

She couldn't imagine they thought this was a good idea.

"They thought I was joking. But I told them I was serious. I want to spend time with my grandson, reconnect with my family. Kids, they grow up so fast."

"I understand that, but why not just take a leave of absence?"

"I thought about that, but… It's time I put my family first."

"What did Chief Russo say when you told him you were leaving the PD to take care of your grandson?"

"He thought I was pulling his leg."

"But you told him you were serious."

The detective nodded.

"Did he ask you to reconsider?"

"He told me to take some time to think about it, to go up to Boston, spend the summer with the family if I wanted, then decide."

"Sounds sensible to me. Why not take him up on it?"

"I already decided."

"So that's it. You're leaving."

The detective didn't say anything.

"When?"

"As soon as they find someone to replace me."

"And what if they don't?"

"I told the chief I'd stay through the summer. Then I was leaving, with or without a replacement."

Guin didn't know what to say. It was like a bad dream, except she was awake.

"And nothing can make you change your mind?"

She was looking right at him.

"No."

Guin felt her heart breaking. This couldn't be happening.

"What about us?"

He didn't answer right away.

"I don't know."

"So that's it? You just leave and it's, 'goodbye Guin, nice knowing you?'"

"I said I didn't know."

But Guin had a feeling he did know.

"What if I said I'd move to Massachusetts?"

He looked at her.

"Do you want to move to Massachusetts?"

"Not really, but…"

Every part of her wanted the detective to ask her to go with him, to beg her, to say he couldn't live without her.

"You should stay here on Sanibel."

Guin felt as though she had been punched in the gut.

Just then the timer on the oven went off. Dinner was ready, but she was no longer hungry.

She turned off the timer and opened the oven, as if in a trance. She reached in to pull out the potatoes, then remembered to put on an oven mitt. She grabbed the cast iron skillet next, then placed the steak on a cutting board. She cut it up and placed several slices on each plate, adding some potatoes. The detective watched her. Then she placed the plates on the island.

"Dinner," she announced.

They picked at their food, neither of them hungry. When they were done, Guin picked up the dishes and placed them in the sink.

"I should go," said the detective.

"You don't have to," said Guin, placing a hand on the detective's arm.

He looked down at it, then up at Guin.

"I have a long day tomorrow."

He got up and headed to the door. Guin followed him. They stopped by the door and looked at each other.

"I'm sorry," he said.

A part of Guin wanted to grab him, beg him not to go. But all she said was, "Me too." Then she opened the door and watched him leave.

CHAPTER 13

Guin slept fitfully that night. She had yet another anxiety dream and woke up at three a.m., her heart racing. It was like the other dreams. She had gone on vacation and had a wonderful time. But when it came time to go home, she was unable to. Either she missed her plane, got on the wrong train, or couldn't find her car. She went to the bathroom, then climbed back into bed. But she wound up staring up at the ceiling.

Finally, she gave up and grabbed the book she kept on the nightstand for just such occasions. It was a thick volume on the flora and fauna of Florida. She found it soothing (and a bit boring). And soon she had fallen back to sleep.

When she arose the next time, it was seven-forty, and Fauna was staring down at her. The cat tapped her with her paw.

"Let me guess, you want food."

"Meow," said Fauna.

Guin nipped to the bathroom, then she headed to the kitchen, Fauna at her heels. She opened a can of wet food and dumped the contents into Fauna's bowl. Fauna lunged.

"Go easy there. I don't want to have to clean up cat puke," said Guin, gazing down at the cat. As usual, Fauna ignored her.

Guin sighed and went to make coffee.

She reached for her phone, only to remember it was still

in the bedroom. She retrieved it and found multiple messages from Shelly, the last one left a few minutes ago, telling Guin to call her. She waited until her coffee was ready, took a couple of sips, then dialed Shelly's number.

Shelly didn't bother to say hello.

"Did you read the email?!" she asked.

"What email?" said Guin.

"The email about Harry Heartthrob, of course!"

Guin frowned. Harry Heartthrob had been a nickname given to Ris when he had been named one of Southwest Florida's sexiest men. Both she and Ris had hated it.

"Check your email," said Shelly. "It was sent late last night by the Shell Museum."

Guin opened her email and saw it.

"You find it?" said Shelly.

Guin nodded.

"I got it."

"You're not going to believe it."

Guin quickly read the email. It was as the woman at the front desk and Bonnie had told her. Ris was the museum's new science director.

She quickly read it again. There was nothing about Ling or a baby. Not that there necessarily would be. Just that Ris was returning to Southwest Florida from a sabbatical in Australia and was thrilled to accept his dream job as science director.

"Hello? You still there?"

"Sorry, I was reading the email."

"Pretty shocking, right? I mean, who even knew Dr. Gutiérrez was leaving?"

"I heard it was a family emergency."

"Wait, you knew?"

"Bonnie told me yesterday."

"And you didn't tell me?"

"I meant to. I guess it just slipped my mind."

"Your old flame returning to Sanibel slipped your mind? Well, I guess that means you're really over him."

She was, but Ris's return still made her nervous. Though she wasn't sure why. Was it guilt for the way she had treated him?

"So he didn't call or text you to give you a heads up?"

"No, why should he?"

"I would have. Just common courtesy."

"Ris doesn't owe me anything."

"Speaking of flames, how did dinner with the detective go?"

Guin frowned.

"Not great."

"What happened? Did he say why he was leaving?"

"He's planning on taking care of his grandson."

"You serious?"

"Yep."

"How old's his grandson?"

"Six months."

"Does he even know how to care for a baby?"

"He'll figure it out."

"I give him two weeks tops, then he'll be begging to get his old job back."

"I thought the same thing, but he says he's committed to helping his son out."

"Did his son ask for his help?"

"No, but Bill feels guilty about not being there for Joey when he was little. And he thinks being there now will make up for that."

"Yeah, right. But why quit your job? Why doesn't he just take some time off, hang out with them, then come back to Sanibel? He can visit with them on vacation."

"That's what I said, but he feels he has to do this. Also, I think it might have something to do with his ex looking after the kid. I think he feels competitive, like he has to show her up."

"Oy. What is it about men? So did he say when he was leaving?"

"As soon as they can find someone to replace him or else at the end of the summer."

"Huh." There was a slight pause. "Did he ask you to go with him?"

"Nope."

"Did you offer?"

"Yep."

"And what did he say?"

"He told me I should stay on Sanibel."

"Ouch. Well, maybe it's a good thing Ris is back."

"Oh no. That relationship is over and done. Besides, he has a fiancée, or maybe she's his wife by now."

"You going to be okay?"

"I'll be fine."

Though Guin didn't feel fine.

"Remember who you're talking to. I'm here if you need me."

"Thanks, but I'll be fine," said Guin, more to convince herself than Shelly.

"Okay. Well, call or text if you need anything."

"I will."

They ended the call and Guin stared out the window. There was a flock of ibis making its way across the backyard and it looked to be another beautiful day. She looked at the clock. It was nearly eight-thirty. Normally, she considered that too late to go for a beach walk. But she needed to clear her head. She took a last sip of coffee, then went to get changed.

Guin was lost in thought, staring out at the Gulf, when she heard someone calling her name.

"Guin!"

There it was again. She turned to see Linda, one of the Shell Fairies who had been at Shelly's, waving and moving quickly towards her. Guin waited for her to catch up.

"Phew!" said Linda, bending over to catch her breath.

"You okay?" asked Guin.

"I'm fine. Just a bit winded." She straightened up and smiled. "Not as spry as I used to be." Guin waited for her to go on. "I heard through the grapevine you were asking if anyone had seen a shell painted with a skull and crossbones."

"That's right," said Guin, wondering how Linda had heard. "Have you seen one like that?"

"I haven't, but I think I know who painted it."

Guin waited.

"She's new to the group. Just moved to Sanibel from up north. Super talented. A real artist."

"And does this artist have a name?"

"Oh, yes, sorry. It's Stephanie."

"And you think she painted a shell like that?"

"Pretty sure."

"Pretty sure?"

Linda glanced around, making sure no one could hear them.

"I overheard her talking about it."

"About the shell?"

Linda nodded.

"I was having lunch with my friend Irma over at the Sanibel Sprout. And Stephanie and this other woman were having lunch next to us. And I heard Stephanie saying to the other lady, 'I still can't believe someone swiped my shells!'"

"Someone stole her shells?"

"That's what she said."

"And did she mention a shell with a skull and crossbones?"

"Sort of. Her friend asked her which shells were stolen, and I heard her mention one with a pirate flag on it."

"Did she happen to say where the shells had been stolen from?"

"She said from the Community House."

"When was this?"

"Sometime early last week, I think. I wasn't paying that close attention."

"Do you know if the shells were for the treasure hunt?"

"I don't know. Maybe? Though we're not supposed to talk about those shells with anyone."

Guin was processing what Linda had told her. Did Mary Ann know about the stolen shells? If they were intended for the treasure hunt, she'd have to. Guin would need to phone her later.

"Well, thanks for letting me know."

"Of course!" said Linda. She looked down at her watch. "Oh! Gotta run! I have bridge at ten!"

Guin watched as Linda made her way off the beach. She should probably head back too.

Guin was headed home along West Gulf Drive when she saw a truck with "Martín Landscaping" printed on the side. Several men were busy trimming trees and attending to the grounds of one of the palatial properties. Guin wondered if Mr. Martín was there and went up to one of the men.

"Excuse me," she said. "Is Mr. Martín here by any chance?"

The man turned and pointed to another man a few feet away who was talking to one of the workers.

"Thank you," Guin said. She went over to Mr. Martín. "Excuse me, Mr. Martín?"

Mr. Martín turned.

"I am Mr. Martín."

"Hi, Mr. Martín. My name's Guinivere Jones, I work for the local paper and…"

Mr. Martín frowned.

"You're a reporter?"

"I am, and…"

"I'm very busy."

"Please, Mr. Martín. If I could just have a minute of your time."

She gave him a pleading look.

He eyed her warily.

"What do you want?"

"It's about Jackson Brennan."

Mr. Martín frowned.

"I understand you met with him last Friday," Guin went on.

Martín continued to frown.

"I was supposed to meet with him, but he never showed up."

"He didn't show up?"

Mr. Martín didn't say anything, just continued to look hostile.

"Did he call to cancel or send you a text?"

"No. Nothing."

"I understand there was some disagreement over money."

Again, no reply.

"Were you giving him a check? That's what his assistant said."

One of his workers came up to him and said something to him in Spanish.

"I need to go."

"Just one more thing. Where were you Friday evening and Saturday morning?"

"At home, with my family. Now if you would excuse me?"

Guin watched as he limped over to the man who had said something to him. Guin followed him, tapping him on the shoulder while he was speaking to the man in rapid-fire Spanish. Mr. Martín turned, clearly annoyed.

"I'm sorry to bother you, Mr. Martín, but how did you injure your leg? Is that why you hired Mr. Brennan?"

"*Sí.*"

"Can you tell me about it?"

"If I tell you, will you let me get back to work?"

Guin nodded.

"One of my clients, she has a big dog. The dog, he's supposed to be locked up. Only the dog escapes, gets loose. Next thing I know, he's attacking one of my men. I go get the dog, and the dog attacks me."

"And that's how your leg got injured?"

Mr. Martín nodded.

"They took me to the hospital. Gave me lots of stitches. I couldn't walk for weeks."

"So you sued the dog owner."

Martín nodded.

"The bills from the hospital were bad. I ask the woman to pay, but she refuse. Said her dog never hurt no one, but Manuel and I are proof."

"So you hired Mr. Brennan?"

Again, Mr. Martín nodded.

"*Sí.* I saw his ads on the billboards. He say he the best. But…"

He frowned.

"But he lost your case."

Mr. Martín nodded.

"Then he send me a bill. But he told me I only pay if he wins."

"What did you do?"

"I told him what he told me, that I only pay if he wins."

"And what did he say?"

"He say I have to pay him."

"But you didn't."

"His bill, it was for a lot of money. I was hoping to talk with him, negotiate."

"And that's why he was coming to see you?"

Mr. Martín nodded.

"But he never showed."

"*Sí.*"

Another worker came over and said something to Mr. Martín. He nodded and turned to Guin.

"I need to work."

"Of course," said Guin. "Thank you for your time."

She watched as he limped over to his truck and yelled something to one of his men. She couldn't imagine this limping man, who stood maybe five-foot-six and weighed maybe 120 pounds, killing six-foot-something Jackson Brennan. She stood watching him for a few more seconds, then turned and headed home.

CHAPTER 14

At one o'clock Guin drove over to the Savoury Spoon.

"Back so soon?" said Nick, smiling at her.

"You know I can't resist your grilled cheese," said Guin, smiling back at him.

"What kind do you want?"

Guin examined the menu.

"I'll have the Brie and Fig *and* the Caprese."

Nick gave her a look.

"I'm really hungry."

"Anything to drink?"

"A Green Flash."

"Coming right up!"

Guin grabbed a table and made a mental note to invite Shelly and a few of their friends the next time.

"Here you go!" said Savannah a few minutes later, delivering the sandwiches and juice to Guin. "You must be really hungry."

"I am," said Guin. Even though she wasn't.

Savannah stood there for a few more seconds, then returned to her spot behind the counter. Guin dug in. She took a bite of the Brie and Fig first. The cheese melted on her tongue, and she loved the sweetness of the fig. So good.

She took a bite of the Caprese sandwich next. Mm... The tomatoes were bursting with flavor, and the pesto tasted slightly salty and fresh.

She had made it about halfway through the two sandwiches when she decided she couldn't eat another bite. She went up to the counter and asked for a to-go box.

"Eyes bigger than your stomach?" Nick asked her.

Guin nodded.

"But I'll eat the rest for dinner or for breakfast tomorrow."

He handed her a box and Guin thanked him.

Guin put the box in the refrigerator as soon as she got home. She was still feeling full from lunch and wanted to take a nap. But she needed to type up her notes. A short time later she was done. One more visit to the Savoury Spoon—with Shelly and their friends—and she'd be able to write the review. Even though she already knew what she would say. But Ginny insisted her reporters visit a restaurant three times before reaching a judgment, which Guin thought was fair.

Next, she pulled up her notes on Jackson Brennan. She mentally kicked herself for not asking the detective about the case while he was there and chastised herself for letting her emotions once again interfere with work.

She reviewed what she had written but didn't really know much more than she had a couple of days ago. Though she ruled out the landscaper as a suspect. That is assuming Brennan hadn't in fact killed himself. It was still a possibility, but one Guin was loath to accept.

Even if Brennan had killed himself, why do it at the Bailey Tract? And why then? Had something happened that Friday to put him over the edge? She needed to find out.

She had already spoken with Wanda, who claimed to have no idea what Brennan was up to Friday night or Saturday. But maybe his new partner, this Tom Dewey, would know. And there was Beth. No doubt the police had already spoken with both of them. Would the detective tell her if she asked? Only one way to find out.

She took out her phone and texted him.

"You speak with Tom Dewey and Brennan's wife?" Though she couldn't imagine he hadn't. "And did the medical examiner say when exactly Brennan died?"

She stared at her phone, waiting for a reply. Nothing. Though what had she expected? She turned back to her computer and decided to make a list of potential suspects.

At the top of the list was Anthony Mandelli. Though Audra said he was in the Hamptons at the time of Brennan's death. But she could have lied. Then there was Audra herself. And there was Paris's boyfriend, Marcus. Though Paris said he didn't know about Brennan. But Guin wasn't so sure about that. *Who else?* she thought. She mulled it over. Surely there was someone she was leaving out.

She looked at her phone again. Still no reply from the detective.

She decided to call over to Brennan's office and see if Tom Dewey was available. If anyone knew if Brennan had any enemies, or what he was doing that Friday, it would be his partner.

"Brennan and Associates."

The voice didn't belong to Wanda, which threw Guin off.

"Hi. Yes, uh… Is Mr. Dewey there?"

"He's meeting with a client," said the woman. "Would you like to leave a message?"

"Is Wanda there?"

"She's unavailable. Would you like to leave a message?"

"Yes. Could you ask Mr. Dewey to call Guin Jones? That's G-U-I-N…"

She gave the woman her number, and the woman said she'd have Mr. Dewey phone her back.

Well, that was progress. She ended the call and sat back.

Now what? She typed *Tom Dewey* into the search engine box, then picked up her phone and called Ginny.

"What's up, Buttercup?"

"What do you know about the lawyer who took over Jackson Brennan's practice?"

"You mean that Dewey fellow?"

Guin nodded.

"Yeah, him. I've been trying to see him, but every time I go over there or call, he's in a meeting or busy."

"Well, I imagine things have been a bit busier than usual seeing as his partner just bit the dust."

Ginny had a point.

"What did you want to know?"

"I don't know. You know anything about him? How he happened to get the job or how he and Brennan got along?"

"You asking me for gossip?"

"No, I'm asking you for information."

Ginny sighed.

"I'm afraid I don't know much. Just that he's from up north, young, good looking, and Brennan was lucky to nab him."

Guin frowned. She was hoping Ginny would have something more useful.

"You do a search on him?"

"I was about to," said Guin. "But I figured I'd ask the woman who knows everything that goes on on Sanibel first."

"I'm flattered. But he's been keeping a low profile. Let me know what you find out though."

"Will do."

"Hey, while I have you on the phone, I've got another little piece I need you to do before you fly off to England."

"What is it?"

"Another profile."

"Who this time?"

"Another artist. She's new to the island, and I hear she's very talented."

"Why not ask Angelique to do it?"

Angelique Marchand was the paper's Arts reporter.

"I would, except she went back to Canada. Where have you been?"

"Angelique went back to Montreal?"

Guin knew Angelique was from there, and that her kids were there, but she had no idea she had gone back. Last she heard, Angelique was living at her parents' place, writing for the paper, and dating Jean-Luc Fournier, the owner of Jean-Luc's Bakery.

"I don't know the details. Something about the children. Didn't even give two weeks' notice."

That didn't surprise Guin.

"Well, you can do better."

Guin had been surprised when Ginny had hired Angelique, Angelique not having a journalism background. But she had somehow convinced Ginny that being a patron of the arts made her qualified.

"No doubt."

"You looking?"

"Not right now. No point. I'll start looking at the start of the season. You wouldn't want the position, would you?"

"I've got enough to do. Besides, you know I don't know that much about art."

"You know enough. Which is why I'd like you to interview Stephanie Yates."

"Stephanie Yates?"

"You know her?"

"No. I just know her name." That is, assuming she was the same Stephanie that Linda had mentioned.

"Well, she just moved here a few months ago, and Mary Ann's been telling me I have to do a story on her for the paper. Seems she's a big-time artist up north. Though I never heard of her."

"Is she a member of the Shell Fairies by any chance?"

"Yup."

It had to be the same Stephanie.

"Speaking of the Shell Fairies, did you hear about some shells being swiped from the Community House last week?"

"Mary Ann told me."

"And you didn't write about it?"

"She asked me not to. The shells were for the treasure hunt, and she didn't want word getting out."

Understandable.

"Does she know who stole them?"

"No. And neither did any of the ladies who painted them. They were supposed to be locked up."

"So, you have contact info for Stephanie?"

Ginny gave it to her.

"When do you want the profile?"

"How soon can you get it to me?"

"The end of next week?"

"That's fine."

Guin heard several beeps.

"I've a call coming in," said Ginny. "Talk to you later."

Guin put down her phone and turned back to her computer. She deleted *Tom Dewey* and typed *Stephanie Yates* into her search engine. There were hundreds of results. Ms. Yates was the real deal. She had attended the School of the Art Institute in Chicago and her work had been exhibited in a number of galleries, not just in Chicago but in New York and London.

Guin navigated to her website and took a look at her portfolio. Stephanie's work reminded her a bit of Roy Lichtenstein and Wayne Thiebaud with its Pop Art feel. She wondered what had brought her to Sanibel.

She was about to send her an email but decided to call her instead. The phone rang several times, then a female voice answered.

"Hello?"

"Is this Stephanie?"

"It is. Who's this?"

"Hi, Stephanie. My name is Guinivere Jones. I'm with the *Sanibel-Captiva Sun-Times* and…"

"Guinivere, like in King Arthur?"

"Yes," said Guin.

"Cool. Sorry for interrupting. You were saying?"

"I'm calling because I work for the local paper and my editor would like me to do a profile of you."

"A profile of me?"

"Yup. We understand you're an artist and were painting shells for the National Seashell Day treasure hunt."

"I'm flattered, but…"

Guin sensed her hesitance.

"It would be a great way to get your name out here. Not that you need to," she quickly added. Probably lots of people knew of her work. Just not Guin. "And I love your art."

"You've seen it?"

"I was just on your website. You're really good."

"Thanks. Though I've been in kind of a rut. That's one of the reasons I agreed to move down here. I needed a fresh perspective."

"Well, I'd love to hear all about your work and your impressions of Sanibel. Do you have some time this weekend to meet up?"

"My boyfriend and I are supposed to go away this weekend. That is if he can tear himself away from work. But I could meet you tomorrow morning."

"That would be great. Have you been to the Sanibel Bean?"

"No, not yet."

"Then let's meet there. Say nine o'clock?"

"Sure."

"Great! I'll see you at the Sanibel Bean tomorrow at nine."

CHAPTER 15

Guin still had Stephanie's portfolio up on her monitor. Which reminded her, she needed to follow up with Mary Ann. She sent her a quick text. Mary Ann replied a minute later, asking Guin to call her. Guin did.

"Were you able to find out if one of the Shell Fairies painted that shell I mentioned?" she asked Mary Ann, without mentioning Stephanie.

"About that," said Mary Ann. "It's a bit sensitive."

"Because of the shell being stolen?"

"How did you know about that?"

"Ginny told me," Guin lied. Though it wasn't a total lie. She just didn't want to get Linda into trouble.

"She said she wouldn't say anything."

"It just slipped out. But it's true, several shells were stolen from the Community House?"

"Yes, but we didn't want word getting out. The shells were for the treasure hunt. Though fortunately the clues hadn't been added yet."

"Do you know how it happened?"

"No. They were supposed to have been kept safe. If word got out, it could taint the hunt."

"Any idea who took them?"

"No."

"And no chance one of the Shell Fairies accidentally took them home with her?"

"No, we asked. They all swear they left them there. Though…"

"Though what?" asked Guin.

Mary Ann sighed.

"This needs to be off the record."

"Okay," said Guin. She had no idea what Mary Ann was about to say.

"There was some squabbling among the ladies."

"Squabbling?"

"About the shells. Who got to paint what. Some of the older ladies, the ones who had been in the Shell Fairies a while, were miffed that we had given two of the new members important shells to paint. They thought they should get first dibs."

"I see."

"But it was about who we thought would do the best job, not seniority."

"I understand. So you think one of the senior Shell Fairies might have taken the shells out of anger or jealousy? Were the missing shells painted by the new members?"

"They were. But I can't believe any of our Fairies would be that petty. They knew the shells were for the treasure hunt."

"And was one of the shells that went missing painted with a skull and crossbones?"

"Yes, though your description initially threw me. It was supposed to be a pirate flag. And there was nothing written inside it. The clues were to be added later."

Guin could see how Mary Ann could have been confused. Playing dumb, she asked who had painted the pirate shell.

"A wonderful artist by the name of Stephanie Yates. She's new to the island and was brought to one of our sessions by her friend Candy. Candy's mother is a Shell Fairy, and Candy recently became one too."

Guin wasn't familiar with a Shell Fairy named Candy.

"What's Candy's last name?"

"Kane."

Guin had to stop herself from giggling.

"Her name is Candy Kane?"

"I know. Her real name is Candace, but her mother used to call her her little candy cane when she was little, and I guess it stuck."

If Guin's mother had named her Candace and her last name had been Kane, she would insist on being called Candace or would have changed her name.

"She's a lovely girl," continued Mary Ann. "Works for Audra Linwood."

Could Candy have been the cheerful young woman she had met there? Guin wondered.

"She's also a talented artist. Just moved back here last year to help her mom who was diagnosed with cancer."

"I'm sorry to hear that."

"Norma's in remission, but it was touch and go for a while."

"And you say Candy introduced Stephanie to the Shell Fairies?"

"That's right. They're about the same age. And Lord knows we could use some fresh blood."

"Well, thanks for your help," said Guin.

"No problem," said Mary Ann. "Just promise me you won't print a word about those missing shells. It could spoil the treasure hunt."

"I won't say or write a thing. Though let me know if any of them turn up."

"I will. I still can't believe someone would have taken them. Do you think they were trying to cheat, get a leg up on the competition?"

"It's possible, but I assume you replaced the missing ones. And you said none of them had the actual clues."

"True, but…"

Mary Ann sighed.

Guin thanked her again for her help and ended the call. As she gazed out the window she wondered what it was about Sanibel shells that made people go a little crazy.

Guin was in bed reading when she felt herself dozing off. She reached over to turn off her phone. Still no word from Detective O'Loughlin. She told herself he was just busy, but she didn't really believe that. Clearly, he was distancing himself. But she needed him in order to solve the mystery surrounding Jackson Brennan's death. Which meant putting aside her personal feelings.

Feeling resolute, she sent him a text.

"You up?"

"Maybe," came the swift reply.

Guin couldn't help smiling. She began to type.

"You going to tell me what time Brennan died?"

"You going to stop bugging me if I do?"

"Maybe," wrote Guin, smiling again.

There was a long pause.

"Between 9 and 12 Friday."

"Night?"

No reply. Though it had to be Friday night.

"You find out anything else?"

Again, there was no reply.

"Fine. I'll just ask Craig."

"We found Brennan's keys in the bushes."

Guin's eyebrows went up.

"What were his keys doing in the bushes?"

"They were wrapped in a cloth."

"Doesn't that seem odd? Why would he wrap his keys in a cloth and throw them away?"

No reply.

"Sounds mighty suspicious to me," typed Guin.

Still nothing.

"You still there?" she texted.

"I'm watching the game."

Of course. She should have known.

"You know where Brennan was Friday night?"

No reply.

"You speak with Brennan's partner?"

No reply.

Guin sighed. Clearly, the baseball game took priority. She gave up getting any more information out of him, turned off her phone, and picked up her book. But she couldn't concentrate. Instead, she retrieved her phone, turned it back on, and called her brother.

"Guin? Is everything all right? You haven't been shot again, have you?"

"Ha ha. I'm fine," she replied. "Can't a woman spontaneously call her brother?"

"But it's after ten. You never call after ten. Shouldn't you be asleep?"

It was true Guin typically turned off her phone before ten and went to bed shortly after, but she was still miffed that her brother assumed she'd be in bed. Though technically she was.

"I was feeling restless, and I miss you."

"Aw, I miss you too, Sis."

Ever since they had been little, and especially since their father died, Guin and Lance had been close. But since she had moved to Sanibel, they didn't see or speak to each other as often.

"So, how are you?"

"Busy. Got a lot to take care of before we jet off to London."

"You mean Bath."

"No, I mean London. I have some meetings there before

the big birthday do. Then, after the party, Owen and I are going to Paris, then to the South."

"Of France?"

"*Oui!*"

"Business or pleasure?"

"A bit of both. I have a meeting I need to attend at the Paris office, then Owen wants to check out some new artist in Saint-Paul-de-Vence."

Guin's brother Lance, which was short for Lancelot, owned a boutique ad agency based in Brooklyn, which had recently gone international. And his husband Owen ran an art gallery in Chelsea.

"Rough life."

"I know, but someone's got to live it. You're welcome to join us."

"In France?"

"There's plenty of room in the Paris apartment and in the cottage we rented in the South."

"I'd love to, but…"

"But what? Not like there's a lot going on on Sanibel over the summer."

Why did everyone say that? Guin thought irritably.

"I have a job, Lancelot. I can't just take off for two weeks."

"Why not? You get two weeks of vacation, don't you?"

"I do, but I'm already taking a week off to go to Bath."

"It's July Fourth. That doesn't count."

Guin rolled her eyes.

"Well, if you change your mind…"

"I'll let you know."

"So, anything new with you?"

"The detective's moving back to Boston."

"O'Loughlin?"

"He's the one."

"Why don't you just call him by his first name? I assume he has one."

It was a reasonable question, but Guin always thought of Detective William "Bill" O'Loughlin as "the detective." Though she didn't call him that when she was with him.

"Why's he going back to Beantown? They fire him?"

"No. He wants to help raise his grandson."

"Huh. I didn't reckon him as the type."

"Neither did I. But that's what he says he's doing."

"Why?"

"Guilt mostly. He wasn't there for his son Joey. And he thinks if he takes care of little Frankie, that'll make up for it."

"Good luck with that. How old's the kid?"

"Around six months."

"Can't they afford a nanny?"

"That's not the point. The detective feels he owes it to Joey to be there for him. Though Joey's mom has been taking care of Frankie, and probably doing just fine."

"So O'Loughlin's giving up his job and you to go play nursemaid to a kid who doesn't really need him?"

Hearing Lance say it that way made Guin feel depressed.

"Yup."

"Sorry. That sucks."

"It does indeed."

"Did you say something to him?"

"I did."

"And?"

"He's determined to go."

"What about the two of you?"

"I don't know. He made it pretty clear he's not interested in me going with him."

"Would you go if he asked?"

Guin sighed.

"I don't know."

"Maybe it's for the best."

"Oh? Why do you say that?"

"You guys are so different. And you're always saying how closed off he is."

Guin hadn't realized she had said anything to her brother.

"You should find someone younger."

"On Sanibel? Good luck with that."

Guin yawned.

"Get some sleep, Guin. I'll check on you in a couple of days."

"You don't have to check on me."

"I know I don't have to." There was a pause. "Thanks for calling. I'm looking forward to seeing you."

"Me too," said Guin.

They said good night and ended the call. And this time Guin kept her phone off.

CHAPTER 16

Guin arrived at the Sanibel Bean promptly at nine and looked around for Stephanie but didn't see her. A minute later, a young woman on a purple bicycle turned into the lot. Even with the helmet, Guin recognized Stephanie from the photos on her website.

She walked over to the bike rack and introduced herself.

"Nice to meet you," said Stephanie.

"I like your bike and your helmet," said Guin, admiring them. They had both been painted with bright graffiti-like flowers. "Did you paint them?"

"I did. I couldn't resist."

"You could probably make a small fortune painting bikes and helmets here on Sanibel."

Stephanie smiled.

"Thanks, but if I did it for a living, it wouldn't be as much fun."

Guin understood.

"Shall we get some coffee and something to eat?" she asked the artist.

"Sounds good to me!" Stephanie replied.

They went inside the café and ordered, then found a quiet table on the screened-in porch.

"So I looked at your website," said Guin. "Some of your pieces reminded me of Roy Lichtenstein and Wayne Thiebaud's work with their playful Pop Art vibe. Though other pieces had a definite Photorealistic feel and others felt almost Surreal."

Stephanie grinned.

"I'm impressed. You study Art History?"

"No, I just spent a bunch of time on the internet doing art research. Though I knew about Lichtenstein and Thiebaud from growing up in New York near the Whitney."

"Well, you're more knowledgeable than some of the supposed art experts who've tried to categorize my work. And for what it's worth, you pretty much nailed it."

"I did?"

Stephanie nodded.

"I love playing with different styles, never doing the same thing twice. But it makes it hard for people—or critics—to categorize my work. Not that I mind. It just makes it a bit harder to sell."

Guin liked this young woman. It also made her think about her own work. Lately, she had been feeling as though she had been writing the same thing over and over again, none of it very interesting.

They sipped their coffee and picked at the muffins they had ordered.

"So had you ever painted shells before moving to Sanibel?" Guin asked Stephanie.

"No. But I loved the idea."

"How did you hear about the Shell Fairies?"

"My friend Candy. She works for the real estate agent who helped us find a place here. Her mom's a Shell Fairy. She is too. And when she heard I was an artist, she suggested I check out the group."

"What brought you to Sanibel? I can't imagine it was the gallery scene, though we have some very nice galleries here."

Stephanie smiled.

"My boyfriend. He got a job here, and I thought, what the heck? Not like I was loving winter in Chicago."

"Do you miss it? Chicago, that is."

"Some. Though I was ready to try someplace new. I had grown up and gone to school there."

"At the Art Institute."

Stephanie nodded.

"And do you plan on staying on Sanibel for a while?"

"As long as Tom's here, or until I get bored."

"Your boyfriend's name is Tom?"

"Tom Dewey. He just took over a law practice here. Kind of a crazy story. The man who hired him just died. They say he killed himself. Totally freaked Tom out."

Guin knew she was staring. But there couldn't be two lawyers named Tom Dewey on Sanibel, could there?

"Are you by any chance referring to Jackson Brennan?"

"Yes! Did you know him?"

"I hired him to help me with a real estate matter a while back, and I'm covering his death for the paper. Had you met him?"

"Tom and I had dinner with Jack and his wife a couple of times. They were very nice to us."

Guin wanted to ask Stephanie if Brennan had ever made a pass at her, as Stephanie was an attractive young woman. But she felt it would be inappropriate, so didn't say anything.

"I imagine Mr. Brennan's death must have been a big blow."

"It was. Especially after what happened to Tom's sister."

"His sister?"

"Tom's older sister committed suicide when Tom was in middle school. She was a lot older than him, but they were super close. Tom was devastated."

"I'm so sorry."

"Yeah. Tom and his family don't like to talk about it. It took me over a year to find out about it. Now someone else close to Tom has committed suicide, and I…" She shook her head. "I asked him if he wanted to talk about it, thinking it might help. But he's just thrown himself into work."

"Actually…" said Guin. "I've been trying to reach him, but he hasn't gotten back to me."

"Like I said, he's been very busy. Though it's not like him to not get back to people. I'll tell him you've been trying to reach him and have him call you."

"Thank you. I'd appreciate that. Now, how about we get back to your art? You okay if I record our conversation?"

Guin withdrew her microcassette recorder from her bag and placed it on the table.

"Wow," said Stephanie looking at it. "Do people still use those things? Isn't there an app for that?"

"There is, but I prefer the old-fashioned way," said Guin. "So is it okay if I record the interview?"

"Record away!"

"Well, that should do it," said Guin around twenty minutes later.

The two had talked about Stephanie's work as well as her influences and art in general. Guin had enjoyed their conversation and wondered if maybe she should try her hand at being the paper's Arts reporter. Though she quickly dismissed the idea.

She put the microcassette recorder away, then looked over at Stephanie.

"I do have one more question."

"Shoot."

"Did you paint a shell with a skull and crossbones or a pirate flag for the National Seashell Day treasure hunt?"

"How did you know?" said Stephanie. "It was supposed to be a secret."

"I understand the shell went missing."

Stephanie nervously glanced around.

"No one's supposed to know that either. You're not

going to include that in your article, are you?"

"No. I was just curious. Do you know why someone might have swiped it?"

"Maybe someone was trying to get a leg up on the treasure hunt? Though the shells didn't have the clues in them."

"Do you think it could have been one of the Shell Fairies?"

"I'd hate to think so."

Stephanie's phone, which she had placed upside down on the table, began to vibrate. She picked it up and frowned.

"I need to go."

"Of course," said Guin. "Thank you for your time."

They walked out together and Guin handed her a card. Stephanie looked at.

"I'll have Tom call you."

"Or he can text me. Whatever's easier."

Stephanie put the card in her pocket.

"Do you know when your story on me will run?"

"I'm not sure, but I'll let you know as soon as I do."

"Thanks."

They said goodbye and Guin watched as Stephanie peddled away.

Guin arrived home a short time later and began transcribing her interview.

Transcribing was the least favorite part of her job as a reporter. Even though she was a pretty fast typist, it took forever (or felt that way) to make sure she didn't miss a word. And it was after noon by the time she had finished.

She went into the kitchen and fixed herself something to eat. Then she went back to her office. She had hoped to hear from Tom Dewey, but he hadn't called or left a message. If she hadn't heard from him by the end of the day, she would try reaching him again.

In the meantime, she would try Beth Brennan.

She picked up the phone and called Paradise Found. The same cheery female voice as before answered. Guin asked if Beth was available and was told she should be back around four. Did Guin want to leave a message? Guin said that was okay. She would call back later.

Well, may as well start on that profile, she said to herself.

She had been typing away, her phone turned upside down, when it started to move across her desk. She picked it up and saw an unfamiliar number. Though she recognized the area code. It was from Chicago. She immediately swiped to answer.

"Hello, this is Guin," she said.

"Ms. Jones? This is Tom Dewey."

"Mr. Dewey! Thank you so much for giving me a call."

"I'm sorry it took so long. I actually had no idea you were trying to reach me. I understand you have some questions for me."

"I do. Would it be possible to meet?"

"I'm a bit busy right now."

"I understand, but it shouldn't take long. I'm writing about Jackson Brennan for the paper, and I could really use your help."

There was silence on the other end of the line.

"Mr. Dewey? You still there?"

"Sorry, a client was texting me. Like I said, it's been crazy."

"I'm sure."

"What did you ask me?"

"I asked if there was any way you could give me a few minutes of your time sometime over the next few days."

"You free for breakfast tomorrow?"

"Name the place and the time and I'll be there."

"You know the Island Cow? People keep telling me I should check it out."

"I know it well. What time?"

"Eight o'clock okay? I need to be at the office by nine."

"Eight is fine. Though you're working on a Saturday? I thought you and Stephanie were going away."

"We had to postpone our trip. Duty calls. Speaking of which…"

"I understand. I'll see you tomorrow at the Island Cow."

CHAPTER 17

Guin glanced at the clock on her monitor. It was nearly four. Beth should be back at Paradise Found. Guin thought about calling over there again but decided to just drive over.

There was barely any traffic, so she made it in under fifteen minutes. And there were plenty of spaces in the lot. She parked the Mini and started to head to the boutique when she spotted a familiar red convertible. She stopped and stared at it, then quickly walked the rest of the way to the store.

As she reached for the handle the door swung out and there stood Ris Hartwick, looking as handsome as she remembered.

"Guin!" he said, a smile forming on his face. Guin had nearly forgotten about that smile, the one that revealed his dimples and made her stomach flutter. "I was hoping I'd run into you."

Guin didn't know what to say.

"You going into the boutique?" he said, still holding the door.

"What are you doing here?" Guin blurted.

"I was just saying hi to Fiona."

Guin looked confused, though she knew Fiona was Ris's daughter. Was she still in college or had she just graduated? She couldn't remember.

"She works here."

"Ah."

"Just started a few weeks ago."

"She graduate?"

"Not yet."

They stepped aside to let a couple out.

"How does she like it?"

"Okay. She was going to do an internship in DC for the summer, but when she heard I'd be back, she got a job here."

"I assume she heard about the owner's husband."

"You mean Jackson Brennan?"

Guin nodded.

"He was the lawyer you hired to help with your contractor situation, wasn't he?"

"He was." Though she had never told Ris that Brennan had come onto her. "Did Fiona know him?"

"I think so. Why?"

"What did she think of him?"

"You can ask her yourself. I'm sure she'd love to see you."

Guin wasn't so sure about that. After all, she had dumped Fiona's dad.

"So what brings you back to Sanibel? Last I heard you and Ling were back in Sydney. How is she, by the way? Is she here with you or is she coming later?"

Ris sighed, and Guin got the distinct impression that all was not well.

"Did something happen?"

"Ling lost the baby."

"Oh no! When? How? I'm so sorry to hear that." And she was.

"Thank you. We're pretty sure it happened just before we went back to Australia. Ling was having stomach pains, and I suggested she go see a doctor. But she said she was fine. She had an appointment with her OB right after we got back and said it could wait. But when they did the ultrasound, they couldn't find the baby's heartbeat."

"She must have been devasted. You, too."

He nodded.

"It was pretty bad."

"So did they…?

Ris nodded again.

"And is she okay now?"

"I don't know."

"What do you mean you don't know?"

"After the miscarriage, she said she needed a break."

"A break? From your relationship?"

Another nod.

"But you two looked so happy at the wedding."

"We were, but then… I guess Birdy didn't tell you."

"Tell me what?"

"After you got shot, Ling started questioning our relationship."

"But why?"

Ris looked down.

"After you collapsed, it was total chaos at the wedding venue, people screaming and running around. I should have been making sure the mother of my child was safe, but instead I dashed over to see if you were okay."

Guin didn't know what to say.

"Birdy told me he had it covered and that I should be with Ling, but I felt paralyzed seeing you there lifeless with all that blood.

"Later, Ling accused me of not being over you. Then the miscarriage happened and…" He ran a hand through his hair.

"I'm sorry," said Guin. "I had no idea. But surely you two can get past this?"

He shook his head.

"I thought so too, but Ling withdrew. Said she needed time to think. I thought if I gave her some space… Then she sent me back the engagement ring I had given her, and I knew it was over."

"I'm so sorry," Guin repeated, gently laying a hand on Ris's arm.

"Thanks," he said. "So when I heard about the opening at the Shell Museum, I figured it was a sign."

He was looking at her, and Guin felt uncomfortable.

"Well, I'm sure the women of Southwest Florida are happy to have you back," she said jokingly.

"Guin, I…" He laid a hand on her arm.

"I need to go inside and speak with Beth."

"Of course," said Ris, removing his hand from her arm. "I didn't mean to keep you."

They stood there awkwardly for a few more seconds, then Guin opened the door to the boutique.

"Well, good luck with the new position!" she called. Then she closed the door behind her. She had not been prepared to see Ris again.

"Guin?"

Guin turned to see Fiona grinning at her.

"Hey, Fiona."

"I saw you speaking with my dad. Did he tell you about Ling?"

"He did."

"I know I should feel bad, and I do, about the baby. But I'm not sorry to have dad back here. I really missed him. Does that make me a bad person?"

"No, it makes you human."

Fiona smiled again.

"I wasn't a big Ling fan. I liked you way better. Mom did too."

Guin didn't know what to say. Didn't Fiona know Guin had dumped her father? Best to change topics.

"Um, is Beth around?"

"She's in back, but she's super busy."

"Could you see if she could spare me a few minutes?"

"I'll call her."

She picked up the phone.

"Hey, Beth, I have Guinivere Jones here from the paper. You have a minute to speak with her?" She listened, then nodded. "Okay, I'll tell her." She hung up and turned to Guin. "She's just finishing something. She'll be up in a minute."

"I'll just have a look around while I'm waiting," said Guin, not wanting to discuss Ris further with his daughter.

A few minutes later, Beth found her.

"You wanted to speak with me? Is this about our one-year anniversary?"

"No, I'm afraid it's about your husband. I had a few more questions. But I told Ginny we should do an article on the store's anniversary," she quickly added. "So we can talk about that too."

Beth looked like she was mulling it over.

"Okay. Let's go back to my office. But I don't have a lot of time."

"Understood."

Guin followed her back to the cramped office, and Beth closed the door behind them.

"So, what are your questions?"

"First, why don't you tell me about your anniversary?"

That seemed to relax Beth a bit.

Guin listened and took notes. When Beth was done, Guin complimented her on the store's success. Then she switched gears.

"Do you know where your husband was Friday night?"

Beth frowned.

"No."

Guin found that surprising.

"So you have no idea where he was that evening?"

"All I know is that he had some dinner thing."

"Do you know where or with whom?"

"No."

"And you weren't concerned when he didn't come home?"

"No."

"Why not?"

Beth tilted her head.

"I was used to Jack getting home late."

"But when you didn't see him the next morning..."

"I thought he had gone to work early."

Guin found that a bit odd.

"So you weren't at all worried when you didn't see or hear from him?"

Beth was looking at her.

"You knew my husband, didn't you?"

"I did," said Guin, not sure where this was going.

"Did he flirt with you?"

Guin didn't know how to respond.

"Come now. Don't be shy. Did Jack flirt with you? You're an attractive woman. And Jack... Let's just say Jack had a way with women."

Guin felt distinctly uncomfortable.

"I... he..."

"I thought so," said Beth. "Did you flirt back?"

"No!" Guin practically shouted. True, Jackson Brennan wasn't the worst-looking man she had ever seen. Some might have even called him handsome. But Guin found him repulsive.

Beth smiled.

"Good for you. You're one of the few."

"Wait, you knew Jack flirted with women?"

"Please. I'm not an idiot. As long as he didn't cross any lines."

"And did he, cross any lines, that is?"

Beth gave her another look, one that Guin interpreted to mean, what do you think?

"You speak with Audra Linwood?"

Guin was confused.

"Audra Linwood?"

"She and Jack were very close, if you catch my drift. Pretty sure he was the reason she divorced that husband of hers."

Guin was trying not to gape. But she just couldn't picture Jackson Brennan with Audra. And if true, and Beth knew, why had she put up with it?

"Well, he was her attorney," said Guin, composing herself. "I imagine that must have required them to work closely at times."

"Not that closely," said Beth.

Guin was struggling. When she had talked to Audra, Audra had had nothing good to say about Brennan.

"But Audra hated him. She was furious with him for blowing the land deal."

"Is that what she told you?"

Guin nodded.

"Figures. No, the reason she hated my husband is because he dumped her."

"He dumped her? I thought she fired him."

"That was after he dumped her."

"I don't understand," said Guin.

Beth sighed.

"Jack had decided to run for Congress. And I told him if he wanted me to stick by him, he needed to clean up his act. No more messing around. And no more Audra."

"I see," said Guin.

"Audra, of course, was furious. Especially after the land deal fell through. So she told everyone she had fired him. But Jack had already told her they were done."

Guin's wheels were turning.

"Do you think Audra could have had something to do with his death?"

"I wouldn't put anything past her."

Guin glanced around and noticed a spreadsheet.

"Did Jack, I mean Mr. Brennan, have a life insurance policy?"

Beth had said the boutique was doing well, but Guin knew that Brennan had been financing it.

"I assume so."

"You don't know?"

Beth sighed.

"Jack was very private when it came to those kinds of things. Told me not to worry about it."

The phone rang and Beth picked up.

"Can I call you back?"

She hung up and turned to Guin.

"I need to get back to work."

"Of course," said Guin. She got up and headed to the door. "Thank you for your time." She had opened the door when she stopped and turned around. "Just one more question. Do you know if your husband had hired someone to run his campaign?"

"I believe he was still interviewing people. Why?"

"Could he have been meeting with one of those people Friday evening?"

"It's possible. You should ask Wanda. Now if you will excuse me?"

Guin nodded and let herself out.

"You have a good chat with Beth?" asked Fiona.

"Yes," said Guin. She glanced around. "Is Paris not working today?"

"She quit."

"Quit? When?"

"Just a couple of days ago. She didn't show up for work. When Beth finally reached her, Paris said she had a new job and asked Beth to mail her a check."

"Wow."

"Right? I could never do that. But it didn't really surprise me."

"How come?"

"Paris was always talking about how this was only temporary, how she was destined for bigger things. Still, she should have given notice."

"So, um, did Paris ever talk about Mr. Brennan?" asked Guin.

Fiona bit her lip.

"What did she say?"

"It wasn't so much what she said, it was how she acted whenever he was in the shop."

"How did she act?"

"She was always flirting with him."

"She flirted with him?"

Fiona nodded.

"Though to be fair, she flirted with all the good-looking customers."

"And did Mr. Brennan flirt back?"

"Oh yeah. It was pretty cringy seeing the two of them together. They were totally into each other."

"Totally into each other how?"

"You know, whispering and touching each other and giggling. It was like I was back in high school."

"Did Beth know or see them?"

"I don't think so. He always seemed to show up when Beth was out."

"Didn't Paris have a boyfriend?"

"You mean Marcus?"

Guin nodded.

"She said she was going to break up with him."

"How come?"

Fiona shrugged.

"Who knows?"

"You ever meet him?"

"He came by the store a couple of times."

"Did he know she was going to break up with him?"

"I don't think so. He certainly didn't act like he knew he was being dumped."

"And did he strike you as the jealous type?"

"Don't know. I only saw him here a couple of times. But you could tell he was really into her."

"You wouldn't happen to know Marcus's last name, would you?"

"It's Ramsay. You can check him out on Instagram. He played basketball for the FGCU Eagles and was their leading scorer. He's like a local celebrity or was."

"Thanks for the info. I should get going."

Guin reached for the door.

"It was nice seeing you," said Fiona.

"It was nice seeing you, too, Fiona."

Guin opened the door to leave.

"You should call my dad," called Fiona.

Guin stopped and turned around.

"Excuse me?"

"He talks about you, you know. A lot. He thinks the breakup was his fault, that he put too much pressure on you."

Guin didn't know what to say.

"I know you've probably moved on, but, well, maybe you could call him? Go grab a coffee?"

"I'll think about it," said Guin. Then she left.

CHAPTER 18

Guin took out her phone. There was a message from Craig, letting her know he and Betty were back. Guin immediately called him.

"How was your trip?"

"Good."

"Catch any tarpon?"

"I was there to observe, not fish."

"Come on. I can't imagine you not fishing for forty-eight hours."

"I may have snuck in a little fishing."

Guin smiled.

"Did Betty have a good time?"

"She didn't want to leave. Though I think she got tired of eating restaurant food."

Guin could picture it.

"Well, I'm glad it was a good trip."

"It was. So, any news on the Jackson Brennan front?"

Guin filled him in on what she had learned.

"Good work."

"It doesn't feel like it. I'm no closer to figuring out why Brennan died."

"You still don't think he killed himself?"

"No. Though I have no proof. But the fact that his keys were found in the bushes, wrapped in a cloth… Why a cloth? Sounds like someone was trying to wipe them clean."

"He could have tossed the keys himself and then locked the car, so no one could rescue him."

"But why the cloth?"

Craig didn't have an answer.

"And I still can't believe he would take his own life. Sure, he lost a couple of cases, but..."

"I may be able to help with that."

"Oh? You hear something?"

"It seems our Mr. Brennan was heavily in debt."

"Did he have a gambling problem? I could kind of picture that."

"No, he had a lifestyle problem. He was living beyond his means and needed money. So he went to our old friend Lou Antinori."

"Lou Antinori aka Big Lou the loan shark and drug kingpin?"

"The same."

Officially, Big Lou Antinori was a real estate developer, one of the biggest in Southwest Florida. Unofficially, he ran a drug trafficking and payday loan operation.

"How much are we talking about?"

"At least a mill."

Guin whistled.

"But why not get a loan from a bank?"

"Don't know. There was probably a reason."

"So was Brennan paying Big Lou back?"

"He was, though he had missed a few installments."

"So you think he got nervous and killed himself before Big Lou came after him or his family? Or... maybe Big Lou put out a hit on him, made it look as though Brennan killed himself."

"Either's possible."

"Speaking of real estate developers, did you have a chance to look into Tony Mandelli? Audra Linwood claims he was in New York when Brennan died, but I don't trust her."

"I'll get right on it. Anything else?"

"I'm meeting with Brennan's partner, Tom Dewey, tomorrow for breakfast. I'm hoping he can give me some insight into Brennan's state of mind and the business at the time of his death."

"Sounds like you've got things covered. You speak with O'Loughlin?"

"Sort of."

"Sort of?"

"I meant to ask him about the case, but I got a bit sidetracked."

"You find out why he resigned?"

"He's leaving to take care of his grandson."

"He is?"

"Yeah."

Neither spoke for several seconds.

"I should go," said Guin. "Talk to you later?"

"Sure," said Craig. "You know you can talk to me any time."

Guin thanked him, then ended the call.

Guin pulled into the lot next to the Island Cow a little before eight and was surprised to see so many cars there. Though she knew it was a popular breakfast spot. She went inside and peered around, but she didn't see Tom Dewey. The hostess asked her if she'd like a table and led her to a booth.

A busboy came over and poured Guin some water, then asked if she'd like some coffee. Guin had made herself a small pot earlier so passed. She glanced around. The Island Cow had a cheerful vibe. Its walls were painted a sunny yellow and were covered with cow-themed artwork.

Guin took out her phone and scrolled through the news while she waited. There was still no sign of Tom by eight-twenty. She sent him a text and decided she'd wait ten more minutes then leave.

Five minutes later he rushed into the restaurant looking frazzled, his hair wet. He went over to the hostess who pointed to Guin's booth.

"Sorry I'm late," he said, taking the seat opposite her. "I didn't hear the alarm go off."

"That's okay," said Guin. "You're here now."

A server came over and offered Tom coffee, which he greedily accepted.

"So, how can I help you? I'm afraid I don't have much time."

Guin opened her mouth to speak, but the server had come back, asking if they were ready to order.

"Could you give us a few minutes?" asked Guin.

He left and Guin turned back to Tom.

"So how did you come to work with Jackson Brennan? From what I read online, you had a promising career in Chicago."

"I always wanted to have my own practice, something small but fulfilling. Though I didn't see it happening for several more years. Then I heard through the grapevine that Jack was looking for a partner, someone to manage his practice while he ran for Congress and possibly take over when he won." Tom smiled. "He was very confident. It was the dead of winter in Chicago, and having my own practice on Sanibel sounded like a dream come true."

Guin smiled. She understood.

"So you sent him your resume and a cover letter?"

"Something like that."

"And he asked you to interview?"

"He did."

"Did he fly you down to Sanibel?"

"We talked on the phone first."

"When was that?"

"January."

"And when did you actually meet with him?"

"In February."

"Did he fly you down?"

"I used miles as I wanted to bring Stephanie."

"Do you know if he interviewed anyone else?"

"Probably."

"And when did he make you an offer?"

"In March."

"And you started…?"

"April first."

"And when was he planning on announcing his run for Congress?"

"I think he was planning on announcing around July Fourth. Wanted to make a big show of it."

Guin could just picture it.

"So had he hired someone to manage his campaign?"

"I don't think so. Though I think he was close."

"And do you happen to know where he was last Friday?"

Tom looked thoughtful.

"I know he was supposed to meet with that landscaper in Fort Myers. Then he had some dinner."

"Do you know who he was having dinner with?"

"He probably told me, but I've been so busy I don't recall. You could always ask Wanda. She was in charge of his appointments."

He let out a yawn, quickly covering his mouth.

"Sorry."

Guin looked over at the young lawyer. He had dark patches under his eyes. She wondered if he was getting any sleep.

"I know you only worked with him for a few months, but did Mr. Brennan seem at all depressed to you?"

"Depressed?"

"Blue… despondent… unhappy…"

Tom smiled.

"I know what *depressed* means. I wouldn't say he was

depressed exactly. Just had a lot on his mind. Things hadn't been going that well for him, professionally and personally, and I think it was starting to take a toll."

"Did you know he had taken out a rather large loan from a local loan shark?"

Tom nodded.

"Though I didn't know that when I agreed to work with him. Had I known…"

"Did you say something?"

"I did. But he told me it wasn't a big deal, that he was paying it back, and that should anything happen to him, I wouldn't be held responsible."

"He said that to you, that if something happened to him, you wouldn't need to pay back the loan?"

Tom nodded again.

"He did."

"When was that?"

"Actually, just a few days before he died. One of Mr. Antinori's associates stopped by the office to have a chat with Jack, and I asked him what that was about."

"And he told you?"

"He said he had it handled."

"And did you have any idea Brennan was planning to take his own life?"

"No. But looking back, the signs were all there. I was just too busy to notice."

"What signs?"

"Well, there was the loan, and he was starting to lose cases, and then there was all that stuff from his past, and his wife divorcing him… It was a lot for any man to handle."

"Wait," said Guin. "Beth was divorcing him?"

He nodded.

"And what stuff from his past?"

But before Tom could answer, his phone started to buzz. He picked it up and frowned.

"I have to go."

"But you haven't had breakfast." *And I have more questions!* she wanted to add.

"I know. I'm sorry, but I have to get to the office."

"Well, thanks for meeting with me," said Guin.

Tom reached into his wallet and threw a ten on the table. Guin tried to give it back, but he refused.

"Any chance you might have a few minutes later this weekend?" she asked. "I still have a few more questions."

"Text me," he said. Then he was gone.

CHAPTER 19

Guin thought about leaving the Island Cow but wound up ordering a small stack of blueberry pancakes with a side of bacon instead. As she ate, she thought about what Tom had said, about Beth divorcing Brennan. Why hadn't Beth mentioned it? She also wondered what Tom had meant about stuff from Brennan's past popping up. Was there some dark secret lurking there, some skeleton in Brennan's closet? She would have to do some digging—and stop thinking in clichés.

She finished her meal and paid, then drove home.

Guin was sitting at her computer, trying to work, but she was distracted by a great egret walking across the lawn in search of prey. She stared at it for several seconds, then turned back to her monitor. She had just started to type when her phone started to vibrate. It was Glen.

"Hey, Glen, what's up?"

"What are you doing later today?"

"Nothing much. Just working. Why?"

"Could you help me out? I'll pay you."

"You don't have to pay me. What's up?"

"My assistant called in sick. And I have this wedding to photograph up at South Seas. And…"

"You know I know next to nothing about photography."

"I can teach you."

"In a few hours?"

"You don't need to know much. It's mostly holding stuff or schlepping it."

"I can do that. Though are you sure there's no one else who can help you?"

"No one. Believe me, I tried. Please Guin, you'd be really helping me out."

Guin sighed.

"Fine. But don't say I didn't warn you. What time and where?"

"The wedding's at five, but I need to take pictures of the bride and groom beforehand. Could you meet me there at two?"

Guin looked at the clock on her monitor. It was a little after ten.

"Sure. What should I wear?"

"Something practical but professional. Subtle. So you blend into the background. And be sure to wear comfortable shoes. The wedding's outdoors, under a tent, but the reception's inside."

Guin wondered what "practical but professional" meant, and if she had anything that would blend into the background. Perhaps a grass skirt? She smiled at the thought.

"Okay. I'll see you at South Seas at two."

"Thanks, Guin. You're a lifesaver. I owe you."

"You say that now, but you may hate me by the time the wedding's over."

"Never."

They said goodbye and Guin looked down to see that Fauna had insinuated herself into her lap. Guin stroked the napping feline.

"You hear that, kitty cat? I'm going to be an assistant wedding photographer."

Fauna softly purred.

Guin spent the rest of the morning working. Finally, at one o'clock, she stopped. She needed to get ready for the wedding. But first, she needed food.

She made herself a peanut butter and jelly sandwich and was eating it at the island when her phone started to vibrate. A part of her hoped it was Glen, saying he didn't need her after all. But it was Ris. She thought about not answering but decided that was childish.

"Hello?"

"It's me, Ris."

"Hi, Ris."

"It was great running into you the other day, and I thought… By any chance are you free later?"

"Sorry, I'm helping out a friend."

"Oh? Maybe we could get together afterward?"

"I don't know when I'll be free. I'm shooting a wedding up on Captiva."

"As in photographing it?"

"I'm just assisting. Glen's actually taking the pictures."

"Glen?"

"My colleague from the paper. His assistant called in sick, and he was desperate."

"That was nice of you to step in."

"Yeah, well."

"Maybe we could catch up another time?"

"Hey, I need to go," said Guin, not wanting to arrange a date with Ris. "Don't want to be late for the wedding!"

"Okay," he said, sounding disappointed.

Guin suddenly felt bad. It must have been rough for him, losing his baby and his fiancée.

"Some other time."

She ended the call and went to her bedroom.

"Something practical yet professional," she murmured, looking through the clothing in her closet. She pulled out a red cocktail dress and immediately put it back. "Definitely not practical."

Guin pulled out several more outfits before finally deciding on a simple blue sundress. Then she went to the bathroom to fix her hair and put on a little makeup. When she was done, she gathered her bag and her phone. It was just after one-thirty. She sent Glen a quick text, letting him know she was on her way. Hopefully, there wouldn't be traffic and she'd arrive on time.

Guin hadn't realized how big the resort was. And it took her an additional ten minutes to get from the gate to where the ceremony was to take place. She parked the Mini in the lot reserved for the wedding and quickly went in search of Glen.

She found him a few minutes later, looking harried. He quickly set her to work, helping him arrange his equipment and take light readings. There were two separate setups for the affair, one for the ceremony (outside) and one for the reception (inside). That way he didn't have to waste time lugging his equipment around.

He explained how the evening would go, and they did some test shots. Guin felt nervous, worried that she would screw up. But Glen kept telling her she'd be fine. Finally, it was time.

"You ready?" asked Glen.

"No," Guin said. "But I'll do my best."

Glen led her to the room where the bride, whose name was Cassandra, was getting ready. It was a hive of activity. There were three other young women, all of whom looked to be in their twenties, getting their hair and makeup done along with the bride. And over there was the mother of the bride, barking orders at someone. Guin froze. It was Audra Linwood.

Glen went over to the bride, whose mother had just come over to speak with her.

"Cassandra, you look radiant." The bride-to-be smiled.

"You, too, Audra." Audra smiled back at him. Then she noticed Guin.

"What's she doing here?"

"Do you two know each other?" Glen asked. Guin tried not to cower under Audra's withering glare. "My assistant called in sick last minute, and Guin volunteered to help."

Guin wasn't sure *volunteered* was the right word, but she didn't say anything.

"As long as she knows what she's doing," said Audra.

"Don't worry, Guin's a pro."

He gave Guin a wink. Then he turned to the bride.

"So Cassie, would you introduce us to your wedding party?"

Cassie nodded.

"This is my maid of honor, Melissa."

Melissa smiled at Glen, and Glen smiled back.

"And these are my bridesmaids, Libby and Tiffany."

"Nice to meet you, ladies."

Guin heard one of the bridesmaids whisper that she didn't know Cassie had hired such a good-looking photographer, and Guin smiled to herself. Glen was rather good-looking, though she pretended not to notice.

Glen immediately started taking candid pictures of everyone, and Guin wondered if she should be doing something. But he hadn't said anything. So she stood in the background, trying to avoid getting in any of the shots.

"How about a mother-daughter shot?" Glen suggested. He then positioned Cassie and Audra together and took a half-dozen photos. "Got it," he said. He looked over at Guin. "Shall we go see how the groom is doing?"

"Be sure he doesn't make a run for it!" Tiffany called out.

Cassie swatted her friend, and Guin and Glen headed down the hall.

Guin had forgotten how exhausting weddings could be. Even more so when you were photographing one. Glen had kept her busy, having her corral people for photographs, hold up the reflector, give him light readings, and move equipment around.

The ceremony was long over, and they were now inside photographing the reception. Glen had told her she could take a quick break, and Guin was just returning from the restroom when she saw him. She thought about fleeing, but he had already spied her, and she couldn't just abandon Glen.

"I thought it was you," said Tony Mandelli, his over-tan face breaking into a grin. "And you're just as beautiful as I remember."

Guin wanted to throw up.

"I'm working, Mr. Mandelli."

"Please, it's Tony. And I'm sure Mr. Photographer can spare you for a few minutes."

Guin sent a mental SOS to Glen. As if sensing her distress, he turned and came over.

"Is everything all right?" he asked her.

"I was just saying to Mr. Mandelli that I needed to get back to work."

"And I was just saying to Ms. Jones that I didn't think you would miss her."

"I'm afraid you're wrong about that," said Glen.

He placed a hand on Guin's lower back and started to steer her away.

"He your new boyfriend?" Mandelli called. "Does he know you're a cock-tease?"

Guin could feel herself blushing.

"Just ignore him," said Glen.

Guin tried to, but she could feel Mandelli's eyes boring into her.

"What was that about?" Glen asked her when they were a safe distance away.

"Long story."

"Okay, tell me later."

She quickly glanced back and saw Mandelli had his arm around Audra's waist.

A little after nine, Glen said they were done.

Thank God, Guin thought. Her feet were killing her.

She had gone to the restroom again and was surprised to see a familiar face washing her hands.

"Paris?"

The woman turned and looked up at Guin. She was dressed as a server.

"Ms. Jones? What are you doing here? Are you covering the wedding for the paper?"

"No, I'm helping out the photographer. What are you doing here?" Though it was obvious Paris was working. "I went by Paradise Found to see you, but they said you quit."

She didn't reply right away. Just grabbed a paper towel and dried her hands.

"It wasn't really working out for me there."

"Did it have anything to do with Jackson Brennan?"

Guin had been wondering if Paris had lied to her about Brennan after speaking with Fiona. But just then two of the bride's friends came into the bathroom, giggling.

"I should get back to work," said Paris.

Guin had wanted to ask her some questions, but clearly now was not the time.

They left the bathroom at the same time but neither spoke. Then Guin heard a man calling Paris's name—her boss?—and Paris hurried away.

"You ready?" asked Glen.

Guin jumped. She hadn't seen him sneak up on her.

"Everything all packed up?"

"Yup. If you could just give me a hand getting everything into the SUV."

Guin nodded. They brought the equipment to Glen's SUV and began loading.

"That should do it," he said a few minutes later. "Hey, are you hungry?"

Guin's stomach growled in response. She hadn't eaten since before the wedding, and that had been hours ago.

"Come on, I'll treat you."

"But it's nearly ten. Everything will be closed."

"There's always Doc Ford's. Pretty sure the one here's open until ten."

"You think they'll let us in?"

"I'll see that they do. Follow me over."

CHAPTER 20

They drove to Doc Ford's, but the hostess informed them that the restaurant had just closed. However, the bar was still open. They sat and ordered some flatbread and fried calamari, along with a beer for Glen and a club soda with lime for Guin.

"So who was the charmer with the fake tan and slicked-back hair?" Glen asked her. "He looked like something out of *Wall Street*. Though I hear the eighties are making a comeback."

"His name is Anthony Mandelli," said Guin. "He's a real estate developer—and a friend of the mother of the bride. I had a run-in with him a couple of years ago, when I was covering a story. A murder case. He was arrested but got off."

"Is he dangerous?"

"Let's just say, I wouldn't want to be alone with him."

The bartender brought over their drinks and said their food would be right up.

"Is that why Audra was giving you the evil eye?" continued Glen.

"Possibly. Though I think it had to do more with Jackson Brennan."

"Oh?"

"The two of them had some kind of falling out, and I don't think she liked me nosing around."

"You think she could have had something to do with his death?"

"Maybe."

Their food came out, and they ate in silence.

"So, have you given any more thought to my proposal?" Glen asked her when they were nearly done.

"Proposal?"

"The cooking course in Tuscany."

"Oh, that." She took another bite of the flatbread. "It sounds amazing, but…"

"But what?"

"I'm already taking a week off to go to Bath."

"What's another week? You have two, don't you?"

"It's not just that. The course isn't cheap."

"I'd be happy to help."

"I can't let you do that."

"What about Ginny? I bet she'd let you write about it for the paper. And if you did that, the paper might even pay for it."

"I doubt that. Seven days in Tuscany is a little different than paying for three lunches at the Savoury Spoon."

"Just talk to her. I spoke with Bridget. She said she'd hold the spot for another week."

"Just tell her to give it to someone else."

"I'm not going to do that. Look, what about if I spoke with Ginny? You know she can't resist me."

He smiled, and Guin couldn't help smiling back. She knew Ginny had a soft spot for Glen. But if someone was going to speak to Ginny, it should be her.

"I'll speak to Ginny… if I decide to go."

"What's there to decide? It's a week in Tuscany at an amazing villa with all the food you can make—and me!"

Guin laughed.

"You're a good salesman, but I still need to think about it."

"Just don't take too long."

They finished their meal and Glen signaled for the check.

It was a warm evening, though there was a gentle breeze blowing, and the sky was clear. Guin looked up and was amazed by all the stars. Growing up in New York City, you didn't see too many stars, at least of the celestial variety.

"Beautiful, isn't it?" said Glen.

Guin nodded.

They continued to gaze heavenward.

"I should go," said Glen. "I've got a busy day tomorrow. Lots of wedding pictures to go through. Thanks again for your help today."

"You're welcome. I just hope the pictures turn out okay."

"I'm sure they'll be fine."

They stood looking at each other, neither moving.

"Yes, well," said Glen, taking a step away from Guin.

"We should probably go," said Guin.

They headed into the parking lot.

"Thanks for dinner," she said, as they arrived at Glen's car.

"My pleasure. Though I owe you a real meal."

"That food tasted pretty real to me."

"You know what I mean," said Glen.

Guin smiled.

"Well, good night."

"Good night," said Glen.

He unlocked the SUV and Guin headed to her Mini.

It was after seven when Guin got up Sunday. Very unusual for her. And she felt surprisingly calm. For the first time in days, she hadn't had an anxiety dream.

She got up and looked out the window. It was another sun-filled morning. She quickly got dressed and headed to the beach. As she walked along the shoreline, looking for shells, her thoughts strayed. She was thinking about the wedding and about running into Tony Mandelli and Paris.

Had Mandelli really been in New York when Brennan died? He could have easily taken an early morning flight out of Fort Myers that Saturday, after seeing Brennan on Friday. And she could easily picture Mandelli tricking Brennan into swallowing cyanide, even grinning as the life left his body.

She shuddered at the thought.

And what about Paris? Had she really left Paradise Found to work in catering at South Seas? That didn't seem like a step up. And what was her real relationship with Jackson Brennan? She claimed that she wasn't interested in him and that he had tried to rape her. But Fiona said the two of them were always flirting with each other. Of course, both could be true. Maybe she should have another talk with the fickle blonde.

She gazed out at the Gulf. Typically, she went to the beach to forget about work, yet here she was thinking about it. She sighed and tried to put thoughts of work to the side and focus on shells. But it was no use. At least she was getting some exercise.

Guin was back at home by nine and spent the rest of the morning working, finishing her article on Stephanie Yates. She ate lunch, then looked at her to-do list for the coming week. She needed to go back to the Savoury Spoon one more time, but this time she would not go alone.

She picked up her phone and sent a text to Shelly.

"Lunch at the Savoury Spoon this week?"

"Sure," Shelly replied.

"You want to invite Barb and Linda to join us?"

"Is this for a review?"

Shelly knew her too well.

"I'm not at liberty to say."

"I'll take that as a yes," Shelly typed. "When?"

"Tomorrow too soon? Or else Tuesday."

"I'll ask the girls."

"Just don't tell them it's for the paper."

"My lips are sealed."

Though Guin wasn't so sure about that.

Guin had written *Talk to Paris and Fiona* on her to-do list. She thought about texting Paris but decided to wait until Monday and speak with Fiona first, to verify her story. She picked up her phone to text her, then realized she didn't have Fiona's number. But she knew someone who did. Though did she really want to text Ris?

She debated it for several minutes, then picked up her phone again.

"Could I have Fiona's number?" she texted him. "There's something I need to ask her."

"She'll be here for dinner," he replied. "Why don't you join us?"

Guin frowned and was about to write back that she was busy when Ris texted her again.

"We'd both love to see you."

Guin sighed. She couldn't ignore him forever. And she did want to speak with Fiona.

"What time?" she wrote.

"Six-thirty?"

"Fine. Can I bring anything?"

"Just yourself."

Guin stood staring at her closet. Why was she having such a hard time deciding what to wear? It wasn't as though she and Ris were going on a date. The mere idea was ridiculous. They were just having dinner at his place, with Fiona. On a Sunday. He'd probably be wearing his drawstring pants and a loose-fitting button-down shirt, with the top two buttons undone, like he always did.

Suddenly, she was picturing his toned chest.

Stop it, Guin! she admonished herself. Seriously, what was wrong with her? She had no desire to get back together with Ris, but for some reason she couldn't stop thinking about him. Or his body. Had the detective dumping her made her that desperate (or horny)?

She frowned and continued to stare at her clothing.

It was too warm to wear long pants. And she felt shorts and a tee were too casual. Maybe a sundress? She pulled out one with sunflowers printed on it that she hadn't worn in a while.

"What do you think, Fauna?" she asked the cat, who was lying on the bed.

Fauna yawned.

"I don't think it's boring. I'm going to see if it still fits."

She slipped it on and looked at herself in the mirror.

"It'll do," she told her reflection.

She went into the bathroom.

"Ugh," she said, looking at her face. "When did I get so many freckles?" *And when did I start caring?* she silently added.

She got out her makeup bag and took out the bottle of foundation.

"No, I am not wearing makeup," she said aloud, putting the foundation back. "Well, maybe just a little mascara and lip gloss."

She applied the mascara and lip gloss and looked at her face again.

"Now, about my hair…"

After putting it up and then taking it down again several times, she left it down, frizz be damned.

"Enough!" she said.

She walked back into the bedroom and picked her phone up off of the nightstand. It was a little after six. She was going to be late. She sent Ris a quick text, letting him know she was leaving, then headed out the door.

CHAPTER 21

Guin rang the doorbell and waited. A minute later, Ris opened the door. He was dressed just as she had imagined he would be, with his arms and part of his chest exposed. And Guin found herself admiring his lean, tanned, and toned body. *Stop that!* she told herself.

"I was worried you got lost," he said, smiling at her.

"Nope, just forgot how long it took to get to Fort Myers Beach from Sanibel." Only a small lie.

"Well, you're here now. Can I get you a drink? I just opened a bottle of white from Australia."

"You bring it back with you?"

"No, I picked it up here."

Guin followed him to the kitchen where he poured them both some white wine. Fiona was there preparing dinner.

"Hi, Guin!" she said looking up. "I hope you like gazpacho and Mediterranean quinoa salad!"

"I do!" said Guin, smiling at Fiona.

"I don't know if Dad informed you, but we both decided to go vegan for the summer."

"Very noble of you."

"I don't know about noble," she said. "Just better for the planet, you know? And probably us, too. Though I miss cheese."

"There are vegan versions."

"I know. But it's not the same. Though I have a vegan

mac and cheese recipe I'm planning on trying."

"How's your brother?" Guin asked.

"He's okay."

Guin waited for her to go on.

"He's in Miami for the summer, working for some startup with one of his friends," Ris explained.

"But at least Mom has one of us here," said Fiona.

"And John said he'd visit," Ris added.

"Yeah, right. When he needs to do his laundry. Or have Mom do it."

Guin smiled. There was something so nice and normal about hanging out with Ris and Fiona. Would this have been what it would have been like if she had lived with him, as he had wanted her to? Though she reminded herself that while she had enjoyed spending time with Ris, and his kids, the relationship hadn't fulfilled her in other ways.

"So, are you living here with your father over the summer?" Guin asked Fiona.

"She's staying at her mom's," said Ris. "It's closer to work."

"Though I crash at Dad's on my days off."

Guin watched as Fiona made the salad.

"All set!" said Fiona a few minutes later. "You ready to eat?"

Guin nodded.

"Looks great!"

Over dinner, Guin asked Fiona about school and what she planned on doing after she graduated. Fiona said she wasn't sure, maybe take some time to travel? Then Guin asked her about working at the boutique, which led her to ask about Paris.

Had she and Paris gotten along?

Fiona said that they had and revealed that the two of

them had gone to high school together, though Paris was older and had been in the popular group.

Then Guin asked her if Paris and Beth had gotten along.

"I think so," said Fiona. "I wasn't usually there if both of them were."

"And what about with Mr. Brennan? You mentioned at the boutique that he and Paris flirted with each other."

Ris raised an eyebrow.

"Oh yeah," said Fiona. "Though like I said, Paris flirted with all the cute guys."

Did that mean Fiona thought Jackson Brennan was cute? Guin didn't want to go there.

"Why all the questions about Paris?" Fiona asked her.

Guin hesitated. Should she tell them what Paris had told her?

"Paris claimed that Mr. Brennan had behaved inappropriately towards her."

"What do you mean by *inappropriately*?" asked Fiona.

Guin wasn't sure how to answer.

"You mean, like, did he touch her or kiss her?"

Guin nodded.

"Something like that."

Fiona was frowning.

"Is something wrong?" Guin asked her.

"It's just... I know it was none of my business, but I caught the two of them fooling around in Beth's office. And Paris definitely did not seem to be objecting, even though what they were doing was pretty inappropriate."

Guin looked at her.

"Was this recently?"

Fiona nodded.

"It was just a couple of weeks ago, not long after I started. Paris swore me to secrecy and said that Mr. Brennan was helping her."

"Helping her how?"

"She said he was going to help her get a job in Miami and an apartment."

That part jibed with what Paris had told her.

"I see," said Guin. "And did Paris say anything else about Mr. Brennan?"

"What's this all about, Guin?" said Ris.

She turned to face him.

"Paris claimed Brennan tried to rape her the night he died."

"What?!" said Fiona.

Guin looked at her.

"That's what she told me."

"I mean… I guess it's possible," said Fiona. "Paris was pretty upset the next day. She was going on about how you couldn't trust men. I thought she was referring to Marcus." She looked over at the clock.

"Hey, you guys okay if I excuse myself? I can do the dishes later if you need me to. I just told Lauren I'd call her at eight."

"Go ahead," said Ris. "Guin and I can clean up."

"Thanks!" said Fiona. She got up and went over to her father, giving him a noisy kiss on the cheek. "You're the best!" Then she turned to Guin. "Nice seeing you, Guin!"

Guin watched as Fiona headed to her room.

"She's a good kid."

"She is."

They cleared the table and Guin kept Ris company in the kitchen as he washed the dishes.

"So do you think there's a connection between Fiona's coworker and Jackson Brennan's death?" he asked her.

"That's what I'm trying to find out."

They finished cleaning up, and Guin said she should go.

"You don't have to," said Ris, laying a hand gently on her arm.

Guin looked down at his hand, then up at his face. She knew that look.

"Maybe some other time." She put down the dishtowel. "Please thank Fiona for me. Dinner was delicious."

He walked her to the door.

"It was great seeing you."

"It was nice seeing you too."

They stood in the doorway for several seconds. Ris leaned down to give Guin a kiss. But Guin stepped away.

"I should go."

She made her way to the Mini and got in. As she backed out, she saw Ris staring after her. She began to drive, turning onto Estero Boulevard. Then she pulled into a nearby supermarket. She took out her phone and speed-dialed the detective's number. He picked up after two rings.

"You at home?" she asked him.

"I am."

"Can I come over?"

She knew it wasn't a great idea, but she desperately wanted to see him, to find out if things were really over between them.

"It's a bit late.'"

"It's only nine, and I'm close by."

"Suit yourself."

Guin knew she should say never mind and go home. But she didn't. Instead, she said she'd see him soon.

Guin thought about turning around and heading back to Sanibel several times as she drove to the detective's apartment, even as she pulled into the lot next to his building. Instead, she parked the Mini, took a look at her face in the mirror, got out, and jogged up the stairs to his front door. She rang the doorbell and waited. He opened it a minute later, dressed in a pair of old shorts and a t-shirt. He was older and shorter than Ris, and thicker set, more like a boxer than a triathlete (which Ris had been and probably still was). But Guin didn't care. She practically threw herself at him, taking his head in her hands and kissing him.

He was momentarily surprised, then returned the kiss. A minute later, they were frantically making their way to the detective's bedroom.

It was dark when Guin woke up. She had no idea what time it was and had momentarily forgotten where she was. Then she saw the detective lying next to her and smiled. As if sensing her, he rolled over and wrapped an arm around her.

"You awake?" she said.

"No," he replied.

He was spooning her, and Guin could tell at least part of him was very awake.

"Aren't you tired?" she asked him.

He started to stroke her sensitive parts and she gave herself over to the sensation. A short time later, she was lying with her head on his chest, toying with the hair there, which was the same reddish-brown peppered with gray as the hair on his head.

"I ran into Anthony Mandelli this weekend, at a wedding up on Captiva," she casually mentioned.

"He bother you?" the detective said in a gruff voice. "Just say the word and I'll have him arrested."

Guin smiled.

"It was nothing I couldn't handle. But I was wondering, you think he could have had something to do with Brennan's death? The two weren't exactly fond of each other, and he blamed Brennan for that land deal falling through."

The detective didn't say anything.

"You speak with him?"

"You know I can't discuss the case with you."

"You speak with Paris Tisdale?"

"Who's she?"

Guin couldn't believe he didn't know about Paris.

"She works at Paradise Found, Beth Brennan's shop. She might have been having an affair with Brennan."

"And you know this how?"

"You know I can't reveal my sources," said Guin.

He grunted.

"So did you come over here and seduce me in hopes I'd discuss the case with you?"

"Maybe."

"Well, it won't work."

"Oh really?" she said, lowering her hand. "You can't share anything with me?"

She could feel the detective was aroused.

"Shut up," he said, rolling her over.

CHAPTER 22

The detective nudged Guin awake.

"Hm…?" she said. She opened her eyes to see him standing next to her, fully clothed. "Where're you going?" she asked him sleepily.

"Work. I made some coffee."

"Thanks," she yawned. "I should get going too."

"Just lock the door behind you."

He turned to go, and Guin got up and followed him.

"You going to speak with Paris?"

"We'll see," he said.

"I'll take that as a yes. If you do speak with her, could I listen in?"

"You know I can't—"

"Yeah, yeah, yeah. But you wouldn't have known about her unless I told you. So you owe me."

"I owe you?" he said, raising an eyebrow.

"Yes, you owe me."

"If this is about last night…"

"This has nothing to do with last night. It's about the police and the press working together to solve an important case."

The detective frowned.

"Fine. But not a word out of you."

"I'll be as quiet as a mouse."

"You ever hear mice? They squeak. A lot."

Guin made a face.

"I promise I won't say a thing." Though she mentally crossed her fingers as she said it.

"Uh-huh."

They had reached the door.

"Just let me know when you bring her in."

He opened the door to leave but Guin stopped him.

"What?" he said.

"You going to text me later?"

"About?"

"About Paris!"

"I need to get to work."

Guin watched him go down the stairs. Then she shut the door and went to the kitchen.

Guin was staring at her phone. She had forgotten to turn it off, and the battery had drained overnight. Worse, her car charger wasn't working. So she would have to wait until she got home to check her messages. Hopefully, she would make it home without incident.

As soon as she got home, she plugged her phone in and found she had messages from Shelly and Ris.

Shelly had written that lunch was on for Tuesday at noon. And Ris had written to tell her what a nice time he and Fiona had had and that he hoped they could see each other again soon. Guin frowned. She had had a nice time too. But she didn't want to lead him on. Could they just be friends? She wasn't sure that was possible.

She hadn't eaten anything since dinner the night before and was suddenly hungry. *Should have stopped at Jean-Luc's Bakery on the way home*, she said to herself. Well, too late now. She got out a box of cereal and poured herself a bowl, then ate it standing up. When she was done, she went to take a shower and get dressed.

By afternoon, Guin was feeling restless. She hadn't heard back from Tom Dewey, and the detective hadn't called or texted her. Not that she really expected him to. But she wondered if he had contacted Paris. Which reminded Guin, she wanted to speak with Paris's boyfriend. What did Fiona say his last name was? Was it Rollins? No, it was… Ramsay. And she said he had played basketball for the FGCU Eagles and had an Instagram account.

She went to his account and sent him a message. Now what? Should she try Tom Dewey? She knew he was busy, but she had questions that needed answers. Maybe she should just send him an email. But first, she would do a little more digging into Jackson Brennan's past.

She did another online search, but nothing came up that she didn't already know about. Could this so-called stuff from Brennan's past have happened pre-internet, say when Brennan was in law school or college? She would need to dig a little deeper.

She knew Brennan had gone to Syracuse undergraduate and then to law school at Loyola University in Chicago. She had seen both diplomas hanging in his office. She just couldn't recall when he had graduated. She did a quick search and discovered Brennan was forty-eight. So he had attended college and law school in the nineties, back when the internet was in its infancy.

If something had happened when he was still in school, perhaps there would be something in the campus or local newspaper. It was worth a shot.

She found *The Daily Orange*, an independent local newspaper run by Syracuse University students, and typed Brennan's name into the search box. Success! It turned out Brennan had been on the men's basketball team. Interesting. But basketball scores were not what she was after.

She scrolled through the search results and—bingo! She found what she was looking for. During Brennan's senior year, he had been accused of raping an underclassman. Her name wasn't given. She was only referred to as Jane Doe. But it had made the news. No doubt because of Brennan being on the basketball team.

Per the article, Brennan had allegedly raped her while she was passed out at some fraternity party. She had sworn it had been him, and there had been a witness. But Brennan's teammates and fraternity brothers said it couldn't have been him, that the girl was drunk.

The article wasn't very long and didn't say what had happened to the girl or Brennan, so Guin looked for a follow-up piece. She finally found it. But again, it didn't say much. Just that the university had found no wrongdoing on Brennan's part, and that Jane Doe had left campus. Guin wondered what had happened to her, and if this could have been the something from the past that Tom Dewey had referred to. She immediately sent Tom a text, asking when they could meet again, saying she had something important to ask him and would prefer to do it in person. Then she got up and stretched.

She went to the kitchen and got a glass of water. As she drank, she wondered if there were more instances of Brennan forcing himself on women. There was a good likelihood of that if he had done it in college and more recently.

She finished the water and went back to her office to see what else she could discover about Brennan's student days. She found the Loyola University student newspaper, but she wasn't able to find anything about Brennan beyond some alumni news. Maybe try the Chicago newspapers? She searched the *Chicago Tribune* but came up empty. She was about to search the *Chicago Sun-Times* when she had a better idea. Craig. He was a crime reporter there in the nineties.

Maybe he'd know something. Though it was a long shot.

She picked up her phone and entered his number.

"So I've been doing some digging into Brennan's past," she explained. "Turns out, he was accused of raping a girl back when he was in college. And I wondered if there were more instances."

"You find anything?"

"No. That's why I'm calling. Brennan went to Loyola University in Chicago for law school. But I couldn't find anything on Loyola's site about him raping anyone or being accused of rape. But I thought Loyola being Catholic, maybe they wouldn't report something like that. But maybe one of the papers ran something. So I did a quick search in the *Trib*, but I didn't see anything. Then I remembered I happened to know someone who was a crime reporter in Chicago back in the nineties and…"

"You thought maybe I could recall something."

"Exactly."

"That was a long time ago, Guin."

"Not that long ago. Only the mid-nineties."

"That's a long time ago."

"I know. But…"

Craig sighed.

"You think this could be important?"

"I do. Tom Dewey mentioned something about Brennan's past catching up with him. Maybe there's something we don't know. I sure didn't know he had been accused of raping someone back in college."

"I take it he got off."

"Yup. He was on the basketball team. And at Syracuse that made you pretty much Teflon."

Craig didn't say anything.

"And speaking of sleazy men," Guin continued, "you find out if Mandelli really was in the Hamptons when Brennan died?"

"I did."

"And?"

"He was, attending some swanky party with a bunch of other obnoxious rich people."

"And you know this how?"

"There was a picture of him in the local paper."

"When was the party?"

"That Saturday."

"He still could have killed Brennan Friday then taken an early flight out Saturday morning."

"Possible but unlikely."

"But we can't rule it out. What about Brennan's run for office? I know he was interviewing campaign managers. But no one seems to know if he had hired anyone or will give me a name. You hear anything?"

"No, but I can ask around."

Guin heard her phone beep. She had a new text message. It could be from the detective or Tom.

"Hey, Craig, I've got to go. Let me know what you find out."

"Will do."

Guin ended the call and immediately opened the text. It was from the detective. He was about to interview Paris. Guin cursed. Of course he would tell her minutes before the interview. No doubt hoping Guin wouldn't get the text until it was too late or wouldn't be able to get over there in time. But she'd show him.

She grabbed her bag and her keys and flew out the door.

CHAPTER 23

Guin arrived at the Sanibel Police Department and told the man behind the protective glass that she was there to see Detective O'Loughlin. A few minutes later, she was buzzed back.

Guin knocked on the detective's door, then poked her head inside. The detective was on the phone. He glanced her way, then turned his attention back to whomever he was talking to.

"I've gotta go," he said. He hung up and looked over at Guin. "You made it."

"I gather you hoped I wouldn't."

"A man can dream."

Guin scowled.

"So, where is she?"

"She should be here any minute."

On cue, the detective's phone rang.

"Have someone escort her back," he told the caller. He placed the phone back, then turned to Guin. "Remember, you're just here to observe."

Guin raised her hand to her mouth and made a zipping motion with her fingers.

Seconds later, there was a knock at the door.

"Come in!" called the detective.

The door opened to reveal Officer Pettit. Just behind him was Paris.

"Leave her," said the detective.

Officer Pettit gestured for Paris to enter. She gave him a look, then turned and entered the detective's office.

"Have a seat."

She went to take a seat, then noticed Guin standing in the corner. She turned and looked at the detective.

"What's she doing here?"

"Observing."

Paris frowned.

"Sit," commanded the detective.

Paris sat, but she did not look happy.

The detective looked down at his notes, then back up at Paris.

"I understand you were working at the Paradise Found boutique at the time of Jackson Brennan's death."

"That's right."

"And that you quit rather suddenly just after."

"Is that a crime?"

"No, I'm just curious as to why you left."

"I found a better gig."

"Working at the South Seas resort."

"That's right."

"Were you interested in a career in catering?"

"I needed the money."

"Yet you were making more at Paradise Found."

Paris looked uncomfortable.

"The base pay might be less, but you can make more with tips."

"I see," said the detective, looking down at his notebook. "So your abrupt departure from Paradise Found had nothing to do with the owner's husband dying and his wife discovering the two of you were having an affair?"

Guin's eyes immediately went to Paris, but Paris remained cool.

"Well?" said the detective when Paris didn't reply.

"Well, what?"

"You don't deny seeing the owner's husband?"

"Sure, I saw him. He was in the store all the time."

"What about outside of work?"

Paris crossed her arms over her chest.

The detective looked down at his notebook again.

"I have an eyewitness who says she saw you having drinks with the deceased the evening he died."

Guin looked again at Paris.

"So, I had a drink with the guy. Is that a crime?"

"I have another eyewitness who says that you and Mr. Brennan were seen together at Mrs. Brennan's boutique being, shall we say, *overly* friendly."

Paris was scowling now.

"Who told you that? Was it Fiona? She was always jealous of me because the customers liked me better."

The detective eyed her.

"You don't deny being friendly to Mrs. Brennan's husband?"

Paris looked ready to explode.

"What was I supposed to do, ignore him? Jack owned the place. So I was nice to him. Is there something wrong with that?"

"You told me he tried to rape you," said Guin, unable to keep silent. "Was that a lie?"

Paris turned and glared at her.

"Answer Ms. Jones, Ms. Tisdale."

Paris turned back to Detective O'Loughlin.

"Okay, fine. He came to the store that Friday looking for Beth. He was totally pissed about something. I told him she wasn't there. He didn't believe me and went to her office. I followed him."

"Then what?" said Guin.

Paris scowled at Guin, then looked back at the detective.

"I asked him what was up, and he told me I was the only one who really understood him. Then he kissed me."

"Did he force himself on you?" asked the detective.

Paris shook her head, her whole demeanor changing.

"No," she said quietly.

"I'm sorry, I didn't hear that," said the detective.

"I said, no!" said Paris, much louder this time. "You want the truth? Fine, I'll give it to you. Jack and I were in love."

Guin stared at her.

"In love?"

Paris ignored her.

"After he kissed you, what happened?" asked the detective.

"He said we needed to talk. So we went out for a drink."

"Where did he take you?"

"That place just across the Causeway."

"And what did you talk about?"

"He told me that he loved me, but that he couldn't see me anymore. That his wife had somehow found out about us and was threatening to divorce him. And he couldn't have that, not with him about to run for Congress."

"And how did that make you feel?" asked the detective.

"How do you think?" said Paris. The detective waited for her to go on. "I was pissed. He had told me he was going to get me a job in Miami and an apartment."

"But now he wouldn't?"

"He said he'd have to lay low for a while, until things blew over."

"Then what?"

"He drove me back to the boutique, and Marcus was there."

"Marcus Ramsay?"

Paris nodded.

"He saw Jack giving me a kiss goodbye and went apeshit."

"And by apeshit you mean…?"

Paris gave him an exasperated look.

"He told Jack to get his hands off me."

"Did Mr. Ramsay hit Mr. Brennan?"

"He just shoved him a bit."

"What did Mr. Brennan do?"

"Jack told Marcus to take his hands off him or he'd hit him with a lawsuit."

"Did Mr. Ramsay comply?"

"Yeah. Though he wasn't happy about it."

"Then what?" asked Guin.

"Jack got in his car and drove away."

"What about Marcus?"

"We had a few words, then he got on his bike and left."

"You know where he went?" asked the detective.

"No."

"And what time was this?"

"I don't know. Seven? Seven-thirty?"

"I don't understand," said Guin, interrupting. "Why did you tell me Brennan tried to rape you if you were in love with him?"

Paris turned to Guin.

"I panicked, okay? When Jack was found dead, I got emotional, and Marcus got suspicious. He had seen Jack kissing me and assumed there was something between us."

"But why tell him Brennan had tried to rape you?"

"Like I said, I panicked. I couldn't tell him the truth. So I told him I was emotional because I was glad Jack was dead, because he had hurt me."

"And he believed you?"

"I think he wanted to, but he was still suspicious."

"But why tell *me* Brennan tried to rape you?"

"I thought if Marcus heard me telling my story to a reporter, he'd believe me."

Guin shook her head.

"So why did you quit? Was it because you couldn't face Beth?"

Paris nodded.

"Don't you see? He killed himself because of me."

That was not the answer either Guin or the detective was expecting.

"Because of you?" said the detective, looking at Paris.

"He was in love with me, and the thought of not being able to see me was too much to bear."

"So you left the boutique without giving any notice."

"A friend said they desperately needed help up at South Seas, doing events and stuff, and that I could make a lot in tips. And no way was I going back to the store."

"Getting back to the night in question," said the detective. "Did you see or hear from Mr. Brennan after he left you at Paradise Found?"

"No," said Paris.

"Do you know where he went?"

"To some dinner."

"You know where the dinner was?"

"Somewhere on the island. He didn't say."

"Do you know who the dinner was with?" asked Guin.

"No, but I assumed it was important. Otherwise…"

"Otherwise what?"

"Otherwise he wouldn't have been in such a hurry to leave."

"And how did Mr. Brennan seem to you that evening?" Guin asked.

"What do you mean?"

"I mean, did he seem anxious or depressed?"

"Of course he was depressed! I told you, he was heartbroken about us having to end things!"

The detective ran a hand over his face.

"Can I go now?" Paris asked him. "I'm late for work and don't want my pay docked."

The detective picked up his desk phone.

"Send someone back to my office to escort Ms. Tisdale out."

A minute later, there was a knock at the door and an older officer poked his head in. The detective nodded and looked at Paris.

"You're free to go, Ms. Tisdale."

Paris got up and followed the officer out. When she had gone, Guin turned to Detective O'Loughlin.

"Well, what do you make of that?"

The detective looked lost in thought.

"Hello? Anybody home?" Guin said, waving a hand in front of him.

"Hm?"

"You believe her story?"

"That Brennan was madly in love with her and killed himself because he couldn't see her anymore? No."

Guin smiled.

"Me neither. But I think she believes it."

"Young people. They think the world revolves around them."

Guin didn't disagree.

"So, who's the eyewitness who saw Paris having drinks with Brennan?" The detective was giving her that look. "Wait, don't tell me: you can't say. What about the boyfriend, Marcus? Do you think he could have had something to do with Brennan's death? Did the medical examiner say anything about bruises?"

"Nothing that would have resulted in death."

Guin frowned.

"You think he really did kill himself?"

"The evidence would seem to suggest…"

"Forget the evidence," said Guin, interrupting him. "What do *you* think?"

"I think it's time you left, and I got back to work."

But Guin wasn't done.

"You want to grab a quick bite to eat?"

"Thanks, but I need to finish up."

"I can wait."

The detective looked up at her.

"You should go. I could be here a while."

Guin paused. She thought about offering to pick something up for him, but he was already typing away on his computer as if she wasn't there.

"Fine, I'm going," she said.

The detective continued to type.

"Will you let me know if you find out anything?"

No response.

Guin watched him for a few more seconds then saw herself out.

CHAPTER 24

Guin replayed her and the detective's conversation with Paris as she drove home. Could Paris really have been in love with Jackson Brennan? Guin was finding it hard to believe. Though she could believe the young woman loved the idea of the older man getting her a job and a place to live in Miami.

And what about Brennan? Had he been in love with Paris? She couldn't picture Brennan being in love with anyone other than himself. Though she had no problem picturing him lusting after Paris. But to kill himself over her? No way.

But could something have rattled Brennan so much that evening that he decided to take his own life? It was theoretically possible. But what? Guin gripped the steering wheel. She would need to speak with Beth and Tom again. Try to jog their memory. See if there was something she might have missed. She would also have a chat with Marcus Ramsay, assuming he ever replied to her Instagram message.

Guin sent Marcus another message as soon as she got home. Then she texted Beth and Tom. If no one got back to her, she would visit their workplaces.

Feeling a bit better, she made herself some mac and cheese and watched a mystery on Hallmark. It was a new one, about a photographer who helps solve crimes in her small town. As Guin watched, she mused that in nearly all of these mysteries the amateur sleuth was almost always an attractive single woman, and the detective officially in charge of solving the case was almost always a hunky single man, and after butting heads the two of them would usually wind up together. Just like her and the detective.

She watched the movie till the end, even though she had already figured out who had done it. Then she headed to bed.

Guin slept fitfully that night. She dreamed again that she was lost, unable to find her way. She knew what the dream meant. She just didn't want to admit it to herself.

When she finally got up, she was exhausted and went into the kitchen to make herself some coffee. She leaned against the big kitchen island as she drank it, staring out at the backyard. She thought about the cooking class in Italy. She longed to go, but she felt it would be irresponsible. Still, she wasn't ready to say no.

Guin finished her coffee and rinsed out her mug. She should probably eat something, but she wasn't hungry. Besides, she would be meeting Shelly, Barbara, and Linda at the Savoury Spoon in a few hours, and she'd need to have a good appetite.

She took a shower and got dressed, then went to her office.

At eleven-forty-five, a reminder popped up on her screen, informing her she had a lunch date at noon. She removed Fauna from her lap, where she had been napping, then grabbed her bag and keys and headed out.

Guin arrived at the Savoury Spoon to find Shelly, Linda, and Barbara already there.

"Have you been waiting long?" asked Guin.

"We just got here," said Shelly.

They went inside and stared up at the menu.

"Ooh, the Brie and Fig sandwich sounds delicious!" said Linda.

"I think I'll get the Caprese," said Barbara. "What about you, Shell?"

"Hmm… I'm thinking either the OG or the Cuban. What about you, Guin?"

"You want to get the Cuban, and I'll get the OG? Then we can share them."

"Sounds good to me!"

"And how about we get some smoothies?"

They placed their order then grabbed a table outside.

"So, I've been meaning to ask all of you," Guin began. She lowered her voice. "How did those shells you were working on turn out? Are they going to be used in the treasure hunt?"

"I can't speak for Linda or Shelly, but I was very pleased with how mine turned out," said Barbara. "And I assume they'll be used in the hunt, though Mary Ann wouldn't say."

"It's supposed to be top secret," said Linda. "No one actually knows which shells or how many will be used."

Right, Guin remembered. She had temporarily forgotten. Which reminded her…

"Do you know if any of the missing shells have turned up?"

Barbara was looking at her friend, and Guin realized she probably wasn't supposed to know about the missing shells.

"Not as far as I know," said Linda.

"Missing shells?" said Shelly. "I hadn't heard about any shells for the treasure hunt going missing. Did something happen?"

Guin blanched. It was supposed to be a secret. Well, too late now.

"A bunch of shells meant for the treasure hunt disappeared from the Community House," she informed Shelly. "Though no one was supposed to know."

"You knew," said Shelly. "So, were they stolen?"

"They're not sure."

Guin was spared any more explaining by Savannah arriving with their smoothies.

"Here you go, ladies! I'll be right back with your sandwiches!"

Over lunch, Guin only half-listened as Shelly, Barbara, and Linda gossiped. She was too busy surreptitiously taking notes about their meal, hoping the others wouldn't notice.

"You making notes for your review?" asked Barbara.

Guin looked up.

"Don't worry, I won't tell."

"Was it that obvious?"

All three ladies nodded their heads, and Guin sighed.

"You think Nick and Savannah know?"

Shelly glanced inside.

"I don't know. They look pretty busy. Though does it really matter? Not like they would do anything differently."

True, thought Guin.

They finished their meal and tossed the remains in a nearby bin.

"We should get going," said Barbara and Linda. "Thanks for including us!"

Guin watched as they headed to the lot. Now it was just her and Shelly. Shelly gently laid a hand on Guin's arm.

"Everything okay? You seemed a bit distracted. And I don't think it's because you were taking notes."

"Everything's fine."

Shelly wasn't buying it.

"What?"

"It's okay to admit you're upset about Detective O'Loughlin."

"I'm not upset. I mean, I was. But there's no point, right? He's made his decision, and there's nothing I can do about it."

"You could always go to Boston."

"No."

"Why not?"

"You know why not."

"Explain it to me again."

"He doesn't want me there."

"Did he say that?"

"Not in so many words, but he made it pretty clear. Besides, I don't really want to move to Massachusetts."

"So, what do you want?"

"That's the problem. I don't know. I mean, I want Bill to stay, obviously. But…"

"But?"

Guin sighed.

"In a way, I'm envious of him, starting a new life."

Shelly looked at her.

"I love Sanibel, but lately I've felt in a rut, like I've been doing the same thing over and over again."

"Like in *Groundhog Day*."

"Yes, like that."

"So, do something different!"

"It's not that easy."

"Sure it is. Just figure out what you want to do and do it."

Easy for Shelly to say.

"Look, you're going to Bath. Sounds like you could use a vacation."

"Bath isn't a vacation."

"It's not? Sure sounded like it to me."

"A vacation is when you go someplace where you don't

have to make the bed or cook—and don't have to spend nearly every waking hour dealing with your family."

"So, take a real vacation."

"I can't."

"Why not?"

"I'm going to Bath."

"That's only for a week, right? Don't you get two weeks?"

"I do, but…"

"So, go to Paris or Italy! You'll already be over there."

"I've thought about it, but I don't think Ginny will let me."

"Did you ask her?"

"No, but…"

Shelly was giving Guin her best schoolmarm look.

"You know what they say, don't ask, don't get."

"You sound like Glen."

"I always liked him."

"Did I tell you he invited me to go do this weeklong cooking course with him in Tuscany?"

Shelly stared at her friend.

"No, you did not! Please tell me you said yes."

"I said I'd think about it."

"Are you crazy? What's there to think about?! It's perfect. Pick up the phone and tell him you'll go!"

"I told you, I don't think Ginny will let me take two weeks off."

"But you haven't asked her! At least talk to the woman. Sanibel's dead in the summer. She probably wouldn't care." She paused. "If you're worried, tell her you'll write about it for the paper."

"That's what Glen said."

"See! Great minds!"

Guin pursed her lips.

"Oh, come on, Guin! The worst she can say is no. And I bet she won't."

Guin wasn't so sure.

"Promise me you'll talk to her."

Guin sighed.

"I'll think about it."

"Don't think, do."

Shelly's phone was buzzing. She looked down at it.

"I've got to motor. But don't blow off Tuscany. Maybe this Italy trip is just what you need. Heck, if you don't want to go, I'll go." She got up and gave Guin a kiss on the cheek. "Arrivederci!"

Guin had planned on driving over to Jackson Brennan's office but went to the *Sanibel-Captiva Sun-Times* instead. The front door was unlocked, but there was no one at the front desk, and the place was eerily quiet. Maybe they were all out to lunch.

"Hello?" she called.

There was no answer.

Guin went down the hall to Ginny's office. The door was closed, and she thought she heard music. She knocked.

"I'm eating!" yelled Ginny. "Unless the building's burning, it can wait."

Guin thought about leaving but forced herself to stay.

"It's Guin," she called. "I need to talk to you."

"Oh, it's you," Ginny called back. "Come on in."

Guin opened the door to find Ginny at her desk, eating a salad while looking at something on her computer.

"You sure it's okay?"

"I was almost done. Have a seat."

Guin removed a pile of papers from one of the chairs and sat.

"So, what can I do you for?"

"I, uh…" Guin didn't know why she was suddenly tongue-tied.

"Just spit it out!" Ginny commanded.

"Glen invited me to do this cooking course with him in Tuscany. It sounds amazing. And we thought we could do a piece on it for the paper. But it would mean me taking another week off and…"

Wait, why was Ginny grinning?

"So, you and Glen, eh?"

"It's not like that, Ginny."

"No, of course not," said Ginny. But she was still smiling.

"Anyway…"

"I think it's a great idea."

Guin stared.

"You do?"

Ginny nodded.

"Glen mentioned the class to me. Sounded great. You should do it. You can send me daily dispatches, and we can post them on the website. Then you can do a longer piece for the print edition. Our readers will eat it up."

Guin couldn't believe her ears.

"You're serious?"

"Absolutely."

"And the paper will pay for me to do the course?"

"Let's not get carried away," said Ginny. "We'll give you a stipend, but you'll have to come up with the rest."

That sounded fair. Still, Guin couldn't believe Ginny would actually go for it.

"Did Glen put you up to this? What did he promise you?"

"He didn't have to promise me anything. I know a good idea when I hear one. And I've been thinking about adding a travel column. Consider this a trial balloon. Now, is there anything else? What have you found out about Brennan? They still planning on ruling it a suicide?"

Guin caught Ginny up on the latest developments.

"And Craig and I are still trying to see if Brennan had hired a campaign manager. No one seems to know."

"You talk to Bradley Malloy?"

"Who's Bradley Malloy?"

"He's the local kingmaker. Helped Rick Scott get elected."

"You think Brennan talked to him?"

"He'd be a fool not to have."

"Great! So how do I find this Bradley Malloy, maker of kings—and Congressmen?"

Ginny gave her a look.

"They teach you nothing up there in New York?"

"I know I can Google him. I just thought maybe…"

"I don't have his private number if that's what you're after. But he has a place in Naples. Search for him there."

"Thanks, I'll do that."

Guin got up to go but stopped at the door.

"You really mean it about Italy?"

Ginny gave her that look again, the one that said, are you questioning me?

"I'll let you get back to work," said Guin. Then she let herself out and closed the door behind her.

CHAPTER 25

Guin thought again about driving over to Jackson Brennan's office, but Tom hadn't gotten back to her, and she didn't want to incur Wanda's wrath. She'd wait until the end of the day. Then, if he hadn't gotten back to her, she'd go over there tomorrow.

Guin sighed. So now what? She could always drive over to Paradise Found. (Beth also hadn't gotten back to her.) But first, she'd call. The phone rang several times, then Fiona picked up. Guin asked if Beth was in and was told she was. She thanked Fiona, not leaving her name or a message, and headed over.

The wind chimes jingled as Guin opened the door to the boutique.

"Hi, Guin!" said Fiona, giving her a big smile.

"Hi, Fiona. Is Beth available?"

"She's in the back."

"You think it's okay if I go see her?"

"I should probably check."

"I can just go back and knock."

Fiona bit her lip.

"Is she expecting you?"

"I sent her a text."

"I guess if you knock…"

Guin smiled at her.

"I promise not to bother her if she's busy."

"I should probably call, just in case."

"Excuse me, Miss."

There was a customer with a question. Fiona turned to help the woman and Guin made her way back to Beth's office.

Guin knocked on the door.

"Yes?"

Guin opened the door and poked her head inside.

"Hi, Beth. Do you have a minute?"

Guin noticed that there were papers everywhere.

"I'm a bit busy."

"It'll only take a minute."

Beth sighed.

"This better be about our one-year anniversary celebration."

"I'm afraid it's about your husband."

Beth frowned.

"I already told you everything I know."

"You didn't tell me you were planning on divorcing Mr. Brennan."

"Who told you that?" she snapped.

"Is it true?"

"Does it matter? Jack's dead. It's a moot point."

"But could that have been why he took his life?"

Beth snorted.

"Please. When I told Jack I would divorce him if he didn't clean up his act, you know what he said?"

Guin shook her head.

"He said, 'You know I'm a lawyer, right? You try to divorce me, and you won't get a penny.'"

"He said that to you?"

"Word for word."

Guin looked at Beth Brennan. That sounded like a motive for murder. Likely, she got everything in the event her husband died. Though Brennan was supposedly in debt. But did Beth know that? Probably not if she was planning on divorcing him. Or maybe she didn't care and just wanted him out of her life.

"So did you know he was having an affair?"

"Please. I'm not stupid, Ms. Jones. Jack and I had an understanding. As long as he kept his private life private, out of the public eye, and didn't bring home anything, he could do what he wanted."

Guin tried not to be shocked.

"Then he had to go get involved with Audra."

"They were having an affair?"

"He denied it, but there was clearly something going on between them. Whatever it was, I told him to break it off. Then Audra threatened him."

"Threatened him how?"

"She claimed to have dirt on him."

"What kind of dirt?"

"The kind of dirt that could tank Jack's political aspirations."

Guin waited for her to go on.

"Audra found out he was having an affair with a younger woman. She saw the two of them together at some restaurant and couldn't wait to tell me. I didn't believe her at first. Then I looked at the footage and…"

"Footage?"

"We have security cameras positioned around the boutique. Jack insisted. A bit ironic, considering."

Guin continued to listen.

"And there they were… in my effing office."

So Beth knew about Brennan and Paris.

"Did you say something to him?"

"I sent him a text, telling him to end it or else."

"Did he reply?"

"He denied it. Said I was crazy."

"When was this?"

"I don't remember."

But Guin had a feeling that Beth was lying. *Could this had been the reason Brennan had gone looking for Beth at the store that Friday?*

"What about Paris?"

"She quit before I could fire her."

"You think she knew that you knew?"

"I think she suspected."

Just then Beth's cell phone rang. Beth looked down at it and answered.

"Can I call you right back?"

She hung up and looked at Guin.

"I need to go. I trust you can see yourself out?"

Guin knew her time was up, so she thanked Beth and left. On her way out, Fiona stopped her.

"Everything okay?" she asked.

"Everything's fine," Guin lied.

Guin leaned against the Mini, checking her phone. No messages. She opened her browser and searched for *Bradley Malloy Naples*. She immediately found him and called the number listed on the screen. A woman picked up.

"Hi there," said Guin. "My name is Guinivere Jones. I'm a reporter with the *Sanibel-Captiva Sun-Times* working on a story about local political consultants, and I was hoping to arrange an interview with Mr. Malloy."

(Guin had decided it was best not to mention Jackson Brennan upfront.)

"Mr. Malloy's very busy, Ms. Jones. Who did you say you worked for again?"

"The *Sanibel-Captiva Sun-Times*."

She had been tempted to say the *New York Times* or the *News-Press*.

"I'll ask Mr. Malloy, but as I said, he's quite busy."

Guin then gave the woman her phone number and email address, and the woman said Mr. Malloy would be in touch.

"Yeah right," said Guin, after the call had ended. Maybe Craig would have better luck.

She immediately called him, but the call went right to voicemail. She wondered what he was up to and left a message, asking him to call her.

Guin was driving home when she passed the sign for Linwood Real Estate and did a U-turn.

Candy was sitting at her desk, doing something on her phone. However, when she saw Guin, she quickly put it away and plastered a smile on her face.

"May I help you?"

"Is Ms. Linwood available?"

"I'm sorry, she's out with a client. Did you have an appointment?"

"No, I was just in the neighborhood and thought I'd stop by."

"She should be back soon if you'd like to wait."

Guin thought about it. She needed to write her review of the Savoury Spoon, but it could wait.

"Thank you. I'll do that."

"You can have a seat over there," said Candy, gesturing to the seating area.

Guin took a seat and picked up a magazine. Then she remembered that Candy was a Shell Fairy.

"I understand you paint shells."

Candy turned and looked over at her.

"Hm?"

"I said, I heard you were a member of the Shell Fairies."

"That's right. Are you too? Though I don't remember seeing you at any of the meetings."

"No, I'm a reporter. I'm covering the National Seashell Day treasure hunt."

"That's right. You said you were a reporter. My bad."

"Are any of your shells going to be used in the treasure hunt?"

"I hope so. I painted enough of them."

"I understand some of your shells went missing."

Candy frowned.

"How did you hear that? No one was supposed to know."

"Don't worry, it's not common knowledge." Candy looked slightly less worried. "Do you have any idea what happened to them?"

"No. We were painting over at the Community House, and they said the shells would be safe. Then the next day we found out a bunch of them had disappeared, and Mary Ann had us paint new ones."

"Was one of the shells that disappeared black with a skull and crossbones on it?"

"You mean the pirate flag?"

Guin nodded.

"Yeah. There were actually two of them. Both disappeared."

"Two?"

Candy's face turned pink.

"Stephanie, she's another Shell Fairy, had been assigned the pirate flag. But I thought she was doing it all wrong. So I did one too."

"What do you mean by *all wrong*?"

"I thought she had made it too pretty. So I did one too, and we said we'd let Mary Ann decide which one was better. And then they both disappeared."

"You wouldn't happen to have a picture of those shells, would you?"

"No. Photography was strictly forbidden."

"You didn't sneak a picture?"

Candy shook her head.

"I could have gotten kicked out of the group."

Guin believed Candy was telling her the truth. But she wished the young woman had taken a photo, if only to confirm that her shell had been the one found on Jackson Brennan's body.

"So, how long have you been working for Audra?"

"Nearly a year now."

"So you worked with her at her old firm?"

"I did. Then she asked me to come with her when she started this place."

"And her husband didn't mind?"

Candy's face turned pink again.

"She just told him she was taking me, and that was kind of that."

"I see," said Guin. "So do you like working in real estate?"

"It's okay."

"You have your license?"

"I've been studying for it, but I don't really see real estate as my career."

"How come?"

"Too much work. Not that I don't like work. It's just that I see how hard Ms. Linwood works, and some of the clients she has to deal with…"

"I get it," said Guin. "So did you know Ms. Linwood's real estate lawyer?"

"You mean Mr. Cartwright?"

That must be her new lawyer, thought Guin.

"I was referring to her previous lawyer, Jackson Brennan."

"Oh, him."

"Had you met him?"

Candy nodded.

"Was he here often?"

"Pretty often."

"Would you say that he and Ms. Linwood had a close working relationship?"

"What do you mean by close?"

"Yes, what do you mean, Ms. Jones?"

Guin turned to see Audra Linwood standing behind her, looking annoyed.

"I just spoke with Beth Brennan, and I had a few questions… about her husband."

"Let me guess, she accused me of having an affair with him."

"Is there someplace private we can talk?"

Audra continued to look irritated.

"Come with me to my office. Candy, hold my calls."

CHAPTER 26

Guin sat across from Audra.

"Let me guess," she began. "Beth told you I was screwing her husband, that he dumped me, and that I then told her I had seen him canoodling with a younger woman out of spite."

"Something like that. Is it true?"

"Allow me to set the record straight. Jackson Brennan and I had a business relationship. And at one time I would have even called him a friend. That's it."

"So the two of you weren't having an affair?"

"Maybe Jack was looking for more, but I wasn't interested, even though he was a very good-looking man."

Guin wasn't sure if she believed Audra, but she didn't say anything.

"So it was strictly business."

"Yes."

"Then why would Beth Brennan say all of that?"

"Because she was jealous."

"Jealous?"

"Of all the time Jack and I spent together. She couldn't understand why Jack would spend so much time with me if it wasn't between the sheets. And then when Patrick and I were going through the divorce, and Jack chose me…"

"That's right, you and your husband worked together. That must have difficult, to break up personally and professionally."

"You don't know the half of it. Patrick and I had been partners for years. And Jack worked for both of us. Patrick was the one who hired Jack. But when we split, and Patrick insisted Jack stop working with me, Jack refused."

Guin vaguely remembered reading about their split. It had been in the paper. And it had been messy, as she recalled. Patrick had insisted that all of the firm's clients belonged to him, which Audra had said was ridiculous. And a legal battle had ensued.

"And yet you wound up firing him."

Audra sighed.

"Jack had lost his touch. It was a business decision."

"So why is Beth bad-mouthing you?"

"Because she's a jealous cow. She knew Jack enjoyed my company, and she couldn't stand it."

"But you two were no longer working together. And why tell her her husband was having an affair?"

"I thought she should know."

"But why?"

"The man was about to run for Congress. And as much as Jack and I had our disagreements, I still cared about him." Though Guin found that hard to believe. "And him having an affair with a woman half his age would not have been a good look."

"Do people still care about that kind of thing? I would have thought…"

"In Florida they do, especially around here."

Guin decided to try another subject.

"Tell me about your relationship with Anthony Mandelli."

"What about it?"

"You and he are business partners?"

"We are. He's looking to develop land around here, and I've been helping him."

"And does your partnership go beyond business?"

"What are you implying, Ms. Jones?"

"Nothing. I just saw him at your daughter's wedding and wondered."

"He's a friend of the family."

Guin realized she would not get more out of Audra on that subject, so she decided to shift gears once more.

"And how would you characterize the relationship between Mr. Mandelli and Mr. Brennan?"

Audra sneered.

"Do you think the two of them were having an affair?"

Guin blushed slightly.

"No, I meant, did the two of them get along?"

"Hardly. But then what do you expect when you put two alpha males together?"

"I understand Mr. Mandelli blamed Mr. Brennan for the land deal falling through."

"We both did. Tony was furious when he found out SCCF had secured the land. What's your point?"

"Was he furious enough to kill Brennan?"

"Possibly, but as I told you before, he wasn't here the day Jack died. And didn't they rule Jack's death a suicide? Though Jack was the last person I would think would kill himself."

"Speaking of the night Jack died, where were you that evening?"

"Having dinner with a friend."

"Can someone vouch for that?"

Audra looked at her.

"Surely, you don't think *I* had anything to do with Jack's death?"

"I saw you at his office. You looked pretty angry."

"First of all, I was not angry. I was annoyed. Deservedly so."

"Because of some files."

"Exactly. Jack was supposed to have sent all of my files

to my new attorney, Mr. Cartwright, ages ago. But he'd been dragging his feet."

"So you went to personally get them."

"Yes. But his assistant wouldn't let me have them."

"And Mr. Dewey wouldn't help you?"

"As I told you before, the man's been impossible to reach. And now, Ms. Jones, I must ask you to leave, so I can prepare for my next appointment."

"Just one more question. Do you happen to know who Mr. Brennan was having dinner with the night he died?"

"How should I know?"

"I thought you had seen him earlier."

"I did. But he left before me. And now I really…"

Guin knew the interview was over and got up.

"Well, thank you for speaking with me, Ms. Linwood."

She had her hand on the doorknob when Audra called out, "And be sure to tell Ginny to send her real estate reporter here next time!"

Guin spent the rest of the afternoon working on her review of the Savoury Spoon. Although the article only needed to be around five hundred words, she wanted to make sure she captured not only the food but the spirit of the place and the owners.

Finally, a little before seven, she had finished the first draft. Though it was more like the second or third draft, she had tweaked it so many times. She got up and stretched, then went to make herself dinner.

As she was eating her omelet, her phone began vibrating. She had an email from Mary Ann. It was a list of the shells that had gone missing. And sure enough, "Pirate Flag" was on the list. Though, of course, there wasn't a picture. Guin immediately thanked Mary Ann and finished eating.

After she had cleaned up, she went over to the couch in

the living room and turned on the TV. She flipped through the TV guide, but nothing interested her. So she flipped over to Netflix and watched a documentary about an art heist.

Guin had just climbed into bed and was checking her phone one last time before she turned it off. Still nothing from Tom or the detective or even Craig. She thought about texting Craig, but it was too late. She would do it in the morning.

She turned off her phone and placed it in the drawer of her nightstand. Then she picked up her book and began to read.

Guin slept a bit better that night and woke up feeling not as tired. She stretched and went over to the window. It was still dark out, though the sun would be rising soon.

She wanted to go over her restaurant review one last time before sending it to Ginny. But that could wait until after her beach walk.

By the time she reached the shoreline, the sun was just visible over the horizon, and the clouds looked like cotton candy. She pulled out her phone from her back pocket and took a picture. She loved this time of day when the world was just waking up. She closed her eyes and breathed in the sea air. Then she gazed out at the Gulf.

As she stood there, her eyes fixed on the horizon, she felt something furry rub against her leg. She looked down to see a golden retriever smiling up at her.

"Why, hello there," said Guin, returning the smile.

"Sorry about that," said a man who appeared to be somewhere in his sixties. No doubt the retriever's human as there was no one else around.

"That's okay," said Guin. "She's a beauty. What's her name?"

"Taylor. My daughter named her after Taylor Swift. She

can't sing though. The dog, that is. Though my daughter can't sing either."

Guin laughed.

"Is it okay if I pet her?"

"Go right ahead," said the man.

"I'm Guin, by the way."

"Van."

"Van?"

"Like Van Morrison. And before you ask, I can't sing either." Guin smiled. "So, you a sheller?"

"I am. How about you?"

"Not so much. I like shells, but I don't have the patience to go look for them."

"What about Taylor?"

"She prefers sticks."

Guin smiled again.

"Well, have a great morning."

"You live around here?" asked Van, clearly in a chatty mood.

"I do," said Guin. "Just moved here recently. What about you?"

"Been living here eight years now."

"Well, nice to meet you, Van."

"You too, Guin. I'm sure we'll see you around. Taylor and I are out here most mornings."

Guin waved goodbye, then began combing the beach for shells.

She arrived back at the house a little before nine, feeling sweaty from her walk, the temperature already in the eighties. She could use a shower, but first, coffee. As she was waiting for her coffee to steep in the French press, she received a text from Craig. Finally.

She immediately called him.

"Hey, everything okay? I was getting worried."

"Sorry. I was having issues with my phone."

"So, were you able to speak with Bradley Malloy?"

"I left him a message."

Guin frowned.

"So did I, but I got a feeling he wouldn't be calling me back."

"Well, I have a feeling he'll call me back."

"Oh?"

"You speak with O'Loughlin?"

"Not recently, why?"

"I heard he questioned that girl's boyfriend."

"Marcus?"

"That's the one."

"And? He find out anything?"

"You should ask him."

Guin frowned.

"Can't you just tell me?"

"I don't know what was said."

Guin thought she heard Betty calling Craig in the background.

"Hey, I've gotta go."

"Where are you off to? Going fishing?"

"No, I've got a doctor's appointment."

"Is everything okay?"

Craig had been diagnosed with prostate cancer the year before, though he was supposedly in remission.

"Yeah, it's just a checkup. But you know how Betty is."

Guin did.

"Hope the doctor says you're good to go. And tell Betty I said hi."

"I will. Catch you later."

They ended the call and Guin looked over at her French press. The coffee would be cold by now. Of course, she could always microwave it. But it wouldn't taste as good. She debated what to do, then finally poured the coffee into a mug and stuck it in the microwave. A minute later she removed it and took a sip. She made a face and poured it into the sink.

She made a fresh pot and drank it right away. Then she picked up her phone and called the detective. But he didn't pick up.

"It's Guin," she said into his voicemail. "I heard you had a chat with Paris's boyfriend, Marcus. Care to enlighten me? Give me a call or send me a text."

CHAPTER 27

After she had finished her coffee, showered, and gotten dressed, Guin took a seat at her desk and reviewed her article on the Savoury Spoon. She made a few more tweaks then sent it off to Ginny.

A short time later, Ginny replied, thanking Guin for the article and asking if she had spoken with the organizers of the treasure hunt. Guin hadn't. She had been so busy with the Brennan case and the restaurant review it had slipped her mind.

Guin immediately sent an email to her contacts at the Lee County Visitor & Convention Bureau and the Sanibel & Captiva Islands Chamber of Commerce suggesting they talk or meet to finalize details about covering the treasure hunt as it was just a couple of days away. Then she leaned back and stared at her computer monitor. Still no word from Tom. And the detective and Bradley Malloy hadn't gotten back to her either. She frowned, then picked up her phone and called the Sanibel Police Department. She asked to speak with Detective O'Loughlin and was told he was unavailable. *No kidding.* She asked to be put through to his voicemail and left a message.

Next, she called Jackson Brennan's office, but her call went straight to voicemail. She hung up without leaving a message. Maybe she should just drive over. She had nothing better to do. And it wasn't as though she hadn't tried to make an appointment. She grabbed her bag and her keys and headed out. But when she got to Brennan's (or really Tom Dewey's) office, there was a sign on the door saying they were closed, and the lights were off. Guin frowned. Had something happened?

She texted Tom, asking if everything was okay. She waited several minutes but did not receive a reply. Then she texted Stephanie. Again, no reply. She sighed and put her phone back in her bag and headed back down the steps to the Mini.

Guin sat in her office and stared out the window. She had been feeling restless all afternoon. No one was getting back to her. And until they did, there wasn't anything she could do. At least work-wise. Well, she could always ogle the photos posted on the Tuscan cooking course's website. She had been doing that a lot recently.

Finally, she texted Shelly.

"You want to grab a drink?"

"Is that a trick question?" came the immediate reply.

Guin smiled.

"No," she typed back.

"When and where?"

"Say Cip's Place at 5:30?" That was an hour from now.

"See you then!" Shelly typed back.

Guin put down her phone and did a crossword puzzle on her computer. By the time she had finished, it was nearly time to go. She looked down at what she was wearing. Cip's wasn't fancy, but Guin didn't want to go there in shorts and a t-shirt.

She went into her closet and changed into a sundress. Then she went into the bathroom and gazed at her face in the mirror. Her hair was pulled back in a ponytail. She removed the ponytail holder and shook it out. Her curls immediately sprang out around her face. And were those more freckles? She clearly needed stronger sunblock.

She attempted to tame her hair, then applied mascara and lip gloss and regarded her reflection. She had just returned to her bedroom when her phone began vibrating on her nightstand, where she had left it. "Ris" flashed up on the Caller ID. She frowned. Should she ignore him? She thought about it then swiped to answer.

"Hello?"

"Hey, I'm about to leave the museum and was wondering if you were available for a drink."

"Sorry, I was just heading out to meet Shelly at Cip's."

"That's perfect! I'd love to see Mrs. Silverman. I'll meet you over there."

Guin groaned inwardly. She should have kept her big mouth shut.

"Are you sure? You know me and Shelly. You'll probably be bored."

"I doubt that. And this would be the perfect opportunity to talk to her about doing more volunteer work. We miss her over at the museum."

Oh great, Guin thought.

"I just need to finish up here, then I'll see you at Cip's."

"Okay, but don't feel you need to rush. And if you change your mind…"

"Nonsense. I'll be there in half an hour tops."

They ended the call, and Guin wondered if she should say something to Shelly. But she was now running late. She tucked her phone in her bag and headed out.

Guin arrived at Cip's fifteen minutes later and found Shelly seated outside. Shelly waved when she saw her, and Guin waved back.

"Sorry I'm late," she said, taking a seat.

"You're not late," said Shelly. "I only got here a minute ago."

A waiter came over and asked what they wanted to drink.

"Margarita on the rocks, no salt," Guin told him.

"And I'll have a Cosmo," said Shelly. Then she turned to Guin. "Something up? You only order a margarita when something's up."

"I'm just frustrated," said Guin.

"We talking work or personal life?"

"Both."

"You want to talk about it?"

"Not really."

"Shelly! Guin!"

The two women looked up to see Ris Hartwick beaming down at them. Shelly looked from Ris to Guin.

"May I join you?" asked Ris.

Shelly nodded, still looking at him. Then she looked over at Guin.

"I take it you didn't tell her I'd be joining you," said Ris, smiling as he looked at Guin. Guin shook her head.

"Is there something going on that I should know about?" said Shelly, looking from one to the other.

"Nope," said Guin. "Nothing at all."

Shelly smiled.

"I see. Well, always a pleasure to see you, Dr. Hartwick."

"Please, call me Ris."

Shelly beamed.

Just then the waiter came over with Guin and Shelly's drinks. Guin immediately picked hers up and took a healthy sip.

The waiter turned to Ris.

"May I get you something, sir?"

"I'll have a mojito."

Guin looked at him.

"A mojito? Since when did you start drinking mojitos?"

"I've always drunk mojitos."

"Not when I knew you."

"Well, maybe not when I'm in training. But back in the day…"

"So, *Ris*," said Shelly, clearly enjoying herself. "What's it like to be back at the museum? Do you have anything special planned?"

"I'm glad you asked, Mrs. Silverman."

"Please, call me Shelly," said Shelly, leaning over and smiling at Ris. Ris smiled back at her.

"As a matter of fact, the museum has some very big plans. We're not announcing it to the public just yet, but if you promise not to say anything, I'll tell the two of you."

"I promise, I won't say a word," said Shelly.

Guin rolled her eyes.

"The museum is planning a massive, multi-million-dollar renovation. It's going to be incredible. We're going to increase the public space and house live mollusks where the lower level is now."

Shelly stared at him.

"You're turning the museum into an aquarium?"

Ris smiled.

"Not exactly. But instead of having just one live tank, we plan on having over a dozen, featuring different kinds of mollusks, including at least one octopus. You should see the renderings. It's going to be amazing."

"That sounds expensive," said Guin. "Is the museum launching a capital campaign? I haven't heard anything."

"Like I said, we haven't announced anything yet. But yes, there will be a big fundraiser."

"Will the museum have to close?" asked Shelly.

"Briefly. We're working with several firms to make sure the process goes as smoothly as possible."

"And when will the renovation be completed?" asked Guin.

"Optimistically, before the start of the season next year. Though you know how these things go."

Guin did. Construction and renovation on Sanibel often took much longer than planned. She ought to know. Hopefully, the museum had hired a good general contractor.

"Wow," said Shelly. "It sounds amazing. I can't wait to see it."

"Just keep it to yourselves," said Ris.

"I won't breathe a word," said Shelly.

"Does Ginny know?" asked Guin.

"If she doesn't, she will soon."

No doubt, thought Guin. This was big news for Sanibel.

The waiter deposited Ris's mojito and asked them if they'd like something to eat.

"Shall we get some peel and eat shrimp?" suggested Shelly.

"Sounds good to me," said Guin.

"And an order of calamari," added Ris.

"Very good," said the waiter and went back inside.

"Does it ever feel weird to be eating seafood?" Shelly asked Ris.

He smiled.

"Sometimes. I may have to give up octopus as we plan on having a couple of live ones after the renovation."

Shelly smiled back at him and Guin took another sip of her margarita.

"So, Shelly, I haven't seen you around the museum," said Ris, after an awkward silence. "Did you stop volunteering?"

"I didn't want to. But my jewelry business took off and..."

"That's a shame. Is there any way I could convince you to donate a few hours a week?" He was giving her that look. "I know how visitors love you. And everyone misses you."

Guin could see Shelly wavering.

"I guess I could volunteer a few hours a week," she said.

Ris's smile grew wider, and there were those darn dimples.

"Wonderful! And what about you, Guin?"

"What about me?"

She had been taking another sip of her margarita.

"Can we get you to volunteer a few hours a week?"

"Yeah, Guin, how about it?" said Shelly.

Guin gave her a dirty look.

"I'm kind of busy," she replied. "And I'm going to be away."

"Oh, where are you going?"

"I have a family gathering in Bath, then I'm going to Italy for a week."

"You're going to do the cooking course?!" said Shelly. "Why didn't you tell me?"

"You can always start after you get back," said Ris.

"Yeah, you can always start after you get back," echoed Shelly.

Guin shot her friend a withering look, then looked at Ris.

"I suppose I could spare a couple of hours."

"Wonderful! I knew I could count on the two of you."

Guin took another sip of her margarita, which had begun to go to her head.

"Sure, use that super-sexy smile of yours to lure us into volunteering," she mumbled. "I bet you'll have no trouble getting people to donate to your project."

He turned and smiled at Guin.

"You think my smile is sexy?"

"*Super* sexy," corrected Shelly.

Guin could feel her face turning a bright shade of pink.

Fortunately, the waiter showed up just then with their shrimp and calamari.

"Here you go!" he said. "You need anything else?"

A way to turn invisible would be nice, Guin said to herself.

"We're good," said Shelly, smiling up at him.

"May I have some water, please?" asked Guin. If Ris was

going to insist on being charming, she'd need to sober up fast.

When they had finished the shrimp and calamari, Ris excused himself, saying he needed to go. Guin didn't ask where he was going. She was just glad he was leaving. He left some money on the table, more than enough to cover his portion, and said how delightful it had been to see the two of them. Then he was gone.

As soon as he was out of sight, Shelly turned to Guin.

"He totally wants you."

"He does not," Guin insisted.

"I don't know. I saw the way he was looking at you."

"He looks that way at everyone."

"He wasn't looking that way at me."

Guin frowned.

"Just for grins, let's say he wanted to get back together. Would you go out with him?"

"No," Guin immediately replied.

"You seem pretty certain."

"I am. I had dinner with him and Fiona the other night. It was nice, but there was no there there."

"You had dinner with the man and his daughter, and you didn't tell me?"

"I didn't think it was important." Shelly looked insulted. "Besides, things are still unsettled between me and O'Loughlin."

She caught the waiter's attention and signaled for the check.

"Are you mad at me?" asked Shelly.

Guin sighed.

"No, it's just… Seeing Ris put me in a foul mood. Not that I needed any help."

"You could do a lot worse than Ris Hartwick."

"I know that. Believe me. He's a great guy. He's just not the guy for me."

"And the detective is?"

"I don't know anymore. I used to think so. But he's been so mercurial since Birdy came back and the whole wedding fiasco. I thought we were past all of that. But now I don't know."

Shelly put a hand on her friend's shoulder.

"It's going to be okay."

Guin looked up at her.

"How do you know that?"

"Because I'm a mom."

"What does that mean?"

"It means, I've been through this before, with Lizzy and Justin, and these things always work out in the end."

Guin was tempted to bring up Shelly's son, who had tried to kill himself after his girlfriend had dumped him right before finals not that long ago. Fortunately, he had recovered. So maybe Shelly was right. Though thinking about Justin made Guin think of Jackson Brennan. Maybe he had been madly in love with Paris, and it had killed him to end things. She frowned again. No, that was preposterous.

"You okay?" asked Shelly.

"Sorry, I was just lost in thought."

The waiter came over and deposited the check on the table.

"Shall we split it?" said Shelly.

"Sure," said Guin. "We should just deduct what Ris gave us."

She looked at the check, then reached into her bag and pulled out her wallet, taking out a couple of bills. Shelly did the same.

The waiter came back over and asked if they needed any change.

"Nope, we're good," said Shelly.

CHAPTER 28

Guin said goodbye to Shelly, then got in her Mini. But instead of driving home, she drove to the Sanibel Police Department. She knew it was a bad idea, but she couldn't help herself. And likely Detective O'Loughlin wasn't even there.

She pulled in and immediately spotted the detective's car and parked beside it. Then she ran up the stairs.

"I'm here to see Detective O'Loughlin," she informed the woman behind the protective glass.

"Ms. Jones, wasn't it?"

"Yes."

"Is he expecting you?"

"Yes," Guin lied. Well, it wasn't a total lie. She had told him she needed to speak with him.

The woman looked at her suspiciously. Or maybe it was Guin's imagination. Then she picked up her phone and called the detective's extension.

"Ms. Jones is here to see you, sir," she informed him. Guin saw her nod her head. "Okay, I'll tell her." She hung up the phone and looked over at Guin. "He says you know the way."

The door to the back buzzed, and Guin opened it. Then she made her way along the hallway to the detective's office. His door was ajar, and she didn't hear anything, but she knocked anyway.

"Come in," he called.

She opened the door and stepped inside. The detective was seated at his desk, perusing some papers. Guin stood before him and cleared her throat. Finally, he looked up.

"Yes?"

Before she knew what she was doing, Guin had walked around the desk, leaned down, and kissed him. He looked momentarily surprised, then Guin kissed him again. He didn't seem to mind.

"Maybe we should close the door?" he said, a twinkle in his eye.

Guin could feel herself blushing and quickly stepped away from him.

"I don't know what came over me."

She looked down at his desk, at all of the paperwork.

"You're working late."

"Got a lot of stuff to finish up."

"You mean before you leave?"

He nodded.

"What if I came with you?"

"To Boston?"

Guin nodded.

"We went over this."

"I know, but I've been thinking." Though this was purely spur of the moment, inspired by the margarita. "I'm not talking about moving. But I could go with you, stay for a few days, meet the family… see how things go."

"I don't think that's a good idea."

Guin was hurt.

"Why not? You think they won't like me?"

"That's not it," he said, his expression hard to read. "It's just…"

"It's just what?"

"Complicated."

Guin huffed.

"It's always complicated with you." She paused. "Ris is back in town. I just saw him over at Cip's."

"I heard that Hartwick was back at the museum. His fiancée with him?"

"No, they broke up."

"Weren't they expecting?"

"She lost the baby."

"Tough."

"It was. But he seems happy to be back here. He asked me over for dinner."

She was trying to make the detective jealous, but it didn't seem to be working.

"You should go."

Guin stared at him. This was not going as planned. Time to switch gears.

"I heard you questioned Paris's boyfriend, Marcus Ramsay."

No reply.

"What did he have to say?"

The detective was giving her that look of his.

"Oh, come on, Bill. The least you could do is give me some basic information. I know you spoke with Ramsay. Just tell me what he said. Is he a suspect?"

"You're a reporter. Go find him and ask him yourself."

Guin scowled.

"I reached out to him, but he hasn't returned my messages. Come on, give me something."

The detective leaned back, as if thinking it over.

"Fine," he said, leaning forward. "Brennan had dinner at Doc Ford's the night he died."

"Did Ramsay tell you that?"

The detective nodded.

"He followed Brennan after he left the boutique, to have a word with him."

"And?"

"And he said Brennan drove to Doc Ford's. The place was crowded, so he left."

"Without speaking to Brennan?"

The detective nodded again.

"You believe him? He could have waited for Brennan, then ambushed him later."

"He was home at the time of death."

"And you know this how?"

"We spoke to his grandmother."

"His grandmother?"

"He lives with her. So does his sister. They both vouched for him."

"Of course they did."

Guin's bad mood had returned.

"Sorry to disappoint you."

"So what was Brennan doing at Doc Ford's? Do you know who he had dinner with?"

The detective clammed up. Guin knew what that meant. He was done giving her information.

"I need to finish up," he said.

Guin didn't move.

"Go home, Guin. We're done here."

Guin fumed as she drove home. She knew she shouldn't have gone to see the detective. But it had at least yielded some new information. Tomorrow she would go over to Doc Ford's and see what she could find out.

She parked the Mini in her driveway and headed inside. Fauna was there to greet her. The cat meowed, then trotted to the kitchen. Guin knew what that meant. She grabbed the bag of cat food from the pantry and poured some into Fauna's bowl. Fauna immediately began to eat.

Guin watched her for a few seconds, then she opened the freezer and took out a pint of Queenie's Toasted

Coconut ice cream along with a pint of Dutch Chocolate. She placed a scoop of each into a bowl and ate at the counter.

Feeling better, she took out her phone and went to Marcus Ramsay's Instagram feed. She scrolled through and noticed several photos taken at The Eatery by Ryan, a restaurant in Fort Myers popular with the FGCU crowd. It looked like he worked there. She smiled. Well, if he wasn't going to return her messages, she'd just go over there and speak with him in person.

Guin got up a little after six-thirty and thought about going for a beach walk. But she had planned on going to The Eatery by Ryan for breakfast, to talk to Marcus Ramsay. That didn't give her enough time for a walk. She could always go late afternoon and watch the sunset.

She made herself some coffee and read the paper online. Then at seven-thirty, she left.

She arrived at the restaurant a little after eight to find the place closed. It didn't open until nine. She felt like an idiot. Why hadn't she checked? She was about to leave when she saw Marcus inside. She knocked on the door, and he came over.

"We're not open yet."

"I know, but I actually came here to speak with you."

"With me?" he said confused.

"Yes, it's about your girlfriend, Paris Tisdale."

Marcus frowned.

"You a cop? I already spoke with some detective, and I don't have anything more to say."

"I'm a reporter, and I just had a few questions."

"What kind of questions?"

"If you let me in, I'll tell you. They'll only take a few minutes."

He thought it over, then let her in.

"I'm working, so it needs to be quick."

"Shall we sit?" suggested Guin.

They sat at a nearby table.

"So what is it you want to know?"

"Did you know Paris was involved with Jackson Brennan?"

"I suspected something was going on, but she denied it."

"Yet you followed him that Friday, the evening he died, after he dropped Paris off at the boutique."

"I saw the two of them."

"Kissing?"

Marcus nodded.

"Paris said it was nothing, but it didn't look like nothing to me."

"So you followed Brennan. Why?"

"I wanted to find out what was going on."

"Even after he told you to back off."

"I just wanted to talk to him."

"I heard you threatened him."

"He threatened me with a lawsuit."

"But still you followed him to Doc Ford's. You speak with him?"

"No."

"Why not? You had gone all that way."

"The place was packed. And he had already gone inside."

"Did you wait for him?"

"No."

Guin eyed him. She didn't know him well enough to know if he was telling her the truth, but she wanted to believe him.

"So you left and went home?"

"That's right."

"To your grandmother and sister."

"If you already know all the answers, why are you asking me all these questions?"

"I wanted to hear it from you. Did she break up with you?"

"Yeah."

"Because of Brennan?"

"That's not what she said, but I knew the truth."

"Did she tell you that Brennan promised her a job in Miami and an apartment?"

Marcus scowled.

"No, though she did say she was moving there."

"How long had the two of you been dating?"

"Since junior year of college. But ever since we graduated, things have been different. Basketball was my life, but when I got injured…"

"You wanted to play professionally?"

He nodded.

"I would have, too, if I hadn't hurt my knee."

"So after you got injured, Paris lost interest?"

"Something like that."

Guin felt sorry for the young man.

"Do you know where Paris went after you left Paradise Found?"

"I assume she went home. Though she didn't answer her phone."

A man in a grease-stained apron emerged from the kitchen.

"Hey, Marcus, you working or what?"

"Be right there," he called back. "I've got to go," Marcus said, getting up.

Guin followed suit.

"Thanks for speaking with me."

He gave a quick nod and headed back to the kitchen.

CHAPTER 29

Guin checked her phone as soon as she left the restaurant. There was a message from Craig, asking her to call him. She entered his number.

"What's up?"

"We've got a meeting with Malloy."

"How'd you arrange that?"

"I told him I was doing an article on political consultants."

"That's what I said. Did you tell him you were with the *San-Cap Sun-Times*?"

"I may have mentioned the *Tribune*."

Guin grinned.

"So you lied to him."

"Fibbed."

"Is there a difference?" He didn't answer. "So, when's the meeting?"

"This afternoon."

"Wow, that soon? What time?"

"Four o'clock. He's going away for a couple of days but said he would squeeze us in."

"Did you say anything about Brennan?"

"No."

"So you don't know if Malloy was working for him."

"Like I said, if Malloy wasn't, he'll know who was."

"Okay, so what time do you want to head down there? I assume the meeting's in Naples."

"You want to meet me at my place at two?"

"You think it will take that long? I can pick you up at two-thirty."

"I'll drive."

Guin knew that Craig didn't love the Mini and preferred to drive. Though the way he drove, Guin would have preferred to have been in the driver's seat. But she didn't argue with him.

"Okay. I'll see you around two."

They ended the call and Guin checked her phone again. Still nothing from Tom. Or Stephanie for that matter. This was ridiculous. She knew Tom was busy, but how long did it take to send a quick text?

She got in the Mini and started driving. She had just crossed the Causeway when her stomach began to grumble. She thought about ignoring it, then thought better of it and pulled into Sanibel Fresh.

Feeling invigorated after having a Sanibel Sunrise acai bowl and coffee, Guin drove over to Jackson Brennan's office as it was nearby. Maybe Tom and Wanda were back. As she climbed the stairs and looked up at the sign, she wondered if Tom would change it to Dewey & Associates.

She peered through the window. The lights were on, but she didn't see Wanda. She looked down at her phone. It was after nine. She tried the door. It was unlocked. She turned the knob and went in.

"Hello?" she called. No reply. "Hello?" she called again, a little louder this time. She thought she heard the sound of a toilet flush and a minute later Tom emerged from the back. He looked slightly rumpled, as though he had slept there. Maybe he had.

He saw Guin standing there and ran a hand through his hair.

"Ms. Jones, did we have an appointment?"

"No, though not for lack of trying. Is this a good time? I only need a few minutes."

He ran a hand through his hair again, causing some of it to stand up.

"I'm a bit busy."

"Please? Like I said, I'll be quick."

Tom sighed.

"I guess I can spare you a few minutes."

"Thank you."

Guin glanced over at Wanda's desk.

"Did something happen to Wanda?"

"She had to take her father to the doctor. He hasn't been feeling well."

"I'm sorry to hear that. I hope he's okay."

"Me, too. He's the only family she has left."

"They're from Haiti, yes?"

"Yes, and they were lucky to get out."

"Oh?"

"Her father was a religious leader there. And I don't think the government liked what he was preaching. They targeted his family. Wanda's brother was taken away in the dead of night, never to be seen again. And Wanda worried the government would come after them next."

"Wow," said Guin. "I had no idea."

"Yeah. They've been here for a while, but I know her father misses Haiti. But she says it's not safe for them to go back."

"You seem to know a lot about Wanda."

"I like to get to know the people I work with."

"Speaking of which, about Jackson Brennan…"

"Let's go to my office."

Guin followed him down a short hall. His office was much smaller than Brennan's, which was located across from his, and she wondered why he hadn't moved. She glanced around. There were a couple of posters on the walls, one advertising one of Stephanie's exhibits and the other an old-style travel poster of Chicago. He had also hung up his college diploma and law degree.

She looked over at his desk and saw a picture of him and Stephanie on the beach. They looked happy. Near it was a photo of a young Tom with what Guin assumed to be his family.

Tom saw her looking at the photo.

"Is that your family?" she asked him.

He nodded.

"And is the woman next to you your sister?" She was older than Tom, but you could see a family resemblance.

He nodded again.

"Stephanie told me that your sister died when you were in middle school."

He was staring at the picture.

"We had no idea she was still so unhappy."

"Stephanie said she took her own life."

"It was years ago, but it still feels like yesterday."

"It must be hard."

"It is. Not a day goes by when I don't think of her."

Guin's gaze roved from the photo on Tom's desk to the bookcase. Along with a handful of law and other books were several painted shells. Guin went over to look at them.

"These are beautiful. Did Stephanie paint them?"

"She did."

"She's very talented."

"I know."

Guin was still staring at the shells when something tingled in the back of her brain, but she didn't know why.

"I don't mean to rush you," said Tom, jerking Guin out of her reverie, "but I have a ton of work to get through and a client meeting at ten-thirty."

"Of course," said Guin. "Sorry. I'll get right to the point.

Most of the people I've spoken with about your former partner seemed surprised or refused to believe he would take his own life. But not you. Why is that?"

"They didn't know Jack like I did, didn't see what he had been going through the last few months. It was enough to make any man think twice."

"About?"

"Living."

Guin didn't know what to say.

"Jack put up a good front. He even had me fooled for a while. But I began to see the cracks. I think deep down he was very unhappy."

"And you know this how?"

"I'd seen it before."

"With your sister?"

Tom nodded.

"But you were so young."

"Not that young. I was a teenager, and I saw what she was going through, how she tried to put on a brave face and seem okay when deep down she was suffering. Finally, she couldn't pretend anymore, and…"

"And you saw Brennan struggling in the same way?"

"I did. Jack was under tremendous pressure, from his clients, his backers, even his wife. He put on a brave face, but I think it got to be too much."

"What about his run for Congress? I thought he was excited about that and was planning to announce soon. It doesn't make sense."

"I think he was having second thoughts."

"About running?"

Another nod.

"Jack had his hopes pinned on hiring this political consultant. Said he was the man. But I have a feeling the guy turned him down."

"Do you know this consultant's name?"

"I think it was Maloney?"

"Could it have been Malloy?"

"Could be. I've been so busy." He put his hand on the back of his neck. "I'm afraid I didn't really hear half of what Jack said to me lately."

Guin studied Tom's face. He looked tired. Exhausted.

She was about to ask him another question when there was a knock on the door and Wanda poked her head in. She frowned as her gaze fell upon Guin.

"Your ten-thirty is here."

"Thanks, Wanda. Your father okay?"

"Doctor wants to see him again in a week or so if he's not better."

"I hope he doesn't have to. Tell Mr. ..."

"Mrs. Walter."

"Tell Mrs. Walter I'll be with her in a minute."

Wanda gave a curt nod and left.

"I need to go," said Tom.

"Of course," said Guin.

Tom escorted her down the hall.

"Are you planning on hiring someone, another lawyer to help you out?" she asked him as they walked the short distance.

"I'd like to, but I haven't had the time to even write a job description."

They reached the reception area and Tom immediately went over to the elderly woman seated there, a kind smile on his face.

"So good to see you again, Mrs. Walter. Won't you come with me? Would you like a glass of water?"

Guin watched as he led Mrs. Walter down the hall. Then she turned to Wanda.

"I hope your father's okay."

Wanda gave her a quick nod, then Guin saw herself out.

As she drove home, Guin thought about the picture of Tom and his family. They seemed so happy in that photo. Then she pictured her own family. She knew Lance would have been devastated if Guin had killed herself when she was nineteen, just as she would have been devastated if Lance had taken his own life. She wondered if he had ever thought about it. Coming out as a teen couldn't have been easy. Their mother had been far from thrilled. But she didn't kick him out or treat him any differently. And Guin knew her mother loved Owen, Lance's husband.

And what was it about those painted shells she had seen on Tom's bookcase? Something about them rang a bell. But she didn't know why. They had been painted by Stephanie, but why did she feel as though she had seen them before when she knew she hadn't? She racked her brain but couldn't come up with an answer. To distract herself, she turned on the radio.

When she got home, she found a voicemail from Jocelyn, her contact at the Lee County Visitor & Convention Bureau. She was replying to Guin's email. Could they do a conference call later? Guin called Glen to see if Jocelyn had left him a message.

"I was just thinking about you!" he said upon picking up.

"You were? Hopefully, only good thoughts."

Glen smiled.

"Of course."

"What were you thinking?"

"I was thinking that you hadn't gotten back to me about Italy. I spoke to Ginny and…"

"And Ginny told you she had given me her blessing."

"Yup. So I thought it strange I hadn't heard from you."

Guin looked out at the small lake that glittered past her backyard.

"I still haven't decided. I want to go but…"

"But what?"

Guin sighed. She had already told Ginny and Shelly and Ris she was going. Why was she hesitating?

"If it's about the money, I'd be happy to pay for you."

"Thanks, but I can't let you do that. And it's not about the money." Though the course wasn't cheap. "I just haven't had a chance to check flights, or arrange transportation to the villa, or…"

"There's a direct flight from Bristol to Pisa. I'll pick you up and drive you to the villa."

Guin didn't know what to say.

"I checked, and you can change your return ticket to leave from Italy instead of London," Glen continued. "Ginny even said the paper would pay the difference."

"You've got it all covered."

"So what do you say?"

"I promise to let you know by Sunday." Though a little voice inside her head screamed, *Just tell him you'll go!*

Glen sighed.

"Fine. So why did you call me if it wasn't about the course?"

"I got a call from Jocelyn over at the Lee County Visitor and Convention Bureau. She wanted to know if we could do a call later. Did she phone you too?"

"I don't think so. Did she say what time?"

"No. And I'll be unavailable between two and five."

"Could we do the call at five?"

"I can ask her."

Guin would be driving back from Naples, but Craig probably wouldn't mind if she did a call from the car.

"Great. Let me know what she says."

"Will do."

CHAPTER 30

Guin called Jocelyn back, suggesting they do the call at five, and Jocelyn said that was fine and that she would send them the call-in info. That settled, Guin wandered into the kitchen. Although she wasn't hungry, Guin forced herself to eat something. Then a little before two she headed over to Craig's.

He answered the door right away and stepped outside.

"Is Betty home?" Guin asked him.

"She's playing bridge."

He looked over at the Mini and frowned.

"You need to move your car."

"No problem." Was it her imagination or was Craig in a bad mood? "Where should I leave it?"

"On the street."

Guin did as she was told, then watched as Craig pulled his car out of the garage.

"New car?" she asked him. It certainly looked new.

"Yup. Got her last week."

Guin got in the large sedan, which still had that new car smell.

"It's nice," she said gazing around. "Very roomy."

The sedan was twice the size of the Mini.

"You going to put on your seatbelt?"

Craig was definitely in a mood. Guin put on her seatbelt and looked over at him.

"All set!"

They listened to the radio on the drive to Naples as Craig did not appear to be in a chatty mood. Clearly, something was bothering him

"Is something up?" Guin asked him.

"Up?" he replied, glancing her way.

"You seem a bit grumpy. Or grumpier than usual," she said with a smile.

"Mmph," he replied, keeping his eyes on the road.

"You and Betty have a fight?"

"Betty and I never fight."

So it had nothing to do with Betty. Well, that was good. Then she remembered. Craig had recently had a checkup.

"Is it your prostate?"

"No. They removed it."

Craig obviously didn't want to talk about whatever it was, and Guin felt torn. She wanted to know what had put him in a bad mood, but she didn't want to push. They drove in silence for several minutes, then, sensing Guin was going to ask him more questions, Craig spoke.

"The doctor thought he saw something on my lung."

Guin turned to face him.

"What kind of something? Is it cancer?"

"They don't know. I'm going back next week for a CT scan."

Guin didn't know what to say. She wanted to say, "I'm so sorry." But she knew Craig hated pity. Not that she pitied him. She just wanted to let him know she cared and was there for him.

"Hopefully, it's nothing," she finally said.

Though Guin knew that Craig had been a pack-a-day smoker back in the day—and that even if you quit, smoking had a nasty way of catching up to you.

Craig made an indistinct sound.

"Will you let me know the result of the scan?"

He gave a quick nod.

Guin sat back and stared out the window, sending up a silent prayer that Craig was okay.

They arrived at the office of Malloy Consulting a few minutes before four. Craig parked the sedan in the small lot and led them inside.

The office had a modern coastal vibe, with white overstuffed couches, seascapes hanging on cream-colored walls, and bleached wood floors. Not what Guin had expected for the office of a political consultant. (Maybe it had belonged to an interior designer before Malloy moved in?) There was a woman seated at a desk, no doubt the gatekeeper. Craig went up to her and introduced himself and Guin.

"Ah, yes, Mr. Jeffers. Mr. Malloy is expecting you. He's just finishing up a call. Won't you have a seat?"

They sat on one of the overstuffed couches. Craig sank down and looked distinctly uncomfortable. Guin tried not to smile and picked up a magazine. It was the local Naples glossy. She started flipping through it. It was mostly ads and photos of expensive-looking homes. A few minutes later, a door opened and a man who looked to be somewhere in his fifties, with a medium build and a receding hairline, stepped out.

He looked over at the woman at the desk, who looked over at Craig. Then the man walked over and introduced himself.

"Brad Malloy. You must be Craig Jeffers."

"And this is my colleague, Guinivere Jones."

Malloy glanced at Guin, then turned his attention back to Craig.

"Shall we go to my office?" Craig nodded, and Malloy

ushered them into his inner sanctum.

Guin noticed that the office was decorated much the same way as the outer one, though Malloy's desk looked antique and the art on the walls looked more expensive. There were also photos of famous (or infamous) politicians on Malloy's desk and bookcase.

Malloy gestured for them to take a seat then asked how he could help. Craig explained that they were covering the upcoming Congressional race and the role of political consultants in determining a winner. And that he had heard Malloy was the man to talk to.

Malloy preened a bit and told Craig he had come to the right place.

"I understand you've helped many Floridians achieve higher office," said Guin, further fluffing Malloy's ego.

"That's right," said Malloy.

"But you can't help everyone. How do you decide which candidates to take on?"

"Some of it's gut or instinct," replied Malloy. "I can often tell just by meeting with someone if they stand a chance. Other times, I need to do a bit of research. See if they've got what it takes. Running for elected office can be brutal, even on the state level. You need to have a thick skin and a thicker wallet."

"So you need to have a lot of money in order to run, even on the local level?"

"Not necessarily, but it helps."

"As you know, there's an open seat in the nineteenth, your district, which also covers Sanibel," Guin continued. "I'm guessing that there will be a number of people on both sides vying for it."

"You got that right," said Malloy.

"Have any of them approached you?"

He nodded.

"You meet with Jackson Brennan?"

"He came to see me."

"And?"

He turned to Craig.

"I thought you were conducting this interview?"

"I'm mentoring Ms. Jones here. Thought it would be good to let her get in a few questions."

Guin scowled inwardly. Craig had warned her that Malloy was known to be a bit sexist. And that he might prefer Craig interview him. But Guin had insisted on asking at least some of the questions. Craig had replied that was fine, but he suggested that if Malloy objected, he tell him that he was mentoring Guin. Guin had reluctantly agreed but couldn't believe it would resort to that. Sadly, she had been wrong.

"Yeah, I met with Brennan," Malloy replied, still looking at Craig. "But I turned him down."

"How come?" asked Guin.

Finally, Malloy looked at her.

"I tend to stay away from the Brennans of the world."

"What do you mean by that?" asked Craig.

"Guys like Brennan, they're all talk and no action, pardon the pun." (Clearly, he had seen all the "Action Jackson" billboards and late-night TV ads.)

"But he was well known."

"True. But not necessarily in a good way. People tend not to like lawyers, especially ambulance chasers."

As opposed to crooked businessmen, many of whom you had no problem helping, Guin wanted to say. But she held her tongue.

"So how many times did you meet with Brennan?" Guin asked.

"Just a couple," said Malloy. "I had him come in and give me his elevator pitch. Then I asked him some questions. Standard operating procedure."

"When was that?" asked Craig.

"A month, maybe two months ago?"

"You said you met with him a couple of times," said Guin. "So you must have seen something in him."

"I was intrigued, though I didn't think he had a real shot."

"When did you meet with him the second time?" asked Craig.

"A couple of weeks ago? My memory's a bit hazy but Dolores will know."

Guin assumed Dolores was the woman at the desk.

"Where did you two meet?" asked Guin.

"He invited me to have dinner with him on Sanibel."

"Where?"

"That place owned by the mystery writer. Said he knew the guy personally and could get me an autographed copy of one of his books. Like I couldn't get one on my own."

Guin got excited though reined in her emotions.

"And this dinner, could it have taken place on the sixth?"

Malloy looked thoughtful.

"That sounds about right. Why?"

"That's the night Brennan died."

Malloy frowned.

"I didn't realize. Though I saw something in the paper. I guess he took it harder than I thought. Funny, he didn't seem the type."

"The type?"

"You know, the type to kill himself."

"So you turned him down," said Craig. It was more a statement than a question.

"That's right. But he didn't seem that bummed about it. At least at the time."

"He didn't?" said Guin.

"Nope. As a matter of fact, he said he was probably hiring Connie Cordray anyway. I thought he was bluffing or trying to save face since Connie doesn't usually do Congressional races. But I didn't say anything."

"And what time did you two leave the restaurant?"

"Why all the Brennan questions? I thought this was supposed to be an article about me."

Guin and Craig exchanged a quick look.

"It is," said Craig. "But we're doing a sidebar on Brennan and the pressures of running for office."

"And you may have been the last person to have seen him that evening," added Guin.

"You're wrong there," said Malloy. "I saw some people going up to him as I was leaving."

"You didn't leave together?"

"No. I had an early tee time the next morning, and Naples isn't exactly close. Besides, there wasn't anything more to talk about."

"What time did you leave?" asked Craig.

"Maybe nine? I didn't note it in my diary," he said sarcastically. "Now can we please stop talking about the guy?"

"We appreciate you answering our questions," said Guin soothingly. "So have you chosen a candidate to back in the nineteenth?"

"As a matter of fact," he began when there was a knock at the door and his assistant poked her head in.

"I'm sorry to interrupt, Mr. Malloy, but I have an urgent call for you from you-know-who. I told him you were in a meeting, but he insisted on speaking with you now, and…"

"That's okay, Dolores. Tell him I'll be with him in a minute."

Dolores nodded and shut the door.

"I need to take this," said Malloy. "If you want, you can mail me the rest of your questions, and I'll shoot something back to you Monday."

"That's fine," said Craig. He got up and Guin followed suit.

"Thank you for your time," said Guin.

Malloy nodded, then picked up his phone as Guin and Craig saw themselves out.

"So what do you think?" Guin asked Craig when they were back outside. "Was he telling the truth?"

"No reason to lie to us."

He had a point.

"So if Brennan was alive at nine when Malloy left Doc Ford's, what happened? How did he wind up dead at the Bailey Tract later that evening?" She paused. "Do you think the police know that Brennan was having dinner with Malloy at Doc Ford's that evening?"

"You could always ask O'Loughlin."

"Does that mean you don't know?"

"If I did, I wouldn't have dragged us down here."

Guin took out her phone. It was a little after four-thirty, and she had her call with Jocelyn and Glen at five.

"Hey, Craig, I need to make a call at five. It shouldn't take more than fifteen minutes. I can do it from the car, but I was thinking maybe we could hang out and I could do it here? Cambier Park is nearby and…"

"I wouldn't mind getting something to eat," he said. "And I know just the place."

Guin saw the twinkle in Craig's eye. She knew what that meant. Craig wanted something sweet.

"Would Betty approve?"

"What Betty doesn't know can't hurt her."

Or you, Guin wanted to say.

"Okay, let's go check it out. Then I'll do my call from the park."

CHAPTER 31

Craig had led them over to Brambles, an English-style tearoom, which unfortunately had closed at three. He frowned. He had wanted one of their scones. Sensing his disappointment, Guin pulled out her phone and found a place nearby that served sweet treats and coffee. That cheered him up.

He had gotten himself a chocolate chip cookie, and the expression on his face after he had taken a bite could only be described as blissful. Guin instantly felt guilty. She knew Betty wouldn't be happy if she knew. But Guin reasoned that the cookie was better than Craig's first choice, a chocolate cupcake with a big dollop of frosting.

Guin had also gotten a cookie, an oatmeal raisin one, along with a decaf coffee, and they took their treats and coffee to Cambier Park.

They ate and drank in silence until Guin announced she needed to do her call and stepped away.

Jocelyn and Glen were chatting about something when Guin joined in.

"What were you two talking about?" she asked.

"Italy," Glen informed her.

"Such a marvelous place," said Jocelyn. "My husband and I went to Lake Como last summer. I'd love to go back there one day. And the cooking course the two of you are doing in Tuscany sounds divine."

She sighed, and Guin pursed her lips. She hadn't officially said yes to the cooking class.

"Anyway, now that you're both here, I wanted to go over a few things regarding the treasure hunt. Can you believe it's tomorrow?" She paused. "As you know, we are expecting twenty-one teams, in honor of the first day of summer, each with up to four people. And the hunt kicks off at eight a.m."

Guin knew all of that, but she listened patiently.

"Glen, we'd like you to take shots of all the teams at the Visitor Center before they head out. Then we'd like you to get some photos of them at the various hiding spots. I'll be emailing the two of you a list of where all the clues are hidden along with a map. We know you won't be able to get to every location, but if you could do a half-dozen or so and then take some photos of the winning team after they've found the treasure, that would be wonderful."

"Of course," said Glen. "Though what happens if more than one team finds the treasure?"

"Then they split it."

"And what would you like me to do?" asked Guin.

"Interview some of the teams, including the winners, of course."

"Of course."

"We could cover the course together," Glen suggested to Guin. "That is if you don't mind leaving the Mini at the Visitor Center. Or I could pick you up."

"You don't need to do that," said Guin. "I'm fine leaving the Mini at the Visitor Center. Anything else we should know, Jocelyn?"

"Just keep the map hidden and make sure no one follows you. We don't want anyone accused of cheating."

That reminded Guin…

"Jocelyn, remind me about the clues. The Shell Fairies didn't write them inside the shells, did they?"

"No, they did not. Technically, no one *wrote* them. The

clues were typed on small pieces of paper, like the kind you find in fortune cookies, then pasted inside the shells."

"By someone at the Visitor Center?"

"Yes, who was sworn to secrecy."

Guin frowned. So who had written *Time's up!* inside the shell left outside of Brennan's office? Was it meant as a warning?

"Guin, you still there?"

It was Jocelyn.

"Sorry, what did you say?"

"I asked if either of you had any other questions."

"I have one," said Glen. "Will there be people monitoring the treasure hunt, to make sure no one cheats?"

"Oh yes. We have several volunteers positioned along the route. Though the teams won't know who they are. They're supposed to blend in or hide."

"Hide?" said Guin.

"We didn't want to make it obvious where the shells were hidden. So we asked all volunteers to discreetly conceal themselves or not make it obvious why they're there."

Guin was curious to see how well that worked.

"Sounds like you've got it covered," said Glen.

"We've tried. Though it's going to be a challenge. We've never done a treasure hunt before, and something's bound to go wrong. We just hope it all works out in the end."

Guin thought of something else.

"What if someone figures out where the treasure is without finding all of the clues?"

Jocelyn smiled.

"In order to be awarded the treasure, you must produce all of the clues or shells. Otherwise you forfeit."

"And do the teams get to keep all of the painted shells they find?" asked Glen.

"They do. They also receive a bag of favorite Sanibel shells and a certificate of participation. Anything else?"

"Not from me," said Glen.

"I'm good," said Guin.

"Good. Then I'll see you two at the Visitor Center bright and early tomorrow, say seven-thirty?"

"That's fine," said Guin.

They said their goodbyes and ended the call.

Guin had wandered away from where she and Craig had been sitting and frowned when she returned to find him not there. She glanced around, but there was no sign of him.

"Craig?" she said, calling his name.

She spotted a couple at a nearby bench and asked them if they had seen a man fitting Craig's description, but they shook their heads. Now Guin was worried. She took out her phone and entered his number. The call went straight to voicemail.

He wouldn't have left without her, would he? She thought about going to his car, but what if he wasn't there either? Obviously, she could call for a car to take her back to Sanibel, but...

She stood there, wondering what she should do when she spied Craig a short distance away walking towards her.

"Thank goodness you're okay!" Guin said, hurrying over and hugging him.

Craig stared down at her.

"What's that for?"

"I thought something happened to you."

"I just went to the restroom."

Guin felt her face turning pink.

"Sorry. I guess I overreacted."

"You sure you're okay?" he asked.

She nodded.

"I'm fine. Shall we go?"

"Yeah. Let me just let Betty know I'm running late."

"Did you two have dinner plans?"

"Nah. I just don't want her to worry."

Guin waited while Craig talked to his wife. As she stood there, she felt her own phone vibrating. She looked at the Caller ID. It was her mother. She thought briefly about answering then let the call go to voicemail.

They arrived back at Craig's a little after six-thirty. Craig invited Guin to join him and Betty for dinner, but Guin declined. She wanted to get over to Doc Ford's and see what she could learn about Brennan's last supper.

She drove over, going several miles per hour above the 35 mph speed limit, and parked the Mini in the lot. Even though it was off-season, the restaurant was busy. No doubt the treasure hunt was partially responsible. Guin waited in line to speak with the hostesses, two young women who looked to be in their twenties.

"Hi, there," Guin said when it was her turn. "I'm wondering if one of you could help me. I'm looking for information about something that happened here back on the sixth."

"The sixth, as in, like, two weeks ago?" said the shorter one.

Guin nodded.

"It was a Friday."

"We don't work weekends," said the other hostess." Guin looked deflated. Though she knew it had been a long shot to find someone who had worked that evening and remembered Brennan. "But Mina should be here around three tomorrow if you want to stop by then. I think she worked that weekend."

Guin immediately perked up.

"Okay, I'll do that. Thank you."

She left the restaurant, determined to go back the following afternoon, after the treasure hunt.

CHAPTER 32

Guin woke up Friday to sunlight streaming in through the cracks in her shades. Fauna was still asleep, curled up next to her, and Guin did her best not to disturb the feline as she rose. She got up and went over to the window, raising the shade. It looked like a beautiful morning, with barely a cloud in the sky.

She turned on her phone and checked the forecast. The treasure seekers were in luck. It wasn't supposed to rain until much later, and the high was predicted to be only around 81 degrees, cool for that time of year.

Guin made her way to the bathroom, then headed to the kitchen, Fauna appearing beside her. (Amazing how the cat always knew when Guin was headed to the kitchen.) Guin opened a can of wet food and deposited the contents into Fauna's bowl, then gave her fresh water.

That done, Guin made herself a pot of coffee. She would need it. Though she knew she shouldn't drink too much, or else she would spend the morning in search of a restroom while the teams searched for the treasure.

She heated water in her electric kettle and poured some freshly ground beans into her French press. Then she went in search of food. She wasn't hungry, but who knew when she would be able to eat something? Best to nourish herself before heading out.

She stared into the refrigerator. Nothing interested her.

She opened the pantry next and frowned. Nothing she wanted in there either. What she really wanted was a croissant, but she didn't have the time or the energy to go to Jean-Luc's Bakery.

She finished preparing her coffee then grabbed a protein bar from the pantry. She was about to open it when she opened the refrigerator again and grabbed the container of yogurt. She would mix it with some granola, raisins, and walnuts. That should tide her over until the treasure hunt was over. Just in case it didn't, though, she tucked the protein bar in her bag.

She finished her breakfast and looked at the clock on the microwave. She would be late if she didn't get a move on. She quickly washed her bowl and mug and went to brush her teeth and get dressed.

Guin arrived at the Sanibel Island & Captiva Island "Francis P. Bailey, Jr." Visitor Center a few minutes past seven-thirty. Glen was already there, speaking with Jocelyn and a man Guin didn't know. She parked the Mini and went over to them.

The man, whose name was Trey (short for Michael Harrington the Third, he explained), introduced himself and explained the rules of the treasure hunt to them, even though Jocelyn had already explained them, twice now, and they had been sent the information via email. But Guin just smiled and nodded her head as Trey mansplained, stealing a glance at Jocelyn who covertly rolled her eyes.

When Trey was done, he asked if they had any questions.

"Nope. Got it," said Glen. Though Guin had a question for Jocelyn.

"Are there any specific locations you'd like us to cover?"

"Actually," said Jocelyn, preempting Trey, "as you know, most of the shells or clues are hidden outside beloved

Sanibel or Captiva businesses, many of whom are sponsors
of the treasure hunt. So it would be great if you could include
them in your article."

"We probably won't be able to get to all of them," said
Glen. "Are there any ones in particular you want to make
sure I photograph?"

Jocelyn looked thoughtful and seeing his opening, Trey
spoke up.

"You should definitely go to Congress Jewelers. They're
one of our top sponsors."

"And I was thinking it might be nice to include the
Watson MacRae Gallery," said Jocelyn.

"Absolutely," said Guin.

Jocelyn smiled.

"And maybe On Island."

"And the Island Trust Company," said Trey. "We can't
forget about them."

"And maybe the Shell Museum?" said Jocelyn.

"Got it," said Glen. "What about up on Captiva?"

"The Bubble Room," said Jocelyn and Trey together.

Glen smiled.

"I just wish we could have photos of all the locations,"
sighed Jocelyn.

"Unfortunately, I can't be everywhere," said Glen.

"I know," said Jocelyn. "We should have hired two
photographers."

"You know that wasn't in the budget," said Trey.
"Though I agree it would have been nice to have had
pictures of all of the locations."

"Glen and I could split up, and I could take some photos
with my camera phone," said Guin. "That way we'd cover
more territory."

"Is it an iPhone?" asked Trey.

"No, it's a Samsung."

Trey frowned.

"It takes really good pictures," said Guin. "Here, let me show you."

She pulled up her Instagram feed and showed him some of her photos.

"They're not bad," he sniffed. "I guess we don't have much of a choice. Just make sure you're both at the lighthouse."

That was where the treasure was buried.

"Of course," said Guin.

She and Glen then divvied up the locations. They still wouldn't be able to get to all of them, but they'd make it to more than half. And the paper wouldn't run photos of every location anyway. That would take up too much space.

"Show time!" said Trey, seeing the first teams arriving. He and Jocelyn then hurried over to greet them with Glen and Guin not far behind.

Guin was busy interviewing a group of women in their seventies when she saw a police car pull in. She wondered if the detective was inside. Though this was a marked car and the detective typically drove his unmarked sedan. A few seconds later, Officer Pettit emerged and went over to speak with Jocelyn and Trey. Guin finished speaking with the women, then made her way over to see what was up.

"Is everything okay?"

"Everything's fine," said Jocelyn. "Officer Pettit's just here to make sure everyone behaves."

"And if they don't you'll what, haul them off to the Sanibel PD or fine them?" asked Guin.

Officer Pettit smiled.

"No, ma'am. I'm just here to let people know we'll be keeping an eye on things."

"And giving out speeding tickets," said Trey.

Guin could just imagine. It would probably be a good day for the Sanibel Police Department, at least where speeding fines were concerned.

A little after eight, Jocelyn and Trey called all the teams together, so Glen could take a group photo. When he was done, he and Guin sneaked off while Jocelyn and Trey reminded everyone of the rules. Then the hunt was on.

Guin didn't think anyone had seen her pulling into the Village Shops. But just in case, she parked her purple Mini in the back then made her way to the Watson MacRae Gallery, the second stop on her list. She was surprised to see Stephanie there, speaking with the owner. Though she shouldn't have been that surprised. Stephanie was an artist, after all, and the gallery was always looking for new talent.

Guin greeted Colleen, the owner of the gallery, whom she had met a few times, and said hello to Stephanie.

"I should warn you," Guin said to the two women, "some of the treasure hunters will be here any minute."

"Thanks for warning us," said Colleen.

Guin looked over at Stephanie.

"Are you a volunteer?"

Stephanie nodded.

"Mary Ann asked all the Shell Fairies if some of us could help out, and it sounded like fun. I said I'd keep an eye on the gallery. I hadn't been in here before. It's amazing."

Colleen beamed.

"I was just saying to Stephanie that I'd like to include some of her pieces in the fall show."

"And I was telling her she didn't have to."

"Nonsense," said Colleen. "We're all about showcasing local talent. And I have no doubt your work will sell out."

"That's very kind of you to say, but..." She glanced around the gallery. "You really think people around here will want my work?"

"Absolutely," said Colleen.

She was about to go on, but before she could say another word the three women were interrupted by a group of breathless treasure seekers. It was the three seventy-something ladies Guin had interviewed earlier.

"Is it here?" asked the tall one, who Guin thought to be the ringleader.

"It must be here as she's here," said her friend, looking at Guin.

Colleen gave the women a hard look, and Guin thought she would have made an excellent school principal or nun.

"You ladies should know that none of the clues are hidden inside any of the businesses."

The three women frowned.

Stephanie jumped in.

"But you're very close! I'm sure you'll hit pay dirt if you look outside."

"Check the flowerpots!" shouted the ringleader. The three women turned and ran outside.

Guin couldn't help smiling.

"You gave her an extra clue."

"I couldn't help myself," said Stephanie.

A minute later, they heard a triumphal cry. Guin stepped outside and saw the three women beaming, admiring the shell they had found.

"May I get a quick picture?" she asked them.

"Hurry!" said the ringleader. "We need to find the next clue!"

Guin hurriedly snapped a photo, then the three ladies raced off, which was Guin's cue to race off too. Though seeing the ladies with the shell had reminded her of a question she had been meaning to ask Stephanie. Unfortunately, she had no time.

"Will you be at the lighthouse later?" Guin asked her.

"Maybe," said Stephanie. "I'm not sure."

"Well, if not, may I call you later? There's something I've been meaning to ask you."

Before Stephanie could reply, though, another team came pounding up the stairs towards the gallery.

"I'll text you!" Guin called, racing to the back stairs to avoid being seen.

Guin was mentally exhausted by the time she made it to the Sanibel Light, where the treasure was buried. Less than ten minutes later, the three ladies whom Guin had encountered at the gallery arrived.

"Are we the first?" they asked her.

Guin nodded.

"I supposed you're not going to tell us where it is?" asked the ringleader.

"Sorry, can't," said Guin.

"Can't or won't?" said the short one, squinting at her.

"I don't actually know where it is," Guin replied.

"Leave her alone," said the third lady. "We're wasting time!"

Jocelyn, Trey, and Guin watched as the women frantically searched for the treasure. A minute later, Glen pulled in and got out of his car.

"Good, you're here," said Guin, going over to him. "I was worried I might have to take the final photo, which would surely not have pleased Trey."

Glen smiled.

"I got stuck behind a day-tripper going twenty on Periwinkle."

"Ugh. I hate when that happens. But you're here now."

Glen took a few photos of the women searching for the treasure. Then another car pulled in and out poured a family of four.

"Spread out," commanded the mother. The rest of the family—her husband and two children—did as they were told.

"What was the clue again?" asked the girl, who Guin thought looked to be eight or nine.

"It was a picture of the lighthouse," said her brother, who looked to be around eleven or twelve. "Duh."

The girl made a face.

"No fighting," called the father. "Just seeking."

"I bet I find it first!" said the boy. Then he ran off in search of the treasure.

Guin smiled. She could picture herself just like them, a mother with a husband and two adorable children looking for buried treasure. Sadly, it was not to be.

"I think I found it!" called the boy.

Guin turned to look.

Everyone—the boy's parents and sister, along with Glen, Jocelyn, Trey, and the three ladies who had gotten there first—ran over to where he was kneeling. Guin went to join them. Sure enough, the lad had uncovered a chest that reminded Guin of the ones you saw in pirate stories and movies. Though she doubted that this one had actually belonged to a pirate.

"There's a lock on it," said the boy frowning, unable to open the chest.

Trey and Jocelyn stepped forward.

"In order to open the chest and reveal the treasure, you need to show us all of the clues," said Jocelyn.

"Do you have all the clues, young man?" said Trey, looking down at the boy.

The boy looked over at his mother, who told her husband to retrieve the shells from the car. He dutifully obeyed.

"Here you go," he said a minute later, handing over a bag full of painted shells to Trey.

Trey took the bag and began removing the shells one by one, with Jocelyn checking off each one on her clipboard as the family, the other team, and Guin and Glen looked on.

Then Trey and Jocelyn conferred privately. A minute later, they returned to the group.

"I am pleased to say that The Fantastic Four are the winners of the first-ever Sanibel-Captiva National Seashell Day Treasure Hunt!" said Jocelyn. "Here is the key to your treasure, young man."

She handed the key to the boy, and he immediately used it to unlock the chest. A few seconds later, he popped open the lid, revealing the treasure: dozens of shells, including a perfect junonia, a giant horse conch, a great big lightning whelk, and a bunch of other highly prized shells; costume jewelry that resembled what you might expect to find in a pirate's treasure chest; coupons for a dozen or so stores and restaurants on Sanibel and Captiva; a book on local seashells and beach life; and a check for five-hundred dollars.

"Wow!" said the boy, waving around the giant horse conch. "Check out this big shell!"

"Be careful with that horse conch," said his mother.

"Conk!" said the boy, pretending to hit his sister over the head with it.

"Hey!" said the little girl.

Their mother frowned.

"Put that down, Noah."

Noah reluctantly obeyed.

"Thank you," said Noah's father to Jocelyn and Trey.

"Our pleasure," said Jocelyn.

Glen gathered the family together and took photos of them around the treasure chest. They had big smiles on their faces. Then he took some photos of the family with Jocelyn and Trey—and photos of the three women who had nearly won. They had grumbled at first but were gracious, congratulating Noah and his family.

Finally, it was over.

"You want to grab a bite to eat?" Glen asked Guin as they headed to the parking area.

Guin glanced around. A few of the volunteers had shown up to see who had won, but Stephanie was not among them. She had really hoped that Stephanie would be there, so she could ask her about the shells she had seen on Tom's desk. She would just have to call or text her later.

"Sure," said Guin. "Where were you thinking?"

"Gramma Dot's?"

"Sounds good to me. I could use some coconut curried lobster salad."

Glen smiled.

"I'll meet you over there."

CHAPTER 33

They were given a table outside in the shade, where they could look out at the boats tied up in the marina. Every time Guin had lunch at Gramma Dot's, she fantasized about owning a yacht, like the ones they had for sale just outside the restaurant.

"You ever imagine owning a boat?" she asked Glen.

"We talking yacht or fishing boat?"

"Either."

"I had some friends who owned a yacht. Total money pit."

"Was this when you were living up in New York?"

Glen nodded.

"They took me out on it a few times."

"Must be expensive keeping a boat in Manhattan."

"You better believe it. Part of the reason why I never wanted one. People who say houses are money pits clearly never owned a boat."

"So no boat for you, at least not now."

Glen smiled.

"Maybe if I won the lottery."

Now it was Guin's turn to smile.

They ordered food and admired the view.

Guin was sure Glen would ask her about Italy again, but he didn't bring it up. Instead, he asked her about her family in Bath.

Guin's mother had married her stepfather, Philip, when Guin was a teenager, after her father had died. It had been hard for her at first, but Philip was so easygoing, it was hard to dislike him. His family in Bath, on the other hand, was a bit harder to take. She knew they meant well, but Guin found Philip's sister to be like those village gossips she read about in old British novels and mysteries.

Lavinia was always going on about someone or other who did this or that, which irritated Guin. And she agreed with Guin's mother that being single was possibly the worst fate that could befall a woman.

When she was younger, Guin would get excited about visiting her step-cousins in England. They were roughly the same age and got along well, at least most of the time. And she had loved Bath and the English countryside.

Things changed a bit when they all went off to university and again when they all got married. But they remained friendly.

However, after her two cousins both had children, Guin heard less from them. And to be honest, she communicated less too. Then came the divorce, and the move, and, well…

She told all of this to Glen, who listened patiently.

"So are you nervous about seeing everyone?" he asked when she was done.

"A bit. At least I'll have Lance and Owen as buffers."

"And you'll have Bath. I've always wanted to go there."

"Yeah, Bath is pretty special."

They sipped their drinks, then Guin looked up at Glen.

"But enough about me. Tell me about your big wedding in the Hamptons!"

"First of all, it's not *my* wedding," said Glen.

"You know what I meant," said Guin. "So where is it taking place?"

"On a farm in Amagansett."

"A farm in Amagansett? I would have thought your

friends would have rented out a winery or some big estate."

"Garrett's actually very down to earth and his fiancée runs the farm."

"She does? Farming is hard work."

"I know."

"So if Garrett works in the city and his fiancée runs a farm in Amagansett, how did they meet—and when do they see each other?"

"Bella, that's Garrett's fiancée, used to work on Wall Street, same company as Garrett. They met during orientation. But Bella felt burned out after a while and decided to try something different."

"Running a farm sure is different."

"She didn't run it right away. She apprenticed for a year, then got hired on, then when the owner wanted to retire, she got Garrett and a bunch of their friends to bankroll her."

"Nice to have rich friends."

"She's been paying them back. The farm's done well for itself, and she has a country store now where they sell produce and baked goods and stuff made by local artisans."

"Sounds great."

"It is."

"But when do they see each other? Is Garrett going to commute?"

"Garrett's retiring at the end of the year. Though his boss doesn't know it yet. Then he's going to help Bella develop a line of farm-fresh jams and other products and get them distributed, regionally first then around the country."

"Wow! And will they live in Amagansett?"

"That's the plan."

"Well, I wish them luck. So the wedding's being held on Bella's farm?"

"Yep."

"And where will everyone stay? Not a lot of hotels around there."

"They're setting up tents."

"Tents?! Really?"

"Yep. Though they're probably not the kind of tents you're imagining. It's more like glamping than camping. They also rented out a couple of houses nearby for those who'd prefer not to sleep in a tent."

"How many people are they expecting?"

"Only around a hundred, I think. They wanted to keep it intimate."

Guin's idea of intimate was maybe a dozen people, but she didn't say anything.

"And you're going to take the wedding photos."

"I am, as well as the before and after ones."

"You hire an assistant?"

"Betsy's going to help me."

"Betsy?"

Guin hadn't heard Glen mention a Betsy before.

"She works at Vogue. She's the assistant creative director."

"Wow. An assistant creative director at Vogue is willing to be your assistant? How much are you paying her?"

"Nothing. She's Garrett's sister. And she was more than happy to help out."

Guin made a mental note to check out this Betsy. She also wondered, not for the first time, about Glen's life in New York. From what little she knew, it sounded quite glamorous. Or glamourous compared to her life.

"You done?" he asked.

"Hm?" she said.

She realized he was looking at her plate. She had only eaten half of her salad.

"I guess so. I'll take the rest home."

Glen signaled to their server and got the check and a to-go box.

"This should cover me," he said, putting down two twenties.

"That's too much," said Guin.

"It's fine. I have to get going. Keep the change."

"Where are you off to?"

"Yet another wedding."

"Have fun!"

He smiled and left.

Guin lingered for a few minutes, trying to decide what to do. Mina wouldn't be at Doc Ford's until three, which was over an hour away. Then she remembered about the shells.

She took out her phone and sent a text to Stephanie, asking if she would like to meet at Doc Ford's later for a drink. She waited to see if Stephanie got back to her. But there was no reply. She paid the check and left.

As soon as she got home, Guin went to her office. She knew Ginny would want her article on the treasure hunt ASAP, which meant typing up her notes and transcribing all of the interviews, which would take hours. She groaned. She was tempted to put it off, but the sooner she got started, the sooner she'd be done.

She sat down and took out her microcassette recorder. It was going to be a long afternoon.

A four o'clock she took a break to stretch and get some water. She also checked her phone. There was a message from Stephanie. She'd love to get a drink. What time?

Guin suggested they meet up at Doc Ford's at five-thirty. A few seconds later, Stephanie replied, saying that was fine. She'd see her then. Guin made a mental note to get to the restaurant around five, so she could speak with Mina beforehand. Hopefully, the hostess had been there the night Brennan died and could tell Guin when Brennan had left and if he had been acting strangely.

Guin looked at the clock on her monitor. If she was going to get to Doc Ford's at five, she needed to get ready soon. She looked back at her notes. She should do some more transcribing. She sighed and pressed "play" on her microcassette recorder.

At four-forty, Guin saved what she was working on and went to get changed and put on a little makeup. Then it was off to Doc Ford's.

She parked the Mini in the lot and went inside to the hostess stand. There was a short line. Guin waited until it was her turn. As she waited, she glanced around to see if she saw anyone she knew. She did spy a couple of familiar faces but not any of her close friends. Finally, it was her turn.

She glanced at the hostess's nametag. It read *Mina*. Guin smiled.

"May I help you?" asked Mina. She had glossy brown hair and big brown eyes and was around Guin's height. Guin guessed she was in college or else had recently graduated.

"I hope so. By any chance were you working here the night of June sixth?"

"Did you leave something here that evening?" Mina asked her.

"No. I'm doing a story on Jackson Brennan for the paper, and I understand he had dinner here that evening and that you were working that night."

Guin heard a man clear his throat behind her and turned. There were two parties behind her, clearly eager to be seated.

"Any chance we could speak in private?" Guin asked Mina. "I can wait a minute."

"I'm not sure I can help you, Ms. …"

"Jones. But you can call me Guin. And I just had a few quick questions."

"Go on," said the other hostess. "I can hold down the fort for a few. Just don't let Vic see you."

Mina looked reluctant.

"Please?" said Guin. "Like I said, it'll only take a few minutes."

"Fine," said Mina. "But I don't know how I can help." She stepped away from the hostess stand and told Guin to follow her.

Mina led Guin to an area off to the side of the restaurant. "So what is it you wanted to know?"

"You know who Jackson Brennan is?"

"You mean the guy with those ads and billboards?" Mina pitched her voice low. "You want action? Call Jackson!"

Guin smiled.

"He's the one. So do you remember seeing him here that evening?"

"What day was it again?"

"The sixth. It was a Friday."

Mina looked thoughtful.

"He was with a short, middle-aged, balding guy and…"

"Now I remember!" said Mina. "Yeah, he was here all right. Caused quite a scene."

"What kind of scene?"

"This other guy started yelling at him, real loud. I think he was drunk. Accused Mr. Brennan of all sorts of stuff."

"What did this other guy look like? Do you remember?"

"He was kind of average height, not bad shape, older, with thinning red hair. I think his name was Patrick."

"How do you know that?"

"I heard Mr. Brennan call him that. And I think he worked in real estate. At least that's what someone told me."

Could the man yelling at Brennan have been Patrick Finney, Audra Linwood's ex? He certainly fit the description. Guin asked her.

"I don't know. Maybe?"

"Do you recall what they were arguing about?"

"I think it had something to do with his wife. Patrick's that is. I didn't hear what they were saying. Though several of the servers did."

"What happened?"

"Like I said, there was a bunch of yelling. The Patrick guy got pretty irate, so Vic, she's the manager, had one of the guys escort him out."

"Do you know what time that was?"

"A little after nine? I don't recall exactly."

"And do you know what time Mr. Brennan left?"

The other hostess popped her head out.

"Hey, Mina, we need you back inside."

"I'll be there in a sec." Mina turned to Guin. "I've gotta go."

Guin thanked her and was going to ask one more question, but Mina had disappeared inside. Hopefully, Mina would still be there when Guin finished her drink with Stephanie, and Guin would be able to ask her a few more questions then.

CHAPTER 34

Guin had just sat down at the bar and ordered a white wine spritzer when she felt a hand on her shoulder.

"Is this seat taken?"

She looked up and saw Marty Nesbitt, Sanibel's most eligible sixty- or seventy-something bachelor, wearing one of his signature Hawaiian shirts, his thinning gray hair pulled back in a ponytail, smiling at her. Guin groaned inwardly.

Marty wasn't a bad guy, just annoying. Really annoying. He thought of himself as God's gift to women, Guin included. Though Guin had never given him any sign that she was even mildly attracted to him. However, she suspected Marty couldn't read a sign if it was painted red with the words *Go away* written on it in large type.

"Hey, Marty. I'm actually waiting for a friend."

"I am, too. We can wait together."

Guin realized she was trapped and moved her bag.

Marty signaled to the bartender and ordered a beer.

"So, how're tricks? You over that bird guy yet?" he asked. "I imagine it must have been quite a blow, him going off and leaving you like that."

"For the record, it was the other way around. I broke up with Birdy," said Guin, unable to hide her annoyance.

"Sure, sure," said Marty, patting her arm.

Guin suppressed a growl.

The bartender deposited their drinks and Guin quickly took a sip of her spritzer.

"So, what's up with you?" she asked. Though she didn't really want to know.

"I've been taking tango lessons."

Guin stared at him. She was not expecting that answer.

"Tango lessons?"

Marty nodded.

"I know how you ladies love to dance. So I figured, why not?"

Guin continued to stare. She couldn't help it.

"But tango? Have you ever tangoed before?"

"No, but I met this hot little number from Argentina and…"

"Let me guess, she teaches tango."

"How did you know?"

"Lucky guess. Does she teach here on the island?"

"She does. She and her husband, Federico, took over that ballroom studio."

So she was married. Not that that would discourage Marty.

"And how are the lessons going?"

"Good! There's a group of us doing it. That's how I met Eunice."

"Eunice?"

"My new squeeze."

It constantly amazed Guin that women would go out with Marty. Not that he was the worst specimen she had ever encountered. You lop off that ponytail, put him in regular clothes, and give him some sensitivity training and he wouldn't be so bad. Also, she was pretty sure he had money. Maybe that was the attraction.

"Does she live on Sanibel?"

He nodded.

"Just moved here and was looking to meet people. Good

thing she met me. There are a lot of shifty characters who might want to take advantage of a widow new to the area."

Guin felt a laugh bubbling up but tamped it down.

"Where did she move from?"

"Minnesota."

"What brought her to Sanibel?"

"She has a sister who lives in Estero. That's why she moved here."

"Any kids?"

Guin didn't know why she was asking all these questions. It was like she was on autopilot, unable to help herself.

"Three, but they live all over the place."

"Guin! Sorry I'm late."

Thank God, thought Guin as Stephanie rushed over.

"No worries," she said. She saw Marty sizing up Stephanie and was almost afraid to introduce them. But she couldn't be rude. "Stephanie, this is Marty Nesbitt. He runs one of the local Facebook shell groups."

Stephanie smiled.

"A pleasure to meet you, Marty. I'll have to check it out. I'm a member of the Shell Fairies."

"I've always admired a woman who can paint a shell," he said, ogling her.

Stephanie didn't know what to say.

"Let's go to the back bar," Guin said, gently taking Stephanie's arm. "It's a bit quieter and more private back there." She turned to Marty and smiled sweetly. "Would you excuse us?"

"I get it," said Marty. "You two need to do a little 'girl talk.'" He made air quotes as he said *girl talk* and Guin winced.

"Something like that."

Guin grabbed her drink and whispered, "let's go."

The back bar was much quieter than the one in front. There were just a couple of men, probably locals, nursing beers. Guin and Stephanie took two seats far away from them, and the bartender came over a minute later. Stephanie ordered a mojito, and Guin asked for a glass of water.

"I didn't see you at the lighthouse," Guin said.

"Sorry about that. I got so excited after speaking with Colleen that I went home and started painting. If you hadn't texted me, I'd still be there."

"I'm glad you felt inspired."

"Yeah, me too. It's been tough, especially with Tom being…"

She trailed off.

"What about Tom?"

"He's been so busy since we got here, I feel like I barely see him. Even when he's home, it's like he's not there, like his mind is someplace else."

It reminded Guin of Art, her ex, their last few years together.

"Have you said something?"

"I have, and he's apologized. I just don't think he knew what he was getting into."

"I imagine it must be tough taking over a law practice, especially when your partner suddenly dies."

"I know. And I feel for him. It's just…"

"Lonely?"

Stephanie nodded.

"I mean, I've made a couple of friends, but it's not the same."

"Was he this busy up in Chicago?" asked Guin.

"He was. But it was Chicago. And the whole point of us moving down here was so he'd have more time, so *we'd* have more time."

Guin sympathized.

"I'm sure things will calm down eventually."

"I hope so. Tom is a wreck. He barely sleeps or gets any exercise."

The bartender came over with Stephanie's mojito and she took a large sip.

"Can I get you something?" he asked Guin, looking at her nearly empty glass.

"I'm good," she said. She was tempted to get another spritzer, or something stronger, but she wanted to keep her wits about her.

"Speaking of Tom, I was in his office the other day and noticed some beautiful painted shells on his bookcase. I assumed they were yours."

Stephanie smiled.

"He asked me if he could have a couple to show off to clients. He thinks I should sell them."

"You could, you know."

"Nah, I just do it for fun."

"Do you remember what shells you gave him?"

"Sure, there was one with a hibiscus on it and another with a turtle."

"What about one with a piece of cake on it? It kind of reminded me of Wayne Thiebaud's *Pie Counter* painting."

Stephanie frowned.

"Is something wrong?" asked Guin.

"You say he had a shell with a piece of cake on it?"

"That's right. Did you not paint one like that?"

"I did, but…"

"But what?"

Stephanie continued to frown.

"I painted that one for the treasure hunt. It was the Bubble Room clue."

Guin suddenly understood.

"Was that one of the shells that went missing from the Community House?"

Stephanie nodded.

Neither spoke for several seconds. Finally, Guin broke the silence.

"Maybe he found it?"

"Maybe," said Stephanie. She seemed distracted.

"Speaking of Tom's office, there's a great photo of the two of you on the beach and one of him and his family. They all looked so happy."

"I think they were. It was taken on their last family vacation, before…"

"It must be painful, seeing her looking so happy in the photo, knowing what happened."

"I think Tom keeps it there so he doesn't forget. He worshipped Emma. Even though there was a big age difference, the two of them were very close."

Guin felt for the lawyer. She couldn't imagine what life would be like without her brother.

"Do you know why she killed herself?"

"Emma was raped when she was a freshman in college, and I guess she never got over it. Of course, it didn't help that the guy who raped her got off."

"That must have been hard to take."

Stephanie nodded.

"It was. I would have been furious."

"How old was Tom at the time?"

"Thirteen, I think?"

"And you say Emma was a freshman in college? Where was she enrolled?"

"Syracuse. She took a leave of absence but never went back, even though the guy graduated."

"So he was a senior?"

"And a jock. I think he was on the basketball team."

"Do you know the guy's name?"

"No. I asked Tom once, but he said he didn't know. Though I think he was lying. And his family doesn't like to talk about it."

Guin could understand.

She was about to ask Stephanie another question when Stephanie's phone buzzed. Stephanie picked it up and frowned.

"Everything okay?"

"That was Tom. He says he has to work late again."

"I take it he works late a lot."

Stephanie nodded.

"I'm really worried about him."

Guin understood. She remembered what it had been like when Art was gunning for that first big promotion. He practically lived at the office and barely slept.

"You should tell him to take it easy. Or at least take a weekend off."

"I have. And I know he wants to. We even booked a place for the other weekend. But he had to cancel."

"Can't he hire someone to help out?"

"He says he's too busy to even look. And look, I know my not being busy probably makes things worse. But he's going to work himself into an early grave if this keeps up."

Guin placed a hand on Stephanie's arm and changed the subject.

"Speaking of work, are you going to show some of yours at Colleen's gallery? You said you were painting."

Stephanie brightened.

"Yes! Colleen convinced me to put some pieces in the fall show. She said I could give her some of my existing work, but I told her I wanted to create something new. So I've been playing around."

Guin smiled.

"That's great! And you should reach out to some galleries in Naples. I'd bet at least one of them would be thrilled to carry your work."

"Tom said the same thing. I don't know why I've been so reluctant to put myself out there since we moved here.

Maybe the treasure hunt and meeting Colleen were just the kick I needed."

Stephanie's phone was buzzing again.

"Sorry, I need to take this."

She moved away from the bar. A minute later, she was back.

"I need to go," she said.

"Is everything okay?"

"Everything's fine. I just need to run. Here," she said, taking a twenty for her wallet and laying it on the bar.

"It's my treat," said Guin, handing Stephanie back her twenty.

"You sure?"

"Absolutely."

"Thanks," said Stephanie. She paused for a minute. "We should do this again."

"I'd like that," said Guin. Then she watched as Stephanie hurried down the steps.

Guin paid the bill and headed to the front of the restaurant, stopping near the hostess stand. There were people waiting to be seated, so she waited. Finally, there was a brief lull. She immediately went over to Mina.

"I know you're busy, but I just had a couple more questions."

"Now's really not a good time," said Mina.

"Please? It'll just take a minute. And I'm sure [she read the other hostess's nametag] Hallie can handle things."

Mina looked at Hallie.

"Go on," said Hallie. "Just make it quick."

They stepped outside, and Guin asked Mina if she remembered what Brennan had been like that evening, if he seemed depressed at all.

"Depressed? I don't think so. Actually, he seemed kind of happy."

"Happy?"

"You know how some people get when they drink a bit too much? Some people get mean, others get happy?"

"And Brennan seemed happy?"

Mina nodded.

"And what time did he leave here?"

"I don't remember exactly. It was sometime after nine. He was with some guy."

Guin looked at Mina. Malloy said he had left before Brennan. And Mina said Patrick Finney had been escorted out. So who had Brennan left with?

"You say Brennan left with someone? Can you describe him?"

Mina looked like she was thinking.

"I remember he was cute. Tall, though not as tall as Brennan, with wavy dirty blond hair."

"Young or old?"

Mina looked thoughtful again.

"Younger than Brennan. Maybe in his thirties?"

"Did you catch his name?"

But before Mina could answer, they saw Hallie signaling.

"I have to go," said Mina.

Guin thought about going inside and waiting to talk to Mina again, but people were streaming into the restaurant, so it could be a while, and Guin didn't feel like waiting.

She walked slowly down the steps, wondering who had left Doc Ford's with Jackson Brennan.

CHAPTER 35

That night Guin dreamed she was wandering in the dark, looking for something. But when she woke up she couldn't remember what it was she had been looking for. Only that she had felt frustrated and lost.

She looked at her alarm clock. It was a little after six. She needed to work on the treasure hunt story—and pay a call on Patrick Finney. But first, she needed to clear her head. Which meant a walk on the beach.

She quickly got dressed, fed the cat, pulled on her baseball cap, and left.

It was another beautiful morning. The sky was a pale blue, the temperature was in the low seventies, and there was a gentle breeze. It would be much hotter later, but right now it was perfect.

Guin breathed in the sea air, closing her eyes. She opened them and looked out at the water. It was calm today, with just a few ripples. She watched as a double-crested cormorant dove for its breakfast and a group of brown pelicans flew overhead.

She wondered what it felt like, to fly over the Gulf, feel the sun's rays on your wings. She closed her eyes again and felt the sun warm her skin. When she opened them, she saw two dolphins cresting in the water. This was why she loved Sanibel. And the shells, of course. And the friends she had made there.

She stared out at the Gulf for another minute then started walking west. She kept her eyes downward, in search of shells, but her brain kept going back to her dream. What had she been searching for? It bothered her that she couldn't remember.

She reached down to pick up a banded tulip shell (not that she needed any more), then held it up to get a better look. That's when she saw Lenny. She called his name and waved.

"Morning," said Lenny. "Whatcha got there?"

"Just a banded tulip."

"Looks like a nice one."

"It's okay," said Guin. "I'm probably going to put it back, though. Leave it for someone else to find. I was hoping to find a true tulip."

"I could give you one."

"Thanks, but you know my rule."

"Yeah, yeah, yeah. You only want shells you find yourself."

Guin smiled, and Lenny let out a yawn.

"Late night?"

Though a late night for Lenny meant staying up past nine o'clock.

"As a matter of fact, it was."

"Oh? You have a date?"

"A bridge date."

"With Annie?"

Annie was Lenny's bridge partner. She was married (mostly happily), but her husband had no interest in bridge. So when she had found out Lenny was a bridge player, and a good one at that, she had recruited him to play with her.

He nodded.

"You win?"

"No. Though we could have if I hadn't bid three hearts that last game."

Guin yawned.

"Sorry," she said, quickly placing a hand over her mouth.

"*You* have a late night?"

"No, just haven't been sleeping."

"Oh, how come?"

"Just a lot on my mind, I guess."

"Work?"

Guin nodded.

"Speaking of which, I should head home. Gotta type up the treasure hunt story."

"That's right, it was yesterday. Who won?"

"A nice family calling themselves The Fantastic Four. The boy figured out the last clue."

"They from around here?"

"Cape Coral."

Lenny walked with her.

"You hear about the new detective?"

Guin stopped.

"What new detective?"

"The one from Orlando. I hear she's a real tough cookie."

Guin stared at her friend. She hadn't heard anything about a new detective. Could this be the detective's replacement? Surely he would have said something, wouldn't he?

"I'm surprised you didn't know, considering."

"I've been busy. How did you know?"

"Bert said something last night. But maybe it's not common knowledge yet."

Lenny's friend Bert worked in the City of Sanibel finance department, which was located in the same complex as the police department.

"Is she replacing Detective O'Loughlin?"

"I don't know. Bert just said they'd hired a new detective. You can always ask your boyfriend."

"He's not my boyfriend," Guin snapped.

Lenny held up his hands.

"No need to get testy."

"Sorry. I'm just in a bit of a grouchy mood."

"Not getting enough sleep will do that. When you heading off to England?"

"July third."

"You'll miss the big Fourth of July parade."

"I know, but it can't be helped. Duty calls. You got plans for the Fourth?"

"Just the usual. Getting together with some of the guys for gin and lasagna."

"By gin I'm assuming you mean gin rummy."

Lenny grinned.

"You know what happens when you assume."

"Well, have fun," said Guin.

"I'm sure I'll see you before then." He looked down at his fitness watch. "I gotta getting moving. I'm behind on my steps."

Guin smiled at him and headed home.

As soon as she got back to the house, Guin made herself a pot of coffee. Then she took her mug to her office. It was still too early to call Patrick Finney. But she had plenty to do. She opened the document with her treasure hunt notes and began to type.

A little before eleven, she took a break. She stretched then walked to the kitchen to get a glass of water. When she got back to her office, she called Patrick Finney. The woman who answered the phone said he was on a call. Would Guin like to leave her name and number? Guin asked the woman if Mr. Finney would be around later, and the woman said he should be and again asked if Guin wanted to leave a message.

"That's okay," said Guin. She would go by there later.

She ended the call and went back to her treasure hunt article. She was finding it hard to concentrate, but she forced herself to work on it until she had a first draft. She then saved the document and went to get changed—and pay a call on Patrick Finney, Audra Linwood's ex.

Guin entered the real estate office and was amused to see how similar it looked to Audra's. Actually, all of the real estate offices Guin had been to on Sanibel had a similar look, and she wondered if there was some kind of local statute saying that they all had to be decorated a certain way. She smiled at the thought. More likely they were designed by the same person.

She approached the receptionist and introduced herself, saying she was with the *Sanibel-Captiva Sun-Times* and was there to speak with Patrick Finney. Was he available?

"Are you here about the article?" the receptionist asked.

Guin nodded her head, though she wasn't sure what article the receptionist was referring to.

"I'll let him know. What was your name again?"

"Guinivere Jones. That G-U-I-N-I… Just tell him Guin Jones."

The receptionist picked up her phone.

"He'll be right out," she informed Guin a minute later. "Would you like to have a seat?"

"That's okay," said Guin. She glanced around. "If you don't mind me asking, who decorated your office?"

"Works of Art," said the receptionist. "They do a lot of the real estate offices on Sanibel."

Guin smiled. Theory proved.

She had just sat down and was about to pick up a magazine when she saw Patrick Finney coming down the hall and got back up.

"Ms. Jones," he said. There was a smile on his round face. "A pleasure to meet you. So you're here about the article I take it?"

Guin smiled back at him, but she still had no idea what article he was referring to.

"Come, let's go to my office." He turned to the receptionist. "Hold my calls, Tamara."

He led Guin to his office and indicated for her to have a seat. Then he took a seat behind his desk.

"So what can I tell you other than that I have now been a top producer three months in a row *and* just closed the second biggest sale on the island this year? Not many brokers can say that you know."

So that's why he thought she was here, to interview him about being a top producer. Though that typically merited only a small blurb and was handled by the paper's real estate reporter. Still, she'd play along.

"That's very impressive. I'll be sure to mention all that." She then asked him about his recent sales, which he was more than delighted to tell her about. "And am I right that Jackson Brennan helped you with some of those deals?"

It was an awkward segue, but she wanted to steer the conversation to the real reason she had come there.

"He did, but we parted ways."

"Oh?" said Guin innocently. "Did something happen?"

"Brennan screwed me."

"He screwed you?"

"I hired Jack back when he first came to the island, before all that 'Action Jackson' personal injury nonsense. I helped him make a name for himself. Referred my clients to him. And how does he repay me? He convinces my wife to leave me and start her own practice, that's how."

"That must have made you angry."

"You bet it did. But I should have expected it. Brennan

was a weasel. He would have sold out his mother if there was enough in it for him."

"I see," said Guin. "I understand you saw him the night he died, over at Doc Ford's, and that the two of you had words."

Finney squinted at her.

"How do you know about that?"

"It's a small island. I hear you caused quite a scene."

Finney's face turned pink.

"I admit, it wasn't my finest hour. But he had it coming!"

"What happened?"

"I had just lost another deal to Audra. Then I saw Jack sitting there, looking all smug, and I decided to give him a piece of my mind."

"One of the servers said you threatened him."

Finney scowled.

"I don't remember what I said."

"You allegedly said you'd kill him for what he did to you."

"It was just a figure of speech."

"And yet he was found dead less than twenty-four hours later. Was that a coincidence?"

Finney was now glaring at Guin.

"What exactly are you implying?"

"Nothing. It's just interesting that you were heard threatening Mr. Brennan not long before he was found in his car not far from Doc Ford's."

"I heard it was suicide."

"The police haven't officially stated the cause of death."

"Sure sounded like suicide to me. I heard they found cyanide in his system."

"Someone could have forced him to take it."

Finney snorted.

"No one could ever force Jack to do anything. You're barking up the wrong tree."

"What time did you leave Doc Ford's that evening?"

"I don't remember exactly. I had a bit too much to drink and was escorted out."

"What about Mr. Brennan? Was he escorted out too?"

"No, though he should have been."

"And that was the last time you saw him?"

"No. I saw him just as my taxi pulled up. He was with that partner of his."

"Tom Dewey?"

Finney nodded.

"Did they leave together?"

"I don't know. Looked like he was taking Jack out for a bit of fresh air. Jack was pretty plastered."

"So you didn't see Brennan get into his car?"

"No. Say, why are you asking me all these questions about Jackson Brennan? I thought you were here to interview me for the Top Producer column."

Guin was saved from answering by a knock at the door. It was the receptionist.

"Mr. Finney, your next appointment is here."

"Tell her I'll be right there."

Guin got up.

"Well, thank you for your time, Mr. Finney."

Before he could say anything, Guin slipped away.

CHAPTER 36

Guin went to her office as soon as she got home. She pulled up her notes on Jackson Brennan and began adding her conversation with Patrick Finney. According to Finney, Brennan appeared to be in a good mood that evening, despite his wife threatening to divorce him and Bradley Malloy turning him down. Of course, Finney had been drinking. So he wasn't the most reliable witness. And he did say Brennan had been drinking too. So maybe Brennan was depressed.

But Guin still couldn't believe Brennan would take his own life.

And what was this about Tom Dewey being at Doc Ford's that evening and leaving with Brennan? Why hadn't Tom mentioned that? Of course, Finney could have been confused. It might not have been Tom. Still, it bothered her. She picked up her phone and sent Tom a text.

She waited to see if he would reply, but her phone remained silent. She then sent a text to Detective O'Loughlin, willing him to respond right away. But after a minute, she put her phone down and returned to her notes.

She finished entering everything Finney had told her, then went back and reviewed her previous notes. She was just reading through her conversation with Stephanie about Tom's sister when she stopped. Stephanie had said that Emma had gone to Syracuse but had dropped out after her freshman year, after being raped. Brennan had also gone to Syracuse—and had been accused of raping a freshman his senior year.

Could the Jane Doe in the rape case have been Emma Dewey?

Guin knew it was a long shot, but she had to find out. After all, how many basketball players at Syracuse had been accused of raping a freshman in the early nineties? Only one. At least only one that she knew of. Though there could have been more. Back then there was no social media, and incidents of sexual harassment or abuse on college campuses were typically kept quiet. Still, if Emma Dewey had been raped by Jackson Brennan, and Tom knew, why in heaven's name would he go work for the man?

Guin got a chill. She was starting to form a theory, but… Before she let her imagination run wild, she texted Stephanie, asking her when Tom's sister had attended Syracuse and if she knew whether Tom had been at Doc Ford's the night of June sixth.

No reply. She was probably painting.

Guin stared out the window. She couldn't imagine Tom Dewey, who seemed so kind and well-intentioned, murdering his partner. The very idea was crazy. Had her imagination run away with her? All signs pointed to Brennan having committed suicide. But for some reason, she wasn't buying it.

Guin sighed and read through her notes again. Brennan had had a serious streak of bad luck lately. He had lost cases, money, a potential campaign manager, and possibly his wife. That was enough to cause any man to consider ending it. *But not Brennan*, Guin said to herself.

Guin spent the rest of the afternoon working on the treasure hunt story. Around five, she got up to stretch and checked her phone. Stephanie had gotten back to her. Emma was at Syracuse in 1992. And she and Tom had dined at Doc Ford's that Friday. Why did Guin want to know?

"Thanks," Guin wrote her back.

She thought about texting Stephanie again, to ask whether she and Tom had seen Jackson Brennan that evening, then decided to call her instead.

Stephanie picked up after a couple of rings.

"Why did you want to know if Tom and I had dinner at Doc Ford's that evening?" she asked Guin.

"Patrick Finney said he saw Tom with Brennan there, but Tom had told me he hadn't seen Brennan since earlier."

"Who's Patrick Finney?"

"He's a real estate broker on the island. He was heard yelling at Brennan that evening."

"Oh, him. Yeah, he made quite a scene. They had to escort him out."

"You heard him?"

"Hard not to. Tom went over to see what was up."

"You didn't go with him?"

"Not right away. But when Tom didn't come back, I went over there."

"And how was Brennan? Did he seem upset?"

"Not at all. As a matter of fact, he and Tom were laughing."

Laughing? That didn't sound like a man about to kill himself.

"I heard Brennan had been drinking."

"Oh, yeah. He had definitely had a few."

"And Tom?"

"Just a glass of wine. Tom wanted to drive Jack home, but Jack wanted Tom to stay and have a drink with him."

"And did he?"

"I assume so. I left."

"How did you get home?"

"I drove."

"Did you have two cars?"

"No, just the one. But Tom said he'd grab a cab or walk home. We don't live that far from the restaurant."

"What time did he get home?"

"I don't know."

"You don't know?"

"I was asleep. So why did you want to know when Emma went to Syracuse?"

"Just curious. Did you know that Brennan also went to Syracuse?"

"He did?"

However, before Guin could say another word their conversation was interrupted by several beeps on the line.

"I should get this," said Stephanie.

They said goodbye, and the call ended.

No sooner had Guin put her phone down than it started to vibrate across her desk. She had a text from the detective. He wanted to know if she was free for dinner.

"Tonight?" she replied. It was a bit late to be asking her out.

"Yes, tonight," he wrote back. "You free?"

Guin hesitated.

"When and where?"

"7 at my place."

She frowned. Why was he suddenly eager to see her? Could this have something to do with the new detective? She debated whether or not she should go. But she had several questions about the case.

"OK," she replied. "See you at 7."

Guin couldn't decide what she would wear to see the detective. It was stupid really. They were just eating at his place. And not like he cared. But a part of her wanted to show him what he would be missing if—when—he left. So she had changed. Twice.

Now she stood gazing at herself in the mirror. She was wearing a form-fitting dress with a low neckline and had put on heels.

"You know this is a bad idea, right?" said her reflection.

"I know," Guin replied. "But…"

"Just don't come crying to me when he breaks your heart again."

Guin frowned, and her reflection frowned back at her.

A part of Guin knew she should give up on the detective. After all, he had made it quite clear he was ready to move on without her. And if she was being honest, he had never given her any indication that he was interested in a long-term relationship. In fact, he had made it quite clear he had no interest in getting married again. Not that Guin was hot to get married.

But Guin had allowed herself to believe he was interested in her more than just as an occasional baseball buddy or dinner companion or booty call. However, maybe that was all she was to him.

She suddenly felt depressed.

She looked at herself in the mirror again.

"Snap out of it," said her reflection. "Focus on the case. Now go or you'll be late."

"Okay," said Guin.

Guin stood outside the detective's apartment. A part of her was tempted to turn around, go back down the stairs, and get back in the Mini. But she had come this far. Might as well go through with it.

She rang the doorbell and waited for a reply.

"It's open!" called the detective.

Guin let herself in and followed her nose to the kitchen.

The detective was hovering over the stove but turned to look at her as she walked in.

"You come from a cocktail party?"

"No," said Guin, annoyed.

"You want an apron? Wouldn't want to get fish stew on your dress."

"You're making fish stew?"

He nodded.

"Cioppino."

"One of your grandmother's recipes?"

He nodded again.

"You want a taste?"

He lifted the lid. Immediately Guin's senses were overwhelmed with the fragrance of garlic and tomato, basil and oregano.

"It smells incredible," she said.

"Here, have a taste," he said dipping in a spoon and holding it out for her.

Guin closed her lips around the spoon and moaned.

The detective grinned.

"You know, if this nanny thing doesn't work out, you could always open a restaurant or get work as a private chef."

She was half teasing, but the detective looked serious.

"Restaurants are a lot of work." He glanced over at the counter, where there was a bottle of red wine. "Help yourself to some wine. Dinner's almost ready."

The bottle was open. Guin poured herself a glass and took a sip. Then took another. She had forgotten to have lunch and immediately felt a bit lightheaded.

The detective withdrew a loaf of bread from the oven and placed it on a cutting board.

"You make it?" she asked him.

"No. I was just warming it up." He dipped a spoon in the cioppino and slurped. "It's done," he announced. He grabbed two bowls and ladled fish stew into each one.

"Looks delicious."

"You want to grab the bread and the wine?"

Guin did as she was told.

"Sit," he commanded as she stood next to the dining table.

She sat.

The detective cut several slices of bread and handed her one.

"For soaking up the broth."

He sat, and Guin looked down at her bowl of cioppino.

"Go on," said the detective.

Guin wasn't sure whether to use a fork or a spoon.

"Start with a fork," he said, as if reading her mind. "Then switch to a spoon."

Guin picked up her fork.

"This is really good," she said, after taking several bites.

"Glad you like it."

They continued to eat the stew, neither speaking. Finally, when she was nearly done, Guin broke the silence.

"I heard Tom Dewey was with Jackson Brennan the night he died, and that he may have been the last person to have seen him alive."

The detective finished his soup before looking up at Guin.

"Where'd you hear that?"

"From Patrick Finney and Dewey's girlfriend. Have you spoken with them?"

Though of course he had.

The detective opened his mouth to reply, but Guin already knew what he was going to say.

"I know: It's on a need-to-know basis, and I don't need to know."

"Actually, I was going to say that we had."

Guin stared.

"What did Dewey say?"

"That Brennan was drunk, that he offered to drive him home, that Brennan refused, and that was the last Dewey saw of him."

"Do you think he was telling you the truth?"

"We're checking it out."

"So you think Brennan really did kill himself?"

"It looks that way."

Guin frowned. She was still not convinced, though all of the evidence pointed to suicide. Should she share what she had learned about Tom's sister and Brennan both being at Syracuse? The detective would probably laugh at her. Well, not laugh but give her that look. But if he didn't know...

"Did you know that Dewey's sister killed herself?"

The detective's eyebrows rose slightly.

"She'd been raped her freshman year of college at Syracuse. Passed out at some fraternity party and realized later what had been done to her. She reported it to the school, but the guy got off, and she wound up dropping out. A few months later, she committed suicide."

The detective was silent.

"And did you know that Jackson Brennan also went to Syracuse and was there at the same time as Emma Dewey— and that he was accused of raping a freshman his senior year but got off? No doubt because he was on the basketball team."

Guin now had the detective's attention.

"You think the two are connected?"

"I do."

"You have proof?"

"That Brennan raped Emma Dewey? Not exactly. But you have to admit it's quite the coincidence."

"Syracuse is a big school."

"I know. But the guy who allegedly raped Emma was a senior and an athlete. And the only athlete I found accused of raping a freshman at the time was Jackson Brennan."

"You don't know for sure it was Brennan or that Emma Dewey even knew him."

"I don't, but I plan on asking Tom Dewey."

"I wouldn't do that if I were you."

"Why not?"

"You know why not."

Guin scowled.

"So, I heard the Sanibel Police Department hired a new detective."

"Where'd you hear that?"

"Does it matter? Is it true?" He didn't reply right away. "I'll take that as a yes then. Is she your replacement?"

The detective looked uncomfortable.

"When were you planning on telling me?"

"She just started."

"So?"

He sighed.

"I was planning on telling you."

"Is that why you invited me over?"

He didn't say anything.

"So when were you planning on telling me? Were you going to send me a postcard from Boston giving me the news?"

"Can we not fight for once?"

"When are you leaving?"

"I don't know. A couple of weeks, maybe after. It depends."

"On what? I'm heading to England in a couple of weeks. Were you not even going to say goodbye?"

Again, he didn't answer.

Guin put her napkin down and got up.

"I'm going."

"But you haven't had dessert. I made a cheesecake."

"I'm not hungry."

She took her bowl and headed into the kitchen. The detective followed her.

She rinsed the bowl out, then left it in the sink.

"Thanks for the cioppino."

"Guin…"

He reached out a hand to take her arm, but she shrugged it off.

"Don't touch me."

She grabbed her bag and headed to the door, a part of her hoping he'd run after her, beg her not to go. But he stayed where he was, not saying a word.

CHAPTER 37

Guin stood in the parking lot breathing heavily. Part of her wanted to scream, another part cry. She kicked the front tire, then winced in pain.

"Argh! Why did I even bother?"

She looked up at the detective's building. No sign of him. He was not coming after her. And this time she was done.

She pulled out her phone. There was a text from Glen. She sniffled and opened it. He wanted her to call him. She immediately entered his number.

"Hey," she said, sniffling again. "You wanted to speak with me?"

"You okay?"

"Not really."

"Where are you?"

"In Fort Myers, not that far from your place, actually."

"You want to come over? I just made myself some mac and cheese. You're welcome to share it."

Guin normally wouldn't pass up a bowl of mac and cheese, but she wasn't hungry. And she didn't think going to Glen's right now was a great idea.

"Thanks, but…"

She sniffled again.

"You want to meet me someplace, grab a drink?"

A drink sounded good.

"Okay. But what about your mac and cheese?"

"I'll have it tomorrow."

"You sure?"

"Positive."

"Okay. Where should we meet?"

Glen suggested a place not far from him, and Guin said she could be there in ten. Then they ended the call. Guin got in the Mini and looked in the mirror. Her mascara had run, and she looked like a raccoon. She reached into her bag and pulled out a tissue. She dabbed it under her eyes, then looked in the mirror again. A bit better, but her eyes were still red. She sighed and turned the key in the ignition. Hopefully, the bar would be dark.

Guin sat in the parking lot in front of the bar and looked in the mirror again.

"Pull yourself together, Guin," she told herself. She plastered a smile on her face and got out.

She saw Glen as soon as she walked in. He was waiting for her. And when he saw her, his jaw dropped.

"You look incredible," he said. "You just come from a party? Did something happen?"

"Let's get a table," she suggested.

Glen nodded and they grabbed a table near the bar.

"You want to tell me what's up? Though you don't have to."

"Let's order drinks."

A server came over and Guin ordered a margarita, no salt. Glen ordered a beer.

"I'm sorry about taking you away from your mac and cheese."

"No biggie. I can always have it later or tomorrow. You want to tell me why you look so sad?"

"I thought you said I looked incredible."

Their server came over with their drinks, and Guin

immediately took a sip of her margarita.

"I was feeling a bit sad. And angry. But I'm feeling better already."

She forced herself to smile then took another sip of her margarita.

"You sure you're okay?"

"Totally fine. And I am totally done with Detective O'Loughlin. I mean it this time."

Glen looked confused.

"Detective O'Loughlin?"

"We were sort of seeing each other."

"Oh."

"Yeah."

They each took a sip of their drinks.

"Do you want to talk about it?"

"Not really," said Guin. "I mean, I thought we had patched things up, you know? Then I find out he's moving back to Boston. Didn't say a word."

"He's leaving Sanibel?"

Guin nodded.

"He's going to be a nanny."

"A nanny?"

"He has a new grandson and wants to spend time with him."

"So he's leaving to take care of his grandson?"

Guin nodded.

"Huh," said Glen, taking another sip of his beer.

"I know, right? I mean, it's noble and all. But no one's asking him to do it."

"Why not just take a leave of absence?"

"That's what I said! But he won't listen to reason. Says he owes it to his son to be a full-time grandfather."

"Did he ask you to go with him?"

"Nope."

Guin took another sip of her drink.

"Hey, you want to get something to eat? I'm suddenly feeling hungry."

"Sure," said Glen.

He signaled to the server who brought over two menus.

After finishing her margarita and eating some wings and calamari, Guin was feeling much better.

"So how come you were free tonight?" she asked Glen. "Shouldn't you have been photographing a wedding or something?"

"I was supposed to. But the bride's mother called me this morning to say the wedding was off."

"Did she say why?"

"No, and I didn't ask."

"Did they pay you?"

He nodded.

"They had put down a deposit, and I have a pretty strict cancellation policy. But I only charged them half."

"Very nice of you."

Glen smiled.

"I like to think I'm a nice guy."

Guin smiled back at him.

"You are a nice guy. Speaking of weddings, you looking forward to your friend's?"

"I am. Though it'll be weird to see some of the crew again. We haven't really kept in touch, except for Garrett. Most of them thought I was crazy to leave New York and a high-paying job to move to Fort Myers."

"I hear you. My family still thinks I'm crazy. And I barely hear from my friends up there. Though part of that, I think, is due to the divorce. We had a lot of couple friends, and I don't think they wanted to take sides. And my single friends are too busy dating. I miss them, but I've made new friends here."

"You ever think about moving back?"

Guin nodded.

"I like Sanibel, but I can't picture living here and working for the paper forever. What about you?"

"I'd be lying if I said I hadn't thought about it. But I'm here for as long as my parents need me."

Guin placed a hand on top of his.

"You're a good son."

Glen looked down at their hands then back up at Guin.

"So, you psyching yourself up for step-aunt's birthday bash in Bath?"

"I've been trying to."

"You succeeding?"

"How about we talk about Italy instead?"

She could see the hopeful look on Glen's face.

"I'm in, if it's not too late."

"You mean it?"

"One hundred percent. Wait, it's too late, isn't it? Bridget gave the spot to someone else."

"No, it's yours." Glen looked down. "I signed you up last week."

"You what?!"

Glen looked up at her.

"Don't be angry. Ginny told me to."

"What if I had said no?"

"But you didn't."

"What about the deposit?"

"It's taken care of."

Guin stared at him.

"How much do I owe you?"

"Don't worry about it."

"But I do worry. How much?"

"It's really no big deal."

"Glen…"

"Let's not discuss it right now. I'm just really glad you

decided to go. It's going to be incredible."

"Can I get the two of you anything else?" It was their server.

"Can I get an espresso?" asked Glen.

The server nodded.

"And could I get a decaf cappuccino?" asked Guin.

"I'll have to check."

"If not, just bring me a decaf coffee."

"Any dessert?"

"I'm good," said Guin.

"Me, too," said Glen. "Just the coffees."

The server nodded and went away.

"As I was saying," said Glen. "Everything's taken care of."

"What about my flights?"

"Taken care of."

"But how?"

"Your brother."

"What about my brother?"

"He used his frequent flyer miles."

Guin stared.

"You spoke with Lance, and he just gave you his frequent flyer miles?"

"Technically, he gave *you* his miles."

"But I hadn't said yes!"

"We were both pretty sure you would."

Guin eyed him.

"Pretty sure of yourselves, weren't you?"

Glen didn't say anything, but he was smiling.

"Why didn't Lance tell me?"

"I think he wanted it to be a surprise."

"Well, he surprised me all right."

She made a mental note to call her brother as soon as she got home.

"And you'll pick me up from the airport?"

"Yup. And be your chauffeur."

Guin shook her head. So this was really happening. She would be going to Italy with Glen.

Just then their coffees arrived.

They drank them in silence, then Glen got the check. He wanted to pay, but Guin insisted they split it.

They walked outside. The weather had cooled down and there were barely any clouds. Guin thought there must have been a million stars in the sky.

"What a beautiful evening," she said gazing up. Then she turned to face Glen. "Thank you."

"For what?"

"For being a good friend."

"My pleasure. And you really do look incredible tonight. Not that you look bad normally," he quickly added.

Guin smiled. She had forgotten what she was wearing.

"Well, good night," she said.

"Good night," said Glen.

They stood there looking at each other for several more seconds. Then Guin got up on her toes and gave Glen a kiss on the cheek. He smiled. For a brief, crazy moment she thought about kissing him again, though not on his cheek. It must have been the margarita. Instead, she turned and hurried to her car.

CHAPTER 38

As soon as she got home, Guin called her brother. The phone rang several times. No doubt he was out. She was preparing to leave a message when he picked up.

"You answered."

"Should I not have?"

"I just thought you'd be out."

"Then why did you call?"

"Uh…" She didn't have a good answer.

"You forget already?"

"No, it's just… Why didn't you tell me you bought me a ticket to Pisa?"

"I wanted it to be a surprise."

"But what if I had decided not to go to Italy?"

"Oh, you were going."

"How do you know that?"

"I know you. And Glen told me it was a done deal."

"Oh, he did, did he?"

"Are you not going?"

"No, I'm going."

She knew her brother was smirking.

"You're welcome. Though I had hoped you might go to the South of France with me and Owen."

"You know I would have liked to. It's just…"

"I know."

Guin yawned.

"So what are you doing up so late?"

"It's not late."

"For you it is."

"I told you, I was out with Glen."

"Is there something going on between the two of you?"

"Between me and Glen? We're colleagues, that's all."

"I didn't realize colleagues went out together on Saturday nights."

"Okay, we're also friends."

"And didn't he help renovate your house?"

"Yes, so?"

"Sounds like he's a very good friend."

"What are you getting at, Lance?"

"Nothing."

"Uh-huh."

Guin scowled.

"Can't a man and a woman be good friends?"

"It depends."

"On what?"

"On whether they find each other attractive or not. As I recall, Glen was rather good-looking, in that strapping, wavy blond hair, lacrosse player kind of way that I know you find attractive. See Jones, Arthur."

Guin felt her cheeks growing warm.

"Glen looks nothing like Art." Though he did.

"Uh-huh."

"So what are you doing home on a Saturday night?"

"Who says I'm home?"

"Where are you?"

"At some utterly charming B and B that Owen found in Bucks County."

"Nice. Business or pleasure?"

"Both. Owen's meeting with an artist and suggested we make a weekend of it."

"Well, I hope you enjoy yourselves."

She let out another yawn.

"You should go to bed."

"I will. I just wanted to call, to thank you."

"You're welcome. Have you spoken to Mom recently?"

"No, why?"

"I think she's planning something."

"What kind of something?"

"I think she and Lavinia are planning on setting you up."

"Setting me up? With a guy?"

"No, with a woman. Of course with a guy!"

"With a guy who lives in Bath?"

"He lives in the States, but he's over there visiting his family. He's one of Harry's chums from university."

"She told you this?"

"No, I heard it from Vicky."

Harry and Vicky were Lavinia's children, Guin and Lance's cousins.

"You spoke with her?"

"We messaged."

"Do we know anything about this chum of Harry's?"

"Just that he and Harry went to uni together, and that he's recently divorced."

"Where in the States does he live?"

"Does this mean you're interested?"

"Not at all. It's just reporter's curiosity."

"Uh-huh."

"Really, Lance. I am not interested in being fixed up with anyone, here or in England. And I hope you told Vicky and Mom that."

"And spoil the fun? Besides, you've never dated an Englishman before. Could be fun. I hear they're not all circumcised."

"Lance!"

"Sorry. I may have had a bit too much to drink at dinner."

"Uh-huh."

"Anyway, you should give him a try. He could be a prince."

"Doubtful."

Guin let out a third yawn.

"Get some sleep. And give Mom a call tomorrow."

"Oh, I will. And Lance?"

"Yes?"

"I love you."

"I love you, too, Sis."

They ended the call and Guin realized she hadn't told Lance about her and the detective. Probably a good thing as a) he never really liked the detective, and b) he might try setting her up with someone. She yawned once more then turned out the light.

That night Guin dreamed she was back at the paper, the one she had worked at before she moved to Sanibel. It was as though she had never left. She and her colleagues were standing around discussing their latest assignments. One reporter was meeting with the governor to discuss some important piece of legislation he was trying to pass. Another was meeting with a local business leader about a new initiative that would create hundreds of new jobs. Yet another was reporting on some big fundraising scandal. It all sounded interesting.

Then they asked Guin what she was working on. And when she said that she was covering the opening of a new boutique, they all started laughing.

The laughter got louder and louder until Guin couldn't take it anymore and ran out of the newsroom. Then she woke up. Her heart was racing, and for a few seconds she didn't know where she was. It was dark, so she knew it must be early. She turned and looked at her alarm clock. It was three-thirty. She groaned and leaned back against her pillow.

She tried going back to sleep, but the dream kept replaying in her head. Finally, she gave up and turned on the light. She thought briefly about taking a sleeping pill, but they always gave her a headache the next day. She looked again at the clock. Only fifteen minutes had gone by.

She got up and made her way to the kitchen to make herself some herbal tea. She took a few sips, then brought the mug back to the bedroom. She climbed back into bed and cracked open her guide to Southwest Florida's flora and fauna. A short time later, she felt her eyelids getting heavy. She put the book down and turned off the light.

The next time Guin awoke, it was a little after seven. She sighed with relief. She didn't remember what she had dreamed this time, only that it hadn't been another nightmare. She got up and went to the bathroom. Then she took her now cold mug of tea to the kitchen and made herself some coffee.

Fauna had followed her into the kitchen, and Guin gave her a can of cat food.

As soon as her coffee was ready, Guin poured it into a mug. She drank it at the island, staring out at into her backyard. She needed to get Ginny the treasure hunt article, but she wasn't in the mood. It was all because of that stupid dream. Writing about treasure hunts and restaurant and boutique openings was nothing to be embarrassed about, she told herself. Those articles helped local businesses. But she couldn't help feeling that she was meant to do bigger things. She sighed and headed to her office.

Guin was staring at her monitor. She had begun editing her article. But she kept thinking about that stupid dream. Maybe a walk would clear her head.

She continued to stare at the open document. Then she

gave up and went to put on a pair of shorts and a t-shirt.

She was surprised to find the beach mostly empty. Were people at church? No matter. She loved having the beach to herself.

She walked along the water's edge, searching for shells, but there weren't many to be found, just the usual suspects. But it was another beautiful morning. She took off her sandals and sank her toes into the sand. It felt good.

She carried her shoes the rest of the way, being careful to avoid sharp objects. When she reached the leaning palm tree, she turned around and headed home.

Guin had just turned onto her street when she ran into her neighbor, Sally, walking her new dog, a rescue named Zoey. Guin said hello and stopped to pet the pretty pooch, who looked like a cross between a retriever and a corgi. Sally and her beau, Jimbo, who was a friend of Guin's, were about to head to Maine for a week, Sally informed her. Sally had never been and said she was looking forward to seeing Acadia National Park. Guin had never been to Acadia either and told Sally to send pictures.

They chatted for another minute, then Guin said she needed to go.

Guin took a shower then sat herself in front of her computer. This time, she was able to focus on the article. She gave it one last read, then sent it to Glen, to get his take. If he gave it a thumbs up, she'd send it to Ginny.

She stared out the window. Now she just needed to wrap up her piece on Jackson Brennan. No doubt the police would be wrapping up their investigation soon, if they hadn't already. If only Detective O'Loughlin would let her know. She frowned. Maybe this new detective would be more forthcoming. Though at the thought of a new detective, Guin's heart ached.

Snap out of it, Guin, she told herself.

She forced herself to focus and went over everything she knew about Brennan's last days—and kept coming back to Tom Dewey. Why had he lied to her? She thought about texting him again but instead texted Stephanie.

"By any chance is Tom working today?"

A minute later, Stephanie replied.

"He is. :-(," she wrote back.

This was Guin's chance. Assuming he was working at the office. Well, not like she had something better to do. Before she overthought it, she grabbed her microcassette recorder, bag, and keys.

She got in the Mini and paused, sending Craig a quick text to let him know she was headed to Jackson Brennan's office to see Tom Dewey. Then she put her key in the ignition and started the car.

CHAPTER 39

Guin parked in the small lot and went up the stairs. There were lights on in the office. A good sign. Though she didn't see anyone. She tried the door, but it was locked. She knocked, but no one answered. She knocked again, louder this time. Still no answer. She would try one more time, then try calling Tom.

She was about to pound on the plate glass when she saw him. She waved and called his name. Tom spied her and came over. He looked a mess. His hair was sticking up in places and his clothes were rumpled. Had he slept at the office?

He unlocked the door and opened it a crack.

"Is everything okay, Ms. Jones?"

"I need to speak with you."

"I'm a bit busy right now. Still playing catch-up."

"Please, may I come in? It's about your partner."

Tom sighed.

"I have a feeling you won't take no for an answer." He opened the door. "Won't you come in?"

Guin stepped inside and looked around. There were file folders everywhere.

"I've been doing a bit of housecleaning."

"Isn't that Wanda's job?"

"I felt I should help."

She looked at the young lawyer. He had dark bags under

his eyes. She felt a momentary pang of pity. But she couldn't let that get in the way. She had come here for a reason.

"Why did you lie to me about Brennan?"

He looked bewildered.

"You didn't tell me that you saw him at Doc Ford's the night he died. Why?"

Tom ran a hand through his hair.

"Let's go to my office."

Guin hesitated. No one would be able to see them in his office. But he had already headed down the hall, so she followed.

If the front office looked bad, Tom's office looked worse, with stacks of papers everywhere. He moved one stack off of a chair and offered her the seat. Then he went around his desk and took a seat in his own chair. Guin again thought how tired he looked.

"I didn't mean to lie to you, or the police," he began. "I was just trying to protect Jack… and maybe myself."

"Protect him how? Why did he need protecting?"

"He was quite drunk when I saw him that evening. He could barely stand. Yet he insisted on driving himself home."

Guin wasn't following.

"I let him, don't you see? I should have insisted I drive him, but he wouldn't hear of it, said he was fine. He could have killed someone. Yet I backed down because I didn't want to cause another scene. But I was right. He did kill someone. I just didn't know it would be himself."

Guin didn't know what to say. She had a dozen questions and didn't know which one to ask first.

"But he died from cyanide poisoning."

Tom didn't reply.

"Any idea how he got it?"

"He probably ordered it online. You can get anything online these days."

Guin would check that out.

"Another thing, did you know that your sister and Brennan were at Syracuse at the same time? Brennan was a senior when your sister was a freshman. He was on the basketball team, so she probably knew who he was."

"How do you know that?"

"It's my job to know stuff like that. And Stephanie told me about Emma."

Tom frowned.

"I don't like talking about my sister."

"I understand. What happened to her was awful."

"It was beyond awful. It ruined her life. Literally."

"The boy who raped her, it was Brennan, wasn't it?"

Guin watched as Tom's face went from agonized to angry.

"He was on the basketball team, though he mostly sat on the bench. All the girls were crazy about him, though I have no idea why. Emma met him at some fraternity party. She had had too much to drink and passed out. When she recovered, she realized what had happened and panicked."

"Did she tell anyone?"

"Not at first."

"But she told someone?"

Tom nodded.

"Did she report it?"

"Eventually."

"But they didn't believe her."

"Worse! Brennan and his buddies? They laughed about it! Said Emma had been flirting with Brennan all night and that she should be grateful. Grateful that the guy raped her! And people believed them!"

Guin saw the fury in Tom's eyes. She felt furious too. What Brennan did was… There were no words to describe the horror of it, if it was true. Though knowing Brennan, it probably was.

"Emma dropped out and came home. I had no idea what had happened. My parents wouldn't tell me. I just knew that something was wrong."

"How did you find out?"

"After Emma died, I started asking questions. I knew a bunch of her friends. They didn't say anything at first, but then one of them let something slip. And it had been written up in the paper. So it didn't take much to figure out what had happened."

"I don't understand. If you knew Brennan had raped your sister, why go work for him?"

But even as she said it, Guin had a feeling she knew why.

"I hated Brennan. For years I dreamed of getting back at him for what he did to Emma. So I began following him."

"You followed him?"

"Not literally," he clarified. "I followed his career. I knew he had become a lawyer—a personal injury lawyer. Ironic, no? So I decided I would become a lawyer too, if only to protect people from guys like him."

"But why go work for him?"

"I wanted him to experience the pain and suffering I had."

"But you had a promising career in Chicago. And what about Stephanie? Did she know why you wanted to work with Brennan?"

"She had no idea. I told her that I had always dreamed of being a small-town lawyer, helping my neighbors, and that this was my opportunity to do just that. And it wasn't too hard to convince her to move to Sanibel, especially in January."

"But what about Brennan? He didn't make the connection between you and your sister?"

Tom smiled.

"No. Even though I mentioned that my sister had gone to Syracuse. He just went off on some tangent about those being the happiest days of his life and how he missed it. Made me want to puke."

"I still don't understand though. How were you planning on making him suffer?"

"It was simple. I wanted him to lose what meant the most to him, his career and reputation. And I succeeded."

"What did you do?"

Tom smiled.

"Not that much actually. Brennan made it easy. He had taken out a big loan from a local loan shark to bolster his image, and the interest was killing him. On top of that, he had become lazy."

"Lazy?"

"About doing his job. He was too cheap to hire a paralegal and didn't like doing the grunt work his cases required. He made Wanda do some of it, but she could only do so much. That's part of the reason why he hired me. But no way was I going to help him."

"So you what, gave him wrong information? Sabotaged his cases?"

"I wouldn't say *sabotaged*. If Brennan had been a good lawyer, he would have hired a good paralegal and would have reviewed and double-checked everything Wanda and I gave him before he went to trial. Was it my fault he couldn't be bothered?"

"But he trusted you. As did his clients. Didn't you feel bad for them?"

Tom suddenly looked conflicted.

"I've been trying to make it up to them."

"What about Brennan's wife?"

"She deserved better."

"Did you know he was having an affair?"

He nodded.

"I caught them carrying on in his office."

Guin stared.

"Did you say anything?"

"Of course. But Jack said it was none of my business and to keep my mouth shut."

"But Audra Linwood knew."

Tom smiled, and Guin wondered if Tom had somehow tipped her off.

She glanced over at Tom's bookcase, to the shelf where he displayed Stephanie's shells.

"You stole those painted shells from the Community House, didn't you?"

Tom frowned.

"Wanda said Brennan found that painted shell, the one the police found on him, outside your office."

"So?"

"That shell was one of a handful that went missing from the Community House around the time you were there to pick up Stephanie."

"Must be a coincidence."

"I don't think so. I think you swiped the shell, then planted it outside the office, hoping Brennan would find it and that it would scare him."

"Scare him, with a painted shell?" Tom was playing coy, but Guin wasn't buying his innocent act.

"You knew Wanda would say that the shell was bad luck."

"Has anyone ever told you that you have a fertile imagination, Ms. Jones?"

Guin ignored the comment.

"What about that political consultant, Bradley Malloy? Did you have a hand in convincing him not to take on Brennan?"

"He didn't need any help from me to know that Brennan was never going to win."

"You don't know that."

"Please. Brennan was broke, losing cases, and having an

affair with a woman young enough to be his daughter. You really think people would have voted for him?"

"You clearly haven't lived in Florida for very long." Guin studied Tom. "So what do you get out of all of this?"

"What do I get? Peace of mind, Ms. Jones. Brennan's dead and can no longer inflict pain on anyone."

"Did you kill him?"

"No. He killed himself."

"With cyanide, just like your sister."

"Emma didn't deserve to die. Brennan did."

Guin felt a chill run down her spine, but she was not done asking questions.

"Did you give him the cyanide?"

"I told you…"

But before he could answer they were interrupted by a loud knock on the door. The doorknob rattled. Guin hadn't realized Tom had locked it.

"Mr. Dewey?" Guin recognized that voice. "Sanibel police. Open the door."

Tom frowned.

"I'll be right there," he called.

Guin felt her heart pounding against her chest. Tom wouldn't do anything foolish, would he?

He got up and unlocked the door, opening it.

"Can I help you with something, Detective?"

Guin saw Detective O'Loughlin glance at her, then he focused his attention back on Tom.

"If you would come with us, Mr. Dewey."

"Why?" asked Tom.

"We'd like to have a word with you."

"Can't we have a word here?"

"I'd rather we talked at the police department."

Guin craned her neck and saw two uniformed officers standing behind Detective O'Loughlin.

"What's this about?"

"If you would please come with us."

"You didn't answer my question, Detective."

"It pertains to the death of your partner, Jackson Brennan."

"I already told you everything I know, Detective."

"He's lying," said Guin.

The detective and Tom both shot her a look.

"Officer Pettit, if you would escort the gentleman?"

"Are you arresting me?"

"As I said, we just want to ask you a few questions."

Tom looked like he was going to protest again. But then he seemed to change his mind.

"Fine, I've got nothing to hide. Lead the way."

Guin followed the four of them out and watched as Tom got in the back of the police car. Then she watched it drive away.

Guin pulled out her phone. She was itching to text the detective and ask him what was up. But she knew he probably wouldn't—or couldn't—tell her, at least not right away. She sighed and saw that she had multiple text messages from Craig. Right. She had told him she was heading over to Brennan & Associates and then hadn't gotten back to him. Had he called the police?

She entered his number, and he immediately picked up.

"Guin? Are you okay? I got worried when you didn't reply to my messages."

"I'm fine," she said. "O'Loughlin just took Dewey in for questioning."

"Did they arrest him?"

"Not yet."

"What were you thinking, going over there by yourself?"

"I needed some answers."

"Did you get them?"

"Sort of."

"Well, it was still foolhardy of you to go running over there without telling anyone."

"I told you."

Craig grumbled.

"So did Dewey do it?"

"I don't know. He had motive and opportunity. But I don't know how they can prove he forced Brennan to take the cyanide."

"The police will sort it out."

"Maybe," said Guin.

There was silence for several seconds. Then Craig spoke.

"You going to speak with him?"

"Who?"

"O'Loughlin. You know Ginny's going to want you to interview him."

"Right." There was another pause. "I should probably call her, let her know what's up. Unless you want to?"

"You should call her."

"Though knowing Ginny's psychic abilities, she probably already knows."

They talked for another minute, then Guin ended the call and sent a text to her boss.

CHAPTER 40

Guin didn't realize she had left her phone at home until she had gone to take a photo of a great blue heron. It was standing near the shoreline, just hanging out. She thought briefly about returning home to get it. But the bird would probably be gone by the time she got back, so she continued to walk.

The sun had just come up and the tide was high, making it difficult to walk in spots—or find shells. Not unusual for that time of year. But Guin didn't mind. Well, maybe just a little. But how could she really complain when she was able to walk out her door and be on the beach in less than ten minutes, shells or no shells?

She walked past the leaning palm, then turned around. When she was nearly back at her access point, she ran into Van and Taylor. The golden retriever immediately went up to her and sat, resting her head against Guin's leg. Guin smiled and pet the pretty canine.

"Good morning," she said to Van.

"Good morning yourself," he said.

"Is Taylor always this friendly?"

"Only to people she thinks will appreciate her."

"Well, I appreciate you, Taylor," Guin said, looking at the dog and continuing to stroke her soft fur.

"Nice day," said Van.

"It is," said Guin. "Though not a lot of shells."

"Ah, you're one of those."

Guin smiled. She knew what he meant.

"You not into collecting then?"

"I used to be when we first moved here. But one day I looked around and thought, what am I going to do with all of these things? So I donated them to the Shell Museum. My wife on the other hand… She's got a whole cabinet full of shells."

Guin understood. She often wondered what drove her to continue to collect shells, even though she had several bowls full of them. But she couldn't help herself. Shell collecting was an addiction.

They chatted for a few more minutes, then Guin said goodbye.

As soon as she got home, she set water to boil for her coffee. Then she retrieved her phone. There were messages from Ginny and Craig. Had something happened? She opened Ginny's message first. Tom Dewey had been arrested for the murder of Jackson Brennan.

Guin read Craig's message next. It said the same thing. She looked at the time. It was a little after nine. She thought about who to call first, Craig or Ginny, and entered Craig's number. He picked up right away.

"I just got your message. So they arrested him? When?"

"This morning," said Craig. "Ginny wants one of us to go over to the SPD and get a statement from O'Loughlin."

"You want to go?"

"I think you should."

Guin bit her lip.

"I would but…" Guin sighed. "You're right. I should go."

"You sure? If you really don't want to…"

"No. I can handle it."

"I know you can. You're a pro."

Guin didn't feel like a pro.

"Okay, I'll go over there in a bit."

"Let me know how it goes."

Guin said she would, and they ended the call. Then she phoned Ginny.

"You get my message?"

"That's why I'm calling," said Guin. "And I already spoke with Craig."

"Good. You speak with O'Loughlin?"

"Not yet. I figured I'd call you first. How'd you and Craig even know they arrested Dewey?"

"Got the word first thing this morning."

Guin wondered who Ginny's source in the police department was, but she knew Ginny wouldn't tell her.

"Your source say anything else?"

"Nope. Just that he'd been arrested. So get over there and find out what's up."

"I will."

"Good, and while you're over there, see if you can get a meeting with that new detective they hired. I want to do a profile on her."

"You know her name?"

"Denise Brown. She's from Orlando. A real tough cookie from what I hear."

"Got it. Anything else?"

"You going to send me the treasure hunt article?"

Right. Guin had forgotten all about it.

"I'll email it to you later. I'm just waiting to hear back from Glen."

"Good. And we should discuss Italy. You want to stop by the office this afternoon?"

"Can I stop by tomorrow?"

"Fine. Come by whenever. Though I have a lunch meeting and an appointment with a new advertiser at three." Guin heard someone asking Ginny a question. "I've got to go. Let me know when you've spoken with O'Loughlin. I want a report in my inbox ASAP."

"You got it," said Guin. "And the profile of the new detective?"

"We can discuss it tomorrow."

They ended the call and Guin thought about heading over to the Sanibel Police Department. But it would probably be smarter to call there first. She entered the number and asked the operator to connect her to Detective O'Loughlin but was told he was unavailable. Instead, she left him a message, saying she heard they had arrested Tom Dewey and to call her as soon as possible.

She looked over at her kettle. The water she had boiled had no doubt grown cold. She boiled it again, then poured it into her French press. Five minutes later, her coffee was ready. She took a sip and closed her eyes.

She took a few more sips then sent a text to Stephanie, asking if she was okay. Guin chided herself. Of course she wasn't okay. Her boyfriend had just been arrested. She sent Stephanie a follow-up text, saying she was available if Stephanie wanted to talk or grab a drink later. No reply. She was probably at the police department trying to bail out Tom. Maybe Guin should go over there.

She felt torn. Tom had been through so much and seemed like he truly cared about helping people. The opposite of Brennan. But if he had been responsible for Brennan's death... And Stephanie... She had moved to Sanibel to be with Tom. And now who knew what their future held?

Guin looked down at her phone again. Maybe she should text the detective. She bit her lip. She knew he was probably busy. And she had left him a voicemail. *Oh, what the heck*. She sent him a quick text. Though she didn't expect to hear back from him, at least not right away. But at least she could tell Ginny she had tried to reach him.

Guin was sitting in her office, staring out the window. Neither Stephanie nor Detective O'Loughlin had gotten back to her. She had thought about driving over to the Sanibel Police Department but had stopped herself. No point going there if O'Loughlin wasn't available. She just wished he would call or text her.

She sighed, then turned back to her computer. She should finish up the treasure hunt story.

Glen had emailed her back with a couple of suggestions. She incorporated them, then read through the article one more time. When she was satisfied, she sent it to Ginny, letting her know Glen would be sending her the photos separately.

She picked up her phone. Still nothing from the detective. Should she send him another text? Though what was the point? Well, if he didn't get back to her in another hour, she would just go over there and take her chances. Maybe that new detective would be there, and she could speak with her.

Speaking of Detective Brown... Guin opened her browser and typed *Detective Denise Brown Orlando* into the search box. Immediately, the screen began to populate. Guin clicked on a link and began to read.

Detective Brown had grown up in Philadelphia, but her family had moved to Orlando right before she started high school. That must have been tough, thought Guin. Detective Brown's father was also a detective. He had worked in Philadelphia then had gotten a job with the Orlando Police Department. Hence their move.

Guin continued to read.

Detective Brown's husband was a teacher, and they had two children, a boy and a girl. The boy would be starting high school in the fall. The girl was in middle school.

Detective Brown had been involved in several high-profile cases and had received numerous commendations.

What had brought her to Sanibel? Guin wondered. Maybe she wanted a quieter life? Or maybe her husband had taken a job at the Sanibel School? Guin would have to ask her.

Guin glanced at the clock on her monitor. It was later than she thought. She picked up her phone and checked her messages. Still nothing from the detective. She frowned. Guess that meant she would be camping out at the SPD.

Guin looked at her watch. It was nearly one o'clock. She had been waiting in the small entrance to the Sanibel Police Department for just over fifteen minutes and was beginning to feel claustrophobic. And hungry. She had been told that Detective O'Loughlin was in a meeting. Did she want to come back later? No, she did not. She would wait. The woman sitting behind the protective glass had shrugged and told Guin it could be a while. Guin had said that was fine and that she would be just outside.

The police department was located on the second floor of the municipal complex, and there was a breezeway nearby with a bench. Guin was too antsy to sit, so she paced. It was muggy outside, but Guin didn't care. It was better than waiting in the tiny, enclosed space that passed for a waiting area.

She took out her phone and sent the detective another text, telling him she was at the SPD and wouldn't leave until he came out.

Five minutes later, he texted her back.

"Make it quick."

Guin hurried back inside and told the woman at the desk that Detective O'Loughlin was expecting her. The woman checked then buzzed her back.

Guin made her way to the detective's office. The door was closed, so she knocked. "It's open," he called. She let herself in, then closed the door behind her. The detective was looking at his computer.

Guin stood a few feet away, waiting for him to acknowledge her. When he didn't, she cleared her throat. Finally, he turned and looked up at her.

"I hear you arrested Tom Dewey."

He continued to look at her, not replying.

"Was it for the murder of Jackson Brennan?"

Still no reply.

"What did he say when you arrested him?"

"To answer your questions, yes, and he claims he had nothing to do with Brennan's death, that Brennan took his own life."

Of course he'd say that. What had Guin expected, Tom to confess?

"I assume you have proof to the contrary?"

Detective O'Loughlin gave Guin that look of his, the one that said, what do you think?

"What did you find?"

"Dewey had given Brennan a bottle of headache medicine. We had it tested and found traces of cyanide."

"You found a bottle containing traces of cyanide and didn't tell me?"

The detective didn't answer.

"Where was it?"

"In the bushes, not far from where we found Brennan's keys."

"But how do you know Dewey was the one who gave it to him? Or that it was Brennan's?"

"The bottle had Brennan's fingerprints on it, and one of Dewey's too. And Brennan's assistant gave a sworn statement saying she had seen Dewey giving Brennan the bottle."

"And there were traces of cyanide in it?"

O'Loughlin nodded.

"Still, it will be hard to prove that Tom was the one who put the cyanide in there."

"Maybe," said the detective.

"You have proof that Tom purchased the cyanide and placed it in the bottle of headache medicine?"

The detective didn't reply, and Guin could sense his impatience.

"Can I get a statement for the paper?"

"Do I have a choice?"

She smiled.

"Not unless you want Ginny pestering you too."

"Fine, let's get it over with."

Guin dug out her microcassette recorder from her bag. The detective looked at it.

"You must be the only person who still uses one of those things."

"I know, but I like it. Anyway, shall we?"

He nodded, and Guin asked his permission to record their conversation. He gave it, and she began asking him questions. He didn't tell Guin anything she didn't already know. But at least she had him on the record.

She was wrapping up when there was a knock at the door.

"Come in!" called the detective.

The door opened to reveal Detective Brown. Guin recognized her from the articles she had read online about her.

"I had a minute between meetings and wanted to see if…" Then she noticed Guin. "Sorry. Am I interrupting something?"

"We were just finishing up," said O'Loughlin. "Ms. Jones, this is Detective Brown. She'll be taking over for me."

Guin glanced up at Detective Brown. She must have been at least five-nine.

"Nice to meet you," said Guin.

"Ms. Jones here works for the *Sanibel-Captiva Sun-Times*, our local paper," explained Detective O'Loughlin. "She's also an expert at finding dead bodies."

Guin scowled at Detective O'Loughlin then looked at Detective Brown.

"I'd love to interview you for the paper when you have a few minutes."

"Why?" asked Detective Brown.

"It's not every day Sanibel gets a new detective."

"You mean one who's a Black woman."

Guin didn't know how to reply.

"Do you have some time this week? I only need thirty minutes or so." She dug into her purse and pulled out a card. "You don't have to tell me now. You can text or email me."

"I'm pretty busy this week," said Detective Brown, glancing at Guin's card.

"Of course. Just let me know when you're free. Though I'll be away the first two weeks of July."

The detectives exchanged a look.

"I should probably be going," said Guin, making to get up.

"Hold on," said Detective O'Loughlin. He looked over at Detective Brown. "Could you give us a minute?"

Detective Brown nodded and stepped outside, closing the door behind her.

"Is everything all right?" asked Guin.

Detective O'Loughlin was frowning.

"I thought you were just going away for a week."

"My plans changed. Now I'll be away for two. Glen and I are going to Italy."

That caught the detective's attention, and he didn't look happy.

"Glen?"

"You know, Glen Anderson, the tall, good-looking photographer who works for the paper, the one who helped me with the house?"

The detective was definitely scowling now. Was that a

hint of jealousy Guin detected?

"He enrolled in this cooking class in Tuscany and invited me to go with him. Ginny thought it was a great idea. I'm going to write about it for the paper."

The detective didn't say anything.

Guin got up.

"Well, I should get going. Thank you for your time, detective."

She walked to the door and left without sparing a glance back at him.

EPILOGUE

Guin submitted her story on Tom Dewey and Jackson Brennan to Ginny, glad to be done with it. She had disliked Jackson Brennan. And if she was being honest, she wasn't sorry he was dead. Tom Dewey, however, was another matter. He was out on bail, and a trial date hadn't been set yet. And Guin wondered if he would be convicted of murder. A part of her hoped he wouldn't be. Though if he was guilty…

She had reached out to Stephanie again, but Stephanie hadn't gotten back to her. Did Stephanie blame her for Tom's arrest? Guin hoped not. She had only been doing her job. And it was the police who had found the incriminating evidence.

She hadn't heard from Detective O'Loughlin either. And she hadn't been back to the police department since their interview. She was supposed to have interviewed Detective Brown, but due to scheduling issues, Craig would now do it. Which was fine by Guin. She could use a break from detectives. Though she would no doubt have cause to speak with Detective Brown in the future.

Thank goodness for vacation. She needed these two weeks away from Sanibel to clear her head.

She had just started to pack when her phone started vibrating. She looked down at the Caller ID. It was Ris. He wanted to know if she was free for dinner. She thought about it for a second, then told him she was busy. Not a total lie. She did need to get ready for her trip. She could tell he was disappointed, and Guin felt a momentary pang of guilt. But she didn't want to lead him on.

A few minutes later, her phone started vibrating again. It was Glen. He wanted to go over last-minute details for their trip and suggested they meet up for dinner. Was she free? This time Guin said yes.

The next night, Guin had dinner at Shelly and Steve's. It was the night before her trip, and she had tried to beg off, but Shelly had insisted. Guin had brought over the perishable food from her fridge. And after a quick stop in the kitchen, they headed out to the lanai. Steve was manning the grill.

"I'm not smelling bratwurst," said Guin, taking a sniff.

Steve was known for his bratwurst barbecues. Every year in the fall, he would order a case of bratwurst from a butcher in Wisconsin, near where he'd grown up, and invite his friends on Sanibel over to eat them.

Steve smiled.

"It's too hot for brats. We're having fish."

"You catch it?"

He nodded.

"And there's grilled zucchini and corn," said Shelly.

"Sounds yummy," said Guin.

"You want a drink?" asked Steve. "We've got cold beer and wine."

Steve and Shelly were both nursing beers, so Guin said she'd have one too.

Dinner was ready a few minutes later, and they ate it outside on the lanai.

"Mm…" Guin said, taking a bite of fish. "This is really good. What's it marinated with?"

"His secret sauce," said Shelly. "He won't even tell me the recipe."

She gave him a look, and Steve grinned.

"Well, whatever it is, it's really good," said Guin. "You could bottle and sell it."

"Don't give him any ideas."

Over dinner, Shelly asked Guin a dozen questions about her Italy trip. Guin joked that maybe Shelly should go instead, and Shelly said she would in a heartbeat. Then they talked about Shelly's latest jewelry experiments, Steve's latest consulting gig, and other things. When they were all done, Guin helped clear the table, then said she should be off.

"You all packed?" asked Shelly as she walked Guin to the door.

"Yep. Just need to add my toiletries."

"Remember to put anything important in your carry-on."

"Yes, Mom," said Guin. Then she gave Shelly a kiss and promised she'd write and send pictures.

It was nearly time for Guin to go to the airport. She looked around her house, hoping nothing would go wrong in her absence.

She had taken Fauna over to the Bregmans', her next-door neighbors, earlier. Sadie had volunteered to look after Fauna but asked that Guin leave her at their house. Guin had been reluctant at first, not wanting to stress Fauna out. But Sadie, who had worked at a no-kill shelter for many years and had owned cats before moving to Sanibel, didn't like the idea of leaving the cat alone in an empty house. So they had compromised: Fauna would have a sleepover at the Bregmans', and if that went well, she would stay there while Guin was away.

The sleepover had gone well, so Guin had agreed to leave Fauna with Sadie and Sam—and was amused to see that Sadie had bought Fauna an assortment of cat toys and beds.

She just hoped Fauna wouldn't get too comfortable and not want to come home.

The flight to England had gone smoothly, no delays, and Guin emerged from customs to see her brother waiting for her.

"You have a good flight?"

Guin yawned.

"It was okay."

"I take it you didn't sleep."

"Nope."

"Well, you can rest up when we get to the cottage. You'll definitely want to be alert for later."

"Why? What's happening later?"

"Family dinner. And Lavinia invited Harry's university chum David to join us."

Guin groaned.

"But I just got here. Couldn't they have waited?"

"I told them it was a bad idea, but they wouldn't listen."

Guin frowned. This was not how she wanted to start her trip.

"Come on," said Lance. "Let me help you with your bags." She allowed him to, then followed him out of the airport.

Guin loved the little cottage her brother and Owen had rented, and after a brief nap and a hearty lunch, she was feeling much better. And dinner with the family hadn't been so bad. Everyone had been on their best behavior, except for Harry, who felt the need to tease nearly everyone. Though there was nothing vicious about it.

As for Harry's friend, Guin found David funny and charming. And he had endeared himself to her after telling

Lavinia he had no interest in jumping into a relationship when she had asked him if he was ready to start dating again.

Guin knew her mother and Lavinia had been disappointed, but they would no doubt find someone else to fix her up with.

The rest of the week flew by. Every day there was some group activity or family lunch or dinner. Though Guin, Lance, and Owen managed to sneak away to visit Oxford and the Cotswolds. And before she knew it, Lance was driving her back to the airport.

Now, as she stood in the security line, she felt a bit sad. She had actually enjoyed being with her family and would miss them. What a thought.

The flight from Bristol to Pisa had been considerably shorter than the one she had taken from the States to England. And she didn't feel tired in the least when she deplaned. She rescued her bags from the baggage claim and went in search of Glen. She didn't have to search for long.

He smiled and waved as soon as he saw her, and Guin smiled back. There was something different about him. And she realized it was his clothes. He was dressed in a pair of linen trousers and wore a button-down shirt that was unbuttoned at the top, like he had just flown in from a cocktail party in the Hamptons. Which he probably had.

"How was the flight?" he asked her.

"Good," Guin replied.

He took her larger bag and led her to where he had parked.

"Is that your rental car?" asked Guin, staring at the tiny red convertible that looked barely big enough to fit the two of them, let alone two suitcases.

"You like it?"

"It's very... compact," said Guin, trying to be

diplomatic. "Does it have a trunk?"

"Of course it has a trunk," said Glen, who proceeded to open it.

Guin watched as Glen attempted to fit in her suitcase, barely managing to squeeze it in.

"What about my carry-on?"

Glen frowned.

"Perhaps I should have rented a slightly larger car. But I couldn't resist."

Guin said she would put the carry-on between her legs. Fortunately, it wasn't that big. She got in and had to admit, the car was adorable. Though adorable was probably the wrong word.

Glen got in beside her.

"So, are you ready to start your new adventure?"

"As ready as I'll ever be," Guin replied.

Glen smiled and started the engine. It made a loud noise, and then they were off.

To be continued…

Acknowledgments

First, I'd like to thank *you* for reading this book. If you enjoyed it, please consider reviewing or rating it on Amazon and/or Goodreads—and be sure to tell your friends about the Sanibel Island Mystery series (and my novel *Tinder Fella* too)!

Next, I'd like to thank my first readers, Amanda Walter and Robin Muth, who have been with me from the start of this journey. Their friendship, support, and ability to spot typos mean the world to me. I would also like to thank my mother, Sue Lonoff de Cuevas, a former Harvard expository writing instructor and grammarian, for copy editing this book. Any errors you spotted are my fault, not hers.

And if the cover made you pick up this book, you can thank Kristin Bryant, my talented cover designer. Thanks, too, to Polgarus Studio for formatting the interior and making this and all of my books look as good on the inside as they do on the outside.

Lastly, my eternal appreciation to my husband Kenny, who has read every book, listened to me grouse, and kept me well fed the last four years. Guin should be so lucky.

About the Sanibel Island Mystery series

To learn more about the Sanibel Island Mystery series, visit the website at http://www.SanibelIslandMysteries.com and "like" the Sanibel Island Mysteries Facebook page at https://www.facebook.com/SanibelIslandMysteries/.